Where
FOUND
You

a
heart's
compass
novel

Carrien
Enjoy Callum &
Ellie's Story!

BROOKE O'BRIEN

Visit my website at: www.authorbrookeobrien.com

Where I Found You

Edited by: Roxane LeBlanc, Rox Reads

Proofreader: Julie Deaton, Author Services by Julie Deaton

Cover Design: Najla Qamber, Najla Qamber Designs

Front Cover Photo: Photographed by Lindee Robinson,
Lindee Robinson Photography
Cover Models: Andrew Kruczynski and Daria Rottenberk
Back Cover Photo: Shutterstock

Interior Design: Stacey Blake, Champagne Formats

Dedication

This book is dedicated to anyone who has ever ran from their past, only to find themselves right where they were meant to be all along.

Prologue

Ellie

12 Years Old

SITTING ON THE FLOOR IN MY BEDROOM, I'VE BEEN STAR-*ing off into space for what feels like an hour now. My mom sent me downstairs to play, saying she didn't want to look at me. It's not the first time she's told me she couldn't bear the sight of me, but it hasn't hardened my soul, doesn't lessen the hurt. My thoughts continue to replay the way she was digging through the kitchen cabinets while tears streamed down her face. Her eyes red and her hair a tangled mess as she searched the cupboards for more alcohol.*

"Anything to make it go away," she repeated over and over. She never said what she meant, but I knew.

She wanted to take away the pain she felt after my Dad left us and went to heaven.

I try to stay away from my mom when she's drinking, but it seems like all the time lately. So instead I hide out in my room. It's my safe place.

I can hear my name being shouted from somewhere upstairs. I know my mom isn't home. Coming up empty after a thorough search of all her hiding places, she headed to the store for reinforcements. Only one other person could be yelling for me.

My heart starts to pound as I squeeze my eyes shut and say a prayer. I beg God every night for him to leave me alone. I'm living the same nightmares that keep me up at night.

The dry, hoarse sound of my name being called again brings me crashing back to reality. On shaky legs, I stand while taking a deep breath, trying to calm my racing heart. I want to run, but I know what would come either way, so instead, I leave the safety of my bedroom and head up the stairs. As soon as I reach the landing, the stench of cigarette smoke invades my nostrils, causing my stomach to turn.

I hate the smell of cigarettes. It's not only the scent or how they make my head hurt, but because they remind me so much of him. The two are synonymous and will forever be etched in my memory.

The football game blares on the TV as smoke floats through the air. The curtains and windows are open. A fresh breeze flows and sunlight streams in onto the hardwood floors. I can hear the outside laughter of the neighbor kids, and for a minute, I wish I was like the other kids my age, spending the afternoon riding their bikes up and down the sidewalk or playing hide 'n seek.

I would give anything to be hiding in my room.

Letting out a silent breath I didn't realize I had been holding, I steal a glance out of the side of my eye to see him sitting in his chair in the corner of the living room. The ashtray on the end table is nearly overflowing with cigarette butts. My lip curls in disgust.

"C'mere, sweet girl," he says with a cigarette hanging from his mouth.

I stare at it as if I can somehow will it to fall, leaving burn marks on his skin in the process. Anything to get him to leave me alone for a while.

"Come sit up here on my lap," he commands, the tone forcing my feet to move.

Advancing to stand in front of him, I take in the glassy, bloodshot look in his eyes. I wish I could say it surprises me, but it doesn't. The clear liquid in the glass on the end table confirms what I already know. He's been drinking. Vodka, to be exact.

It's not his first drink today, and I know it won't be his last.

Moving to sit on his knee, I turn to face the TV screen and use the football game to distract me from the way my stomach churns. I tell myself over and over to remain calm and remember to breathe, all while wishing I was anywhere else but here.

Slow breaths, Ellie.

Inhale slowly. Exhale slowly.

He takes a deep drag from his cigarette and stubs it out in the ashtray. The smoke swirls around in front of my face. I hold my breath for as long as I can. He reaches out to pick up his half empty glass of vodka. Just before taking a drink, he tips his glass to me in offering. The grin on his face says it all. He thinks it's funny, like the last time I fell for believing it was water.

That's not a mistake I will ever make again.

Shaking my head, I somberly turn back to the TV. I can feel his chest vibrate against my back as he laughs before throwing back what's left of his vodka. I want to be mad at him but I don't have the strength to fight him.

Not anymore.

Wrapping his arm around my stomach, he pulls me back leaving no room between us. His hand runs along the underside of my chest, and it catches me off guard, causing me to tense. I don't like it when he touches me. I harken my ears for the sound of my Mom's car pulling into the driveway. At least when she's home, he doesn't bother me.

Sweeping my long blond hair away from my face, he leans down pressing his nose against my neck. Running his cheek along mine, the stubble of his facial hair feels like sandpaper against my soft skin. He moves his hand down my stomach, groaning as he presses down, rubbing himself against my butt.

Squeezing my eyes shut, I fight back the tears that threaten to fall. The last thing I remember is the grunting sound he makes and the words my father used to say.

Now they only cause me sadness.

Pressing his cheek against mine, he groans, "That's my sweet girl."

One

Ellie

Today

LOSING SOMEONE CLOSE TO YOU IS ONE OF THE HARDEST things you can go through. The moment reality hits you, knowing you will never see them again can be the most difficult part to accept. The finality of death has a way of chipping away at your heart, bit by bit.

You'd think by now I'd be used to it, I've spent most of my life picking up the broken pieces of my heart. But there is no guide to help you navigate through the stages of grief. Everyone has their own way of working through it, but for me what I wanted was to be left alone.

The solitude of silence.

I guess I've just gotten sick of seeing the look of pity on people's faces and their constant questioning whether I'm okay. What did they expect me to say? It's as if they believe

1

there's a difference in the pain you should feel between losing someone unexpectedly or knowing it's their time. I started to wonder if they even gave a shit. If I were honest and told them how I felt, they'd be in tears. We can just leave it at that.

I've spent the past three hours in the backseat of a cab. I suspected the driver was a lot like me, feeling weighed down by the constant need to fill the silence. If I wanted to waste my time with small talk and pleasantries, I'm sure we could chat about the rain beating heavy on the roof of the cab, or I could thank him for how fast he has managed to get me out of that godforsaken town.

I don't though, because what's the point?

The only sound that fills the silence is the GPS signaling we are approaching our destination. Pulling to a stop, I let out a deep breath as I look out the window taking in the dimly lit cafe.

It's been raining heavily all day, and the winds have started to pick up. Unzipping the front pocket of my backpack, I feel around for my coin purse, pulling out the cash I tucked away before turning to pay the driver. Mumbling a quick thank you, I pull up the hood of my sweatshirt as I open the passenger door.

Rushing around to the trunk, I heave my suitcase onto the ground as I situate my backpack. I have less than an hour before I board the bus out of here. With a seven-hour bus trip ahead of me, I use my time wisely, stopping for a coffee and a quick bite to eat. My stomach growls at the thought.

A bell rings as I open the old wooden door to the cafe. A wooden bar lined with barstools wraps around the front and tables sit around the outside of the room. It's small and quaint.

There's an older man reading a newspaper at a table off

to the side and a couple up at the bar laughing together as the waitress refills their coffee. By the looks of it, the weather must be keeping people away this afternoon.

With a kind smile, the waitress raises her hand motioning for me to seat myself. Pulling my suitcase along behind me, I maneuver myself over to a table in the back corner, the sound of the wet wheels dragging along behind me. Pulling out the chair, I choose a seat closest to the window.

The thunder cracks, drawing my attention back outside. Ominous clouds roll through the sky as another storm is brewing, leaving the sky an angry gray. I just hope the bus departure is not delayed. Another night here is not on my agenda.

I moved in with my Grams when I was fourteen. Rarely would you see me venturing out of my house, much less the small town of Garwood where I grew up. A smile brightens my face as I think back to our talks at her dining table and her hopes that this day would come.

"Ellie, promise me when you graduate high school, you'll get out of here. You'll do everything your father would've wanted for you and that I've hoped for you. Promise me you will no longer be held back by your fears and that you'll follow your dreams."

I always knew I would have to go at some point; I just didn't have the courage to leave her behind. She was the only person I had after my father passed away.

It was nine days ago she, too, left me. You'd think after all the losses I've experienced I would be used to it by now, but laying her to rest was the hardest of them all.

I decided it was time to make good on my promise. I knew if I didn't, my past would eventually come crashing down around me. I've accepted no matter where I am, I will always feel like I'm looking over my shoulder. The fear of the day he's released will always be there.

"These bars will only protect you for so long, Ellie. When I get out of prison, I'll find you. I'll always find you."

It's hard to move on from your past when everywhere you look, people remember what happened. I needed to start over, somewhere far from Garwood.

I hadn't given much thought to where I would go when I finally left. After heading to the library and browsing through Craigslist, I found a fully furnished farmhouse in a small town in Iowa. I don't have enough money to make it much further, but I don't need much to survive. It would do for now, at least until I could save up more money. Using the pay phone outside the library, I made a quick call where I learned not only was the house still available, but the landlord was also looking for someone to work at his store in town.

I remember the sense of calmness that came over me after I hung up the phone. I know my Grams was with me at that moment. The decision felt right.

So here I sit, thirty minutes away from boarding a bus and never looking back.

After I eat and pay the tab for my meal, I stuff my wallet into the front pocket of my suitcase. Making my way outside, I look back and forth before heading down the sidewalk, suitcase still in tow. Thankfully the rain has let up, but storms still threaten.

Nearing the bus station, I take in the short line of buses along the side of the building. Standing beneath the awning, I sling my bag around, taking out the ticket I had printed off yesterday. After checking the time on my iPod, I'm relieved to see I still have about fifteen minutes to spare before the bus pulls out of the station.

Right on time.

The wind has started to pick up, causing my hair to whirl around in front of my face making it difficult to see. Spotting the bus with the EVERTON sign on the front, I make a run for it, keeping my ticket clutched to my chest.

Picking up my step, I rush down the side of the bus where bags are being loaded. Out of nowhere I'm knocked back, losing my footing. Everything's a blur as I'm momentarily disoriented. My foot rolls as I crash into a hard surface just as two strong arms wrap around me.

"Whoa, hey there!" I hear a deep voice rumbled against my ear. I don't even register the words at first, too shocked by the sudden movement.

His hands are splayed against my lower back, pressing me deeper against him. Lifting my head slowly, I am greeted with a small smile and the most piercing blue eyes I've ever seen. My eyes follow the path down his jaw that is thick with dark stubble to the outline of his mouth. For a second, I let myself think about how it would feel to run my hands along his cheek as I checked to see how soft his lips are. If I hadn't already been struggling to breathe, the thought itself would nearly take my breath away.

It's embarrassing really, my immediate reaction to this man. A voice in the back of my head is telling me I should say something. Saying "hi" would certainly be a start, yet here I am just standing gawking at him.

The sound of his throat clearing shakes me from my reverie as he tips his head with a knowing smirk on his face.

"Sorry about that, beautiful. I'm not sure how I missed seeing you standing there." The dark timbre of his voice captures all my attention, causing my heart rate to pick up speed. It takes me a minute before I even register what he said, too busy staring at his mouth, willing him to speak again.

I could get lost in the gravelly way the words come out of his mouth and the feel of his arms around me. "Are you okay?"

"It's okay. I'm fine; it's okay." Realizing in my nervousness I had started to ramble, I mash my lips together to silence my utterings.

Keeping my palms pressed against his muscular chest, I let my fingers slide over his strong body covered in a wet t-shirt. Taking a step back, I break the connection needing to put some distance between us. Just as I do, I lose my footing again, knocking my suitcase over into a huge puddle. The cold water splashing over my feet is like pouring a bucket of ice over my head, waking me up. Two strong hands shoot around me once again as I quickly step forward out of the puddle.

"You sure about that, sweetheart?" he asks, keeping his hands pressed low on my hips.

Working up the courage to meet those beautiful baby blues, I see he is doing his best to fight off a smirk himself.

Asshole.

Nodding my head, I look down as I take a step back needing to separate myself from him. It's near impossible to get my wits about me with my body pressed against him. I can't hide the groan when I turn and find the suitcase full of everything I own, which isn't much clearly, laying on its side in a puddle.

"Ah, shit. Are you kidding me?" I groan, bending down to lift the handle of my suitcase out of the water. The only possession I care about is the one thing I can't replace, the photo I have with my father before he passed away.

Just the thought of ruining it has tears filling my eyes.

Unzipping the pocket, I quickly pull out the wallet as I press it close to my chest. I struggle to contain my tears of relief when I find it to be a bit damp, but certainly not ruined.

"Is everything okay?" he asks again, concern etching his brow, rubbing his hand along my shoulder.

I feel the light rain sprinkling down against my forehead as I keep the wallet pressed against my chest, shielding it from any further damage. My only response is a slight nod of my head as warmth spreads through my body from his connection.

"Here, let me help you," he says, leaning down to zip the front pocket and lifts the suitcase off the ground. I mumble a "thank you" as he steps around me, depositing my bag under the bus. The movement causes the muscles beneath his t-shirt to bulge, and I'm momentarily distracted.

I can hear him talking to the baggage handler. The sound of his laughter mingled with the soft sound of rain pattering against the concrete fills the silence around me. I'm so distracted by this handsome and kind stranger that I don't even pay attention to the rain beginning to pour down on me, leaving my hair matted against my face.

Once my bag is stored safely under the bus, he turns, keeping his head angled down, making his way back to me. When his eyes meet mine, there is a softness to them. It's comforting.

"Let's get you out of this rain, shall we?"

Two

Callum

"**C**ALLUM! I know you can fucking hear me, dickhead. Wake the hell up!"

The sound of knocking in the distance mirrors the incessant pounding in my head. Throwing my arm over my face, I attempt to shield myself from the loud thumping and the sunlight shining through the hotel bedroom window.

"Callum, I'm not kidding! You're going to be late if you don't get up and answer this goddamn door. I'm not driving you back to Iowa if that happens!"

Groaning, I roll over and look up at the alarm clock sitting on the nightstand. The time reads 11:52 and considering the way the sun is burning my eyes, I know I'm fucked. I have less than forty minutes to make it to the bus station, in Chicago traffic much less.

Climbing out of bed, I pull on my pants and head to the door. Swinging it open, I don't even bother to greet my brother as I turn on my heel and head toward the bathroom, grabbing my clothes on the way.

"I'm glad you finally decided to answer, took you long enough," he grumbles, the sound of annoyance laced in his tone.

"Fuck off, bro! I didn't drink myself into a pounding headache last night only to wake up having to listen to you," I yell back at him, sighing as I stare at myself in the mirror. My dark hair is standing up on the side of my head, and my facial hair has grown a little longer than I like to keep it.

After taking a quick leak, I change my clothes, brush my teeth, and throw everything on the sink into my toiletry bag. Heading back into the room, I shove all my clothes back into my suitcase and slide my phone from the nightstand into my back pocket.

"Alright, let's get this show on the road," I shout, pulling my suitcase behind me as I walk toward the door, not even caring whether he's behind me. In fact, I know he is, by the way he's stomping down the narrow hallway.

After the way things went down last night, I don't have the patience to put up with him right now. It had been just over five months since I last saw Mason during the holidays. After he sent me a text last week telling me he was finishing up classes, I decided to take a trip to Chicago to visit him.

I didn't expect my impromptu visit with my brother to turn into a reunion with my father as well.

Steven Reid was a well-known defense lawyer in the state of Iowa when I was growing up. His arrogance and no-nonsense temper made him an asshole in the courtroom. It was always his plan for me to follow in his footsteps and study law. The last time I saw him was when I informed him it wasn't going to happen. Instead, I was going into business with my stepfather, Randy Whitt. Together, we were going to run Whitt Construction back home in Arbor Creek, Iowa.

You could say the news did not sit well with him. He made it apparent how disappointed he was in me for my decision, and I made it crystal clear I wanted to be anything but like him.

Growing up, my mom was always making sacrifices for my father and our family. He would spend most of his day at the office and wouldn't return home until all hours of the night. He threw out excuses, like late client meetings or issues popping up on a case. Most of the time he would stumble in the door drunk off his ass, bitching to my mom about his cold dinner she cooked hours ago.

Listening to him yelling at her down the hall as I lay in bed, left me petrified at night. The way his deep voice would growl as he called her names and smacked her around left me with years of built up anger and hostility toward him.

If this is an example of the man he wanted me to be, I had taken it as a lesson in who I never wanted to become.

It wasn't until my parents separated that I saw the change in my mom. I was only eight years old but I realized it was for the better. The light in her eyes that was often overshadowed by sadness now shined bright. She didn't constantly stress over household chores or making the perfect meal. Instead, her time was spent with me and my brother. When she later met and fell in love with Randy, I saw her happiness in a whole new way. She glowed as if their love was overflowing from inside her.

Waiting for the elevator, my phone vibrates in my pocket. Pulling it out, I hold my thumb down to unlock it. As if on cue, a text message appears from Randy.

Randy: Are you on your way home?

The elevator dings announcing its arrival, as I pull the suitcase behind me, hitting the button for the main floor. While we make our descent, I shoot off a quick text in response letting him know I'm on my way to the bus station.

Randy: Travel safe, son.

He won't ever say it, but sometimes I think he worries just as much as my mom does. Ever since he came into our lives, he treated both Mason and me as if we were his own. My father pales in comparison to the man who raised me. Mason still seeks approval from our dad, and I can't seem to figure out why.

"Are we going to clear the air before you leave or are you going to continue to act like last night didn't happen?" Mason asks, picking up on my attempt to evade him and this impending conversation.

Running my hand down my face, I rub my weary eyes and will away a headache pulsating beneath my skin. I'm pissed my weekend with my brother had been ruined by my father's surprise visit.

Seeing him again brought back all those same feelings, and I couldn't hold myself back from telling him exactly how I felt about him. I know talking about this is going to turn into another argument, and I don't want to go into this right now.

Mason was young when they divorced, but it doesn't justify him always excusing our father's actions.

Deciding I need to avoid this conversation, I change the subject entirely.

"Are you going to tell me what's going on with you and the girl from the bar last night?" I ask, raising my eyebrow at him.

The elevator dings as we reach the main floor, and I move to make my way out. I want to laugh at the look of annoyance on his face. It's the same look he had last night when he saw Brea with her arms wrapped around me.

After having a surprise reunion with our father, I told Mason I needed to get the fuck out of there and get a beer. We ended up downtown at the bar where Mason works serving drinks. Brea approached me as I was throwing them back quicker than the bartender could refill them, wrapping her arms around my neck in a warm embrace. That happened to be the exact moment Mason came walking out of the back room.

It only took her a minute before she realized I wasn't who she thought I was. I'm a little taller than Mason is and, while I keep myself in shape working construction, I'm not quite as broad shouldered as my brother. Her reaction nearly had me bent over laughing. I can't fault her for it and neither could Mason. When we were growing up, we could've passed for twins. She was beautiful with long dark hair, but it was evident in the way my brother looked at her that she was his. Even if I were looking for a relationship right now, I would never make a move on my brother's woman.

"That's what I thought, Mase," I say, passing him, emphasizing the nickname Brea used last night. Mason despises nicknames or pet names, although he calls me asshole and dickhead like it's a term of endearment. The irony is not lost on me.

It's only fitting with the way things went down with my father showing up at Mason's apartment and the ensuing argument, that the end of the weekend would end just as shitty. The pounding still has not eased as I rub my fingers along my forehead, hoping to massage it away. I'm dreading the next seven hours sitting on a bus. It's windy as hell outside, and it's starting to sprinkle, causing rain to pepper against my face.

We arrive at the bus station just in the nick of time. Pulling my phone out of my pocket, I quickly attempt to check my messages, only to find a black screen.

"You gotta be fucking kidding me!" I mutter to myself when I find it dead. When I came back to my hotel room last night in a drunken mess, I remember wasting no time stripping myself out of my clothes, chucking my phone on the nightstand and landing face first on the bed. Not only did I forget to plug my phone in to the charger, but evidently, I left the charger back at the hotel room. With less than five minutes to spare, I am shit out of luck in picking one up before I board the bus.

This is going to be a long fucking ride home.

With my ticket clutched in my right hand, I slide my phone back into my pocket and set out to find my bus, keeping my head down away from the rain as I drag my suitcase along. It doesn't take me long to find it with EVERTON prominently written on the front.

Everton is about thirty minutes out of Arbor Creek and nearly three times the size. Don't let that fool you, though; it still isn't big with a population just shy of 12,000. Since I'm not used to traffic in downtown Chicago, I opted to take a bus out of Everton and left my truck at the station. Trying to follow directions with a bunch of people was not something I wanted to deal with. I'd end up getting my ass lost.

Depositing my bag under the bus, I turn quickly on my heel and am taken back as I collide into someone. It doesn't take me long to realize my arms are around the slender body of a woman.

"Whoa, hey there!"

With my arms wrapped around her lower back, I keep her steady to prevent us both from falling. The smell of her floral perfume and a hint of her fruity shampoo assaults me as I inhale deeply.

Once I know we are both on stable footing, I step back, but my words are caught, left lodged in my throat as I drag my gaze over every inch of her. From her long golden blond hair hanging loosely down her back to the magnetic green eyes and soft skin of her face to the shy smile. The woman standing in front of me is breathtaking in a simple sort of way. I can't help but want to keep her pressed against me. From the way her eyes are eating up every inch of me, I know I'm not the only one appreciating the view, causing me to fight back a grin.

"Sorry about that, beautiful. I'm not sure how I missed seeing you standing there. Are you okay?" The distant look in her eyes makes me wonder if she heard what I said. It only seems to last a moment though before she appears to snap out of it, connecting her eyes with mine.

"It's okay. I'm fine; it's okay." She talks so fast it takes a few seconds for me to catch everything she said. The softness in her voice is so sweet, so innocent it sends a jolt of lust straight to my cock. Now is not a good time, especially with the way her body is molded against mine.

With her hands pressed against my chest, her fingers brush along the defined ridges as if out of habit. It's as if it's the most natural thing in the world for her to be doing. My shirt is wet beneath her hand as the rain continues to fall against us. It almost seems as though she is focused on the way my heart beats rapidly beneath her palm. I don't say anything, feeling so overwhelmed by the way my body reacts to her and the adrenaline coursing through me, instead only responding with a smile.

She takes a step back, and my body aches from the loss of our connection as she stumbles in the process. Acting quickly, I shoot my arms out, grabbing her just above her elbows helping to steady her again.

"You sure about that, sweetheart?" I ask, just as her beautiful green eyes find mine.

That's when I notice her suitcase has fallen over in a giant puddle next to the bus. She bends down quickly to pick it up with a string of curse words flowing out of her mouth. So much for the innocent woman standing in front of me; it makes me want to laugh seeing her all riled up.

I can't help thinking of the sounds she would make along with her cries of passion. My attraction to this woman is instantaneous, as if there is a magnetic pull luring me to her. I don't know her, but something about her makes me wish I did.

"Is everything okay?" I ask. I can tell she is worried, her movements jerky as if she is frantic in her inspection. Running my hand along her shoulder, I try to comfort her just as her head falls back sighing. She doesn't say anything as her eyes meet mine, but I can see the relief pass over her face.

Quickly zipping up her suitcase, I pick it up and move to deposit her bag beneath the bus. Turning around, I find her with a small smile and her hand up shielding her face.

"Let's get you out of this rain, shall we?" I smile back, placing my hand on her lower back. With the rain pelting down on us, I should feel cold, but my body burns when I'm next to her.

I don't even know this girl's name and all I can think about is being near her.

Three

Ellie

ONCE I'M SEATED ON THE BUS AND AWAY FROM THE rain, I unclasp the front of my wallet and slide out the picture I keep tucked away behind my photo ID. Thinking back to the day the photo was taken, I run my finger along my father's cheek. It was one of the happiest days of my life. I remember the smile my father wore on his face as he made my favorite Mickey Mouse pancakes for my birthday. The way he held me on his arm, singing and dancing around the kitchen while the pancakes cooked away.

Blinking through the forming tears, I look back down at the picture in my hand. I've been walking around numb, emotionless since Grams passed. Turning my head, I stare blankly out the window with the photo of my father clutched to my chest, letting the tears stream down my face.

The emotions coursing through me now are threatening

to swallow me whole.

I hate the fact life has taken the two most important people in my life from me, leaving me in this world alone.

Movement next to me jolts me from my thoughts as a strong arm wraps around my back. I can smell him before I see him. It's a new but comforting scent, mixed with the smell of rain. Rubbing my fingers beneath my eyes, I turn and look up and see the man from outside the bus as he envelops me into his arms.

I don't react in the way I normally would. The old Ellie would lock her emotions away, covering up the hurt she is wearing. I would push him away and tell him I'm fine. Everything in my life has taught me not to trust people. I do none of those things because something deep inside me tells me even though I don't know him, I can trust him.

Instead, I let myself feel, and in that moment, God do I feel everything.

I feel the weight of the loss and grief pressing down on me. I feel the betrayal and hurt of all the events that happened after my father passed.

And I feel fear because the fear is always there clawing at me and my conscience.

Pushing it all down, I focus on the feel and sound of his heart beating beneath where my head is laying on his chest. The steady rhythm calms my rapidly beating heart, taking solace in this moment.

I can see him lean back out of the corner of my eye, staring at the side of my face as if he's checking on me. I want to look up at him but I know as soon as I do, the concern will be there and the moment will be over. I fight it off for as long as I can until I feel his mouth press against the side of my head.

"You okay?" he asks. The words are soft as I lean away from him, opening my eyes.

He is staring at my mouth, waiting for me to respond as I run my tongue along my dry lips. I don't speak, I can't form a word, so instead I nod my head.

He rakes his eyes over my face again, until they meet mine. Rubbing my fingers along my cheeks and beneath my eyes, wiping away the mascara in the process. "Oh, God," I cry internally as my cheeks heat in embarrassment

"Don't worry, you still look beautiful," he says. The words coming out of his mouth are spoken with such conviction. My stomach flutters as his eyes bore into me, causing desire to pulsate through me, pooling low in my belly.

I can feel my heart rate increase as I struggle to breathe. The rise and fall of my chest visible. He flashes me a wide smile, cueing me in that he's aware of how my body is reacting to him.

"Thank you…" I say, letting the end hang in the air.

"Callum," he responds, picking up on my question. He holds his right hand between us, which is kind of funny considering his arm is wrapped around my shoulders.

"Ellie," I say, returning his warm smile as I slide my hand into his, shaking it while taking in the feel of his rough skin against mine. The feel does all sorts of funny things to my stomach. "I think I'm just going to lay back and get some rest. We have a long drive ahead of us."

Letting go of his hand, I lean down to pick up my backpack off the floor. Sliding the wallet from my lap, I tuck my picture away before dropping it in my bag, zipping it up, and keeping it between my legs.

"Fine by me, sweetheart. I'll probably get some shut eye

too. I'll wake you when we make our first stop." He smiles, winking at me.

Nodding my head to him, Callum crosses his arms and leans his head back against the seat shutting his eyes. I'm surprised he doesn't move to go back across the row where he'd have more room. A man his size could use more space when he's trying to get comfortable. I don't say anything as I know all too well how vulnerable you can be when you're asleep. I'm relieved to have him close to me.

Pulling my iPod out of my pocket, I settle on a song before I lay my head back against the seat. Once I'm situated, I lean back and angle my head against the window; the cold glass feels good against my warm skin. My thoughts drift to what is waiting for me at the end of the bus ride.

I struggle through the first part of the trip to get comfortable and eventually pull a sweatshirt out of my backpack to use as a blanket. A couple of hours later, a large hand wraps around the top of my knee, jolting me awake.

"I'm sorry to wake you. I just wanted you to know we're making a quick stop before we are back on the road." I look up, seeing him standing in front of me with a warm smile.

"Thanks, Callum," I say, enjoying for a moment the way his name rolls off my tongue. Slinging my backpack over my shoulder, I smile up at him as I leave the bus in search of a restroom. My bladder is practically screaming for relief.

After taking care of business, I take advantage of the opportunity to stretch my legs and get some fresh air, sitting on the bench seat outside the Travelodge. It's early evening, the sun has begun to set, and the humidity isn't helping my already frazzled hair.

"Is this seat taken?" His deep voice vibrates through me,

as I look up to see Callum standing before me. His blue eyes are a stark contrast against his dark facial hair and tan skin.

"Not at all," I say, sliding over giving him more space on the already open bench seat.

We sit here for a few minutes in silence while he eats a slice of pizza. I can't help but admire the way his jaw moves as he chews. It's sexy to watch, and I fight the urge to run my hand along his cheek.

"So where are you headed?" he asks, raising his eyebrow in question. I know he is referring to where I'm going at the end of this trip. The realization of what this fresh start means for me and the fact I don't know this man snaps me back to reality. If my past has taught me anything, it's that the only people I could ever count on have either left me or betrayed me.

"I'm still trying to figure it out," I say, suddenly feeling sad at the thought. I know Callum didn't expect that answer or my reaction.

I don't return the question because I want to avoid where this discussion is going. Instead, I focus on people milling around outside before they board the bus. Callum takes a bite of what's left of his pizza and stands to throw his garbage away. Raising his hands over his head, I watch as he stretches preparing for another four-hour ride.

The movement causes the front of his shirt to ride up, and I can't help the way my eyes take in their fill of Callum. My body reacts to both his nearness and my attraction to him, appreciating the way he moves and the confidence he exudes. By the looks of the deep V hidden beneath his jeans, he spends a lot of time taking care of his body.

I hear him laugh lightly, causing me to divert my attention away from his tan skin back to his face. That smirk is back

in full effect. I can't help but want to roll my eyes at him because it's kind of ridiculous how good looking he is. He really
should come with a warning label, good Lord!

"I hope you don't mind but can I borrow your cell phone
charger on the bus?" he asks, sliding his hands into the front
pockets of his jeans. "I forgot to charge my phone last night
and left mine at the hotel I was staying at."

"Umm… I don't have a phone," I mumble awkwardly,
"But I'm pretty sure I saw chargers for sale over there," pointing my thumb behind me toward the lodge.

His brows furrow, as if he is unsure whether he believes
me. I'm probably the only twenty-something-year-old female
in the state of Illinois or Iowa; I'm not even sure where the hell
I am right now, who doesn't have a cell phone.

"You don't have a phone?" he asks, the surprise evident in
his tone, and I work to suppress my eye roll. "I mean, it's not a
bad thing. It's just most girls I know usually have their phone
attached to their hip. It's not very safe for you to be traveling
alone without one."

I can't help the irritation that seeps through at everything
he just said. Clearly, his first impression of me has been misunderstood. I don't appreciate the fact that he obviously per-
ceives me as a lost, helpless girl.

Like a steel rod in my spine, I'm stick straight as the words
he said sink in. How helpless does this man think I am?

"I appreciate your concern over me back there," I say,
waving my hand toward the bus, "I'm sure it looks like I need
some sort of protection, but I can assure you I don't. I've taken
care of myself for most of my life and have gotten along just
fine. No one gives a shit where I'm going, much less how to get
ahold of me when I get there. So please, save your concerns

and knight in shining armor act for someone else," I spit out defensively. Standing, I adjust my bag on my back and head toward the bus, effectively ending the conversation.

This is exactly why I wanted to be left alone and, as predicted, he didn't know what to say when I unloaded the truth.

People don't know how to react without their sugar-coated bullshit.

It's a little after nine o'clock when we pull into Everton. A small part of me was grateful it had taken this long to get here. The two planned stops ended up turning into three. I am just deflecting because when I think too much about what comes at the end of the trip, it scares the ever-loving shit out of me.

Trying to keep my mind off my future, I spent the rest of the time overthinking how things went down with Callum. I have replayed our conversation in the parking lot back in Chicago a hundred times. I can still feel his touch and how my body reacted to him. I can't help but regret the things I said back at the Travelodge.

I know he didn't mean to upset me. I've worked so hard to hide parts of myself from the outside world. Knowing I had been able to open myself up to him in a way I hadn't in a long time, had me feeling exposed. It's as if he was trying to see who I am beneath it all.

Callum didn't bother trying to talk to me for the rest of the trip. I guess I shouldn't be surprised and I can't blame him after the way I snapped at him. I'm sure he thought I wasn't worth the time.

As the bus pulls into the station, I sit up straight in my

seat hanging back as people begin pulling their bags out of the overhead compartments and moving to get off the bus. Once the coast is clear, I pick up my bag off the floor and quickly shove my iPod and sweatshirt inside. Sliding the straps up my arms, I make my way down the aisle.

The sun has long since gone down, leaving the night sky dark and the air cooler. I can't stop the shudder that passes through me, causing me to wrap my arms around my stomach, and I instantly regret my decision to stow away my sweatshirt. The lights in the parking lot are dim, casting a soft glow on the near black asphalt.

I don't even make it five feet away from the bus when I hear my name being called. The deep voice in an unfamiliar place takes me off guard, as I look around trying to decipher which direction the sound came from. I silently long to hear it again in hopes it was him. When my eyes connect with Callum, I want to sigh in relief at the smile on his face.

Pulling my suitcase along behind me, I head over to him, kicking the pebble rocks on the ground in the process. It distracts me from the imminent conversation and the realization that this is likely the last time I will ever see him.

"Hey!" I say awkwardly, not knowing what to say or why he would even want to talk to me.

Looking up, I let my eyes meet Callum's and don't let the fear of him seeing how nervous he makes me push me away.

"I know you said you were still trying to figure out where you're headed, so I don't mean to offend you." I can tell he is approaching the conversation hesitantly. Nodding, I urge him on.

"I just wanted to make sure wherever you're going that you get there safe. Can I give you a ride somewhere?" he asks, his tone showing a hint of vulnerability.

Callum is dressed in a black hoodie and perfectly fitting dark blue jeans; it's fucking unfair. His arms are stiff with his hands fisted in his pockets, likely to keep them warm. His shoulders are raised up, tense as if he is bracing himself for the way this conversation could go. I know I can't leave with him; I can't even put myself in a position to be alone with a man much less one I just met. Even if I feel like I can trust him.

People continue to shuffle along around us, but it's like nothing else exists as I let my eyes run over his face and take in the way his eyes sparkle under the lights. His hair is pulled back underneath a light gray beanie. The way his jaw flexes reveals the small dimple on his cheek, that's so fucking sexy, it makes what I should say next difficult.

"I appreciate the offer, I do, but my friend is going to be here any minute to pick me up." I lie, the words rolling off my tongue before I can even give myself an opportunity to change my mind.

"Thank you for everything, for you know, back there."

He doesn't even hide his disappointment, picking up on my blatant lie. I've never been good at lying, but I don't allow myself the chance to think about it. Holding my hand out in front of me, I force a bright smile and move to shake his.

"Thank you!"

Callum looks down, studying my hand as his brows crease before he looks back up meeting my eyes. He doesn't hesitate, his strong hand wraps around mine, and I relish the way his calloused fingers rub against the soft skin of my palm. Using our connection, Callum pulls me close to him so we are nearly touching chest to chest and leans down so his mouth is near my ear. His closeness sends waves of heat pulsating through me as I take a deep breath, inhaling him, but also to calm my nerves.

"I'm sorry, Ellie," he sighs. His whispered words against my ear send a jolt through me. My heart is beating wildly, leaving me struggling to breathe. I know he's saying he is sorry for upsetting me back at the Travelodge. I want to say it's okay; I want to tell him I'm sorry, too, but I don't. It's as if every word escapes me at that moment as he steps back releasing my hand.

Without a backward glance, he turns and grabs the handle of his suitcase and walks away. I want to call out after him. My eyes begin to water as they take in the way he moves, how his back flexes, and his strong legs eat up the concrete walking further and further away from me. It isn't until he turns the corner, around the side of the building that my rapidly beating heart drops into the pit of my stomach.

Instinctively, I reach up and clasp my hand in a fist around the compass necklace hanging from my neck. It's as if I'm clutching a lifeline to my Grams. Closing my eyes, I release a deep breath, reminding myself of the promise I made to her before she passed away and how it led me here. I came to Arbor Creek to start over fresh, and I don't think I'd survive if I let him in only to have him leave down the road when he discovered the baggage that came along with me.

"I'm sorry, too," I whisper to myself, opening my eyes as a tear trails down my cheek.

Four

Callum

3 Months Later

"**GOD DAMMIT!**" I SHOUT, HURLING THE WRENCH toward the back wall of the garage. The force behind it causes other tools hanging to clank together as they fall on the tool bench. Clenching my hands into fists, I struggle to regulate my breathing and control the anger coursing through me. Feeling a trickling down the side of my face, I reach around and grab the handkerchief hanging from my back pocket and wipe off the sweat.

I've spent nearly half the day working on my dirt bike engine, and I have come to the realization it's no fucking use. The engine needs a rebuild, and after all the money I've already spent on this thing, I'm screwed.

Hearing a grunt from behind me, I turn to see my

stepfather standing before me with his eyebrow raised in question.

"You better not let your mother hear you taking the Lord's name in vain. After the last time, I can promise I won't be around to hear about that one," he retorts.

I don't say anything, mostly because I can't promise my response wouldn't come off as me being a smartass, so instead, I just nod my head in agreement. Growing up, my mom didn't show any patience when it came to my mouth, and the last thing I need is to piss her off. I've got enough shit on my plate.

"Sorry. It's been a rough day. I'm gonna have to start over on the engine, and I'm not looking forward to throwing more money at it." Grabbing the towel off the workbench, I wipe up the grease and oil from my hands. "Have you heard anything back about the inspection over at the Hepp Property?"

"Elliott was working on it just before I took off. Said that he'd have the notes on your desk before he left today," he says, shoving his hands in his pockets. He knows this isn't the news I wanted to hear, needing to pass the inspection before we delayed the project further.

"Let's head out back to the dock. I have something I need to talk to you about anyway, and I think you could use the break," Randy says, turning on his heel, not even giving me a second to contemplate it.

Following along behind Randy, we make our way down the hill toward the pond. The pond is my favorite part of the property. A pavilion with a picnic table sits just off to the side, near the dock. It's surrounded by trees, secluding it from the rest of the land. Sounds of crickets and birds chirping off in the distance are soothing the thoughts weighing heavily on my mind. Lifting the baseball cap from my head, I run my fingers through my hair. The setting sun is leaving the air cooler, which feels good against my head. I let out a deep sigh, already feeling the stress melt away.

Growing up on the ranch, I started working for Randy, helping with the chores, feeding and grooming the horses, and cleaning up their stalls. I remember after long days like today, I'd come down and sit on the dock. Some days I'd ride my quad or the horses down to the pond, letting them graze while I watched the sun go down.

Randy knew how much I loved this place. When I was older and had enough money put back, I bought a few acres including the pond, and built my house on it. Last summer, my best friend, Wes, and I added a track where we ride our dirt bikes, but nothing beats spending my nights sitting on the dock drinking a cold beer.

The boards creak below us as we walk up the stairs of the pavilion to stand at the railing overlooking the water.

"It doesn't surprise me that you wanted to buy this part of the land from me. As a child, you wanted to spend all your time down here. It was always hard getting you to come back home," Randy recalls, leaning over the railing, looking down at the water as if he is lost in thought. "I remember the night you, Mason, and I had a camp out right here under the moon. Then it started to rain, so we ended up sleeping under the pavilion."

After my mother and Randy married, he took on more of a father figure role like any true man would do. He has always been there for Mason and me. I respect the hell out of him for everything he's done for us.

I know where this conversation is heading, so I just wait for it.

"You gonna tell me what's been going on with you and your brother?" Randy asks. His tone affirming a hint of frustration, so I know he must be asking because of my mother.

Called it.

I haven't talked to Mason since I got back from Chicago three months ago; it's not like we talked every day before. He is busy with school and work; I get it.

Mason had always tried to play a neutral party when it came to our parents. I understand that. Hell, I respect it, too. He was young when our parents separated, which means he doesn't remember the way things went down. I made sure to keep him hidden from some of it, not wanting him to deal with what I witnessed at such a young age.

My problem is how he expects me to move on like nothing ever happened, especially when it comes to my relationship with my father. I didn't expect he would lay such a bomb in my lap, having him show up during my visit.

He texted me a couple of weeks back, but I've yet to respond to him. I don't have much to say to him. The fact that he must have shared this with my mother doesn't surprise me for a second.

"Not much to tell," I say, wanting to avoid this conversation as much as possible. While I knew I was feeding him a line of bullshit, it wasn't something I wanted to entertain. The only good thing that came out of the trip was the ride home.

Remembering the bus trip brings back all the same thoughts. The ones that I haven't been able to get off my mind about Ellie since I ran into her at the bus station. Even the first night home I fell asleep to thoughts of her on my mind, the picture of her smiling face looking up at me while my arms wrapped around her. Her scent was clinging to me like a second skin. There were times since then where I would catch her scent, and I could swear that she was standing right next to me. I couldn't help but want to run my nose up the column of her neck just to get more of her.

It was a lost fucking cause though. Ellie made it clear she wasn't interested and was off to God knows where without even a second glance in the rearview mirror.

"Is that so?" Randy grunts, bringing me back to the present and this painful conversation. "That isn't what your mom thinks, ya know? She heard you haven't been respondin' to your brother. You know how much she hates seein' you two fightin'. Will you just talk to him, even if it's for her?"

We both let out a deep sigh as I run my hand over my face, working out how to even approach this. I knew it was coming. I may have thought I could avoid the conversation, but I should've known better.

"Listen," I sigh, looking out on the water. "I know how she can get, and I don't want her worried. I am not ready to talk to Mason yet. I'll stop by the house tomorrow and talk to her. Alright?" I state, just wanting to get this over with. I know she is upset, and I certainly don't want her to be worrying.

"Alright, son, I understand. I hope you'll come around though. There ain't nothin' that should be causin' you and your brother to be fightin' like that," he voices, clapping me on the back.

My phone rings from my pocket, giving me a much-needed reprieve. Holding my finger against the home screen, I unlock my phone and see a pop up for two missed messages; one from Wes and the other from my ex, Madison. Groaning internally, I click on the message from Wes.

Wes: Going out tonight to celebrate the girls opening their salon. Brodie's at 7.

A second message comes through has me choking on a laugh.

Wes: Kins said you better show or she'll drag your ass there by your boots.

Shooting off a quick text, I let him know I wouldn't miss it. The threat of Kinsley and Halle showing up at my door was enough to convince me to be there. Not to mention, I am in dire need of a beer, music, and friends after the way this day has gone.

"That was Wes," I say, mumbling to Randy. "I guess Kins and Halle are having a celebration down at Brodie's tonight for their new salon opening up on Monday."

"Your mother told me about that. I saw their sign going up when I was driving through town. You tell them both we're proud, will ya?" Wes and I grew up running around together, and Kinsley and Halle were two of our good friends. I wouldn't claim to be well-behaved, especially through my teenage years, but those girls were spitfires getting us into nothing but trouble.

"Listen, I won't keep ya. I know you have things to do. Just think about it, about what I said." Randy grunts. I can tell he doesn't like my decision, but he won't say it. He'll let us work it out like grown men.

"Thanks for stopping by. I'll be over early tomorrow morning to wrap up the invoice for the Kroger project. I'll take a look at the inspection too," I say, as we turn to walk back up the hill toward the house. We stand around in my driveway for a little while, just shootin' the shit before he takes off. Once his truck is backing out, I pull out my phone to check the time and see it's after six.

"Fuck, I need to get my ass in gear," I mumble to myself, realizing I'm gonna need a shower and something to eat before I even think about throwing back a few beers.

Staring down at my phone, I remember the missed text message from Madison earlier as my finger hovers over the unread message. Mad and I have a long history not worth repeating, we'll just put it that way.

Deciding to see what she wants, I open the message.

Mad: In town tonight. Wanna meet up?

It's been awhile since I've slept with anyone. Hell, since that day at the bus station, I haven't even been interested in getting close to a woman. The reminder of Ellie has me wondering where she is or what she is doing as my cock twitches back to life. With that thought, I lock my phone and slide it into my pocket as I head inside.

Five

Ellie

THE FLOORBOARDS CREAK BENEATH MY FEET AS I STEP
out onto the front porch. I quickly check my pockets, feeling for my keys and my iPod before I close the
door, locking it. Jogging down the gravel driveway, I head towards the main street heading into town.

A lot has changed since I moved to Arbor Creek. I've
started to settle in to my new job at Hudson Grocery. It's certainly not something I ever pictured myself doing, but I enjoy
it. I like the people I work with and the customers who come
in regularly. Everyone has always been kind and welcoming.

It's the middle of August, and the summer heat is stifling.
The smell of the country air and the quiet stillness around me
is peaceful. The skies are cloudy and a soft wind is blowing. I
know without even checking the weather, a storm is heading
our way.

The thought of storms takes my mind back three months. Back to the parking lot of the bus station. Back to Callum.

I wish I could say I hadn't thought about him since then. I wish I could say I hadn't done a lot of things when it comes to Callum.

Pulling my iPod out of my pocket, I slide my earbuds in and turn up Sam Hunt. I always look forward to the reprieve I get from music during my morning walk into town. When I get closer to Hudson's, I follow the sidewalks that lead me past the small shops and restaurants. There is a small bakery on the way I often find myself sneaking into even though I know I shouldn't. Time always passes by quickly when I walk, and before I know it, I'm turning the corner in front of Hudson Grocery.

The bell rings as I open the door, and I hear Kinsley before I see her. Her larger than life personality makes her easy to spot, even in a crowd of shouting people.

"There she is! FINALLY," she sighs dramatically. I can't help but want to roll my eyes. You'd think she has been waiting for me to show up all day, yet I'm still ten minutes early.

"I'll be right there," I shout back at her, making my way to the back of the store to clock in.

I will never forget the day I met the Hudsons. It was the day after I moved to Arbor Creek and I woke up to the sound of pounding on my door and Kinsley's infectious laugh. Swinging it open, I didn't bother to hide my tired state or lack of enthusiasm. I'm not sure if it was the fact that my hair was sticking up in different directions or the indication I was still sleeping at one o'clock in the afternoon, but it was clear they were concerned. I've never been much of an early riser. Kinsley was determined to fix that as she brushed past me to prepare a piece of banana bread her Grandma June had made just for the occasion.

Keith, my new landlord and now boss, insisted I call him Hudson as he apologized profusely for waking me. Promising to be out of my hair in a few minutes, he set out to fix my broken sink.

I hadn't even noticed.

Kinsley, on the other hand, was like a tornado the way she moved around the kitchen making herself at home, all while talking a mile a minute. I learned that Kinsley is Keith's granddaughter who also happened to work at Hudson Grocery, at least while she is finishing up college. Kinsley's older and strikingly handsome brother, Kolton, was with them. He didn't bother to introduce himself and instead set out to unload the lawn mower and got to work.

Although their visit turned out taking more than a few minutes, I didn't mind. It didn't take long before I was awake, although I wouldn't say I was nearly as energized as Kinsley. We ended up hitting it off almost immediately and have been close friends ever since. She is the type of person you gravitate toward; people just want to be around her. Her humor, though, I've decided is an acquired taste. I often wonder where she comes up with some of the shit she says.

Moving to Arbor Creek was my fresh start and an opportunity to open my heart again. It's a sad reality when everyone in your life has either walked away or betrayed your trust, in one way or another. It forces you to question the intentions of everyone around you. You learn to keep people at a distance, putting up a wall to protect your heart.

It can be incredibly lonely.

Kinsley has taken the wall I've had up and plowed right

through it. She sees through my front and never fails to call me out. I quickly came to terms with the fact that I needed someone like her in my life. Despite all the bullshit life can throw you, she doesn't let anything get her down.

I pull my name tag out of my pocket and pin it to the front of my shirt as I prepare for my shift and head toward the front of the store.

"Good grief, it took you long enough. Did you get lost back there?" Kinsley asks, rolling her eyes. You'd think she was pissed off if she didn't have a bright smile taking up nearly half of her face.

"Don't even start with me, woman. I wasn't supposed to be here until eleven. I wasn't even late!" I throw back at her. "Kolton told me all about how you use the back room to work on your homework. I know you don't get that many breaks. Wait, are you sure you're not getting lost back there?" I ask, feigning concern as I smother a laugh. I'd be lying if I didn't say I enjoyed throwing it right back at her.

Picking up the towel and disinfectant cleaner, I start wiping down the counters. The store is rarely busy, so I like to find things to do to keep myself occupied. It helps make the time go by faster.

"Watch it, Ells!" she smarts, looking around, making sure no one overheard. "That asshole promised me he wouldn't tell on me."

Kinsley has been busting her ass to wrap up her business degree before the end of the summer, all while preparing for the opening of her new hair salon. I know this because the past two times we've had movie nights, she ended up passed out on my couch.

All jokes aside, I'm excited and proud of her and Halle.

The salon has been our main topic of conversation since we first met and has been a dream of hers since she was young. She has worked hard for this.

"Calm down, your secret's safe with me," I say, winking as I continue to wipe down the counters.

"You're still planning on coming out tonight, right?" she questions, looking at me with concern on her face. "I promise you have nothing to worry about. Wes will be there and a couple of his friends, Reid and Brannon. They are good people. Hell, while we're at it maybe we'll even find you a man," she says, wagging her brows.

Throughout the week, I've struggled with the upcoming plans to go out to the local bar with Kinsley and her friends to celebrate the opening of their salon. The fact that I'll be putting myself in a bar, around people drinking, is difficult enough for me. I know I can trust Kinsley, but I still can't seem to shake this uneasy feeling.

Putting on a brave smile, I say, "You know I wouldn't miss it. Although, I'll have to pass on finding me a man."

Later that night, when I'm home standing in front of my closet getting ready, I kick myself for agreeing to this. Running my palms down my face, I let out a slow sigh of frustration. I don't have much of a wardrobe, even though Kinsley has been dragging me out shopping with her on more than one occasion lately.

Settling on a coral and navy plaid button up and my favorite pair of denim jeans, I sit on the edge of my bed to pull on my tan knee-high boots.

It will have to do!

Spending a little extra time on my hair, I opt to curl it, leaving it cascading in waves down my back. I've never been one to wear a lot when it comes to make-up, so just a little powder, mascara, and lip gloss and I'm ready to go!

It's after seven when I start heading into town, wanting to get there before the sun goes down. It doesn't take long before I'm walking up to the front of Brodie's where Kinsley told me to meet her. Thankfully it's close to Hudson's, not far off my normal path, so it was easy enough to find. Flashing my ID to the guy at the front door, he fastens a pink band on my wrist and waves me in.

Stepping inside, I stand against the wall needing a moment to look around. Considering I don't drink nor do I like being around it, I don't usually find myself in situations like this, yet here I am.

The entrance is off to the side, toward the back of the room. Tables surround the dance floor with a stage in the back for live performances. People are up dancing as Jason Aldean plays overhead. On the opposite side is a bar, taking up the full length of the room with a wall full of glass shelves holding alcohol bottles. The bar is bustling with people who are ordering drinks and talking amongst each other.

Spotting Kinsley chatting with a group of people near the bar, I head to where they are standing. In true Kinsley fashion, when she spots me she shouts my name and runs over to me, throwing her arms around my neck.

"I'm so glad you came," she shouts in my ear, jumping up and down excitedly. "I didn't know if you would or not. I mean, I know you said you would, but I didn't know if you meant it. C'mon, let me introduce you to everyone."

With our arms linked together, we join the group of people standing around the high-top table.

"Hey, everyone! I want to introduce you to my friend,

Ellie." Kinsley shouts over the music. I want to be embarrassed by her excitement as my eyes take in the group of people. That is until my eyes fall on the same blue eyes and dark brown hair that have filled my dreams for the past three months.

He's here. The electricity in the room changes as his eyes leave mine, trailing down my body. I can feel the heat of his stare as his eyes make their way down my length, taking me in. When his eyes return to mine, the desire I find shining back at me holds me captive.

Callum is here.

Callum

She's here. For a second, I question if my eyes are playing tricks on me.

Ellie is here and standing in front of me, and she looks breathtaking.

My eyes travel the length of her body, taking in every inch. Fuck me; she's beautiful.

Her hair looks different than the last time I saw her; longer, curled in waves down her back. It's lighter since I last saw her, making her look like an angel.

I can't take my eyes off her.

Making my way down further, I take in her long legs to the boots that come up to meet her knees. Those legs, damn it those legs. I haven't been able to get them off my mind since the day she stormed away from me at the Travelodge. I fight back a groan as my eyes follow the path back up her body, drinking in every inch of her until I meet her eyes.

The look of surprise on her face says she is just as shocked as I am. There is also something else there, a look of heat and, if I'm not mistaken, longing.

Sweetheart, I am feeling the same way, don't you worry.

I'm in the middle of a conversation with Wes and Brannon about my dirt bike as Kinsley introduces Ellie to the group. Immediately drawn to her, I effectively end the conversation as I shoulder past them and amble over to where she is standing.

"Well, hello there," I drawl with my eyes focused on Ellie, interrupting Kinsley which has Halle bursting out in laughter. I can't help it, though, as my eyes remain zeroed in on her. Kinsley does her best to cut in, not liking for a second being overstepped. Little does she know, her introductions aren't necessary. With a knowing smile, I stretch out my hand in greeting.

"Nice to meet you, Ellie. Callum," I say, tipping my head to her.

Ellie uses her hand, attempting to hide the smile that threatens to break across her face. "Nice meeting you, too, Callum."

That sweet as fuck voice has me fighting a groan. I don't let go of Ellie's hand or take my eyes off her as Kinsley continues to prattle on to her friends.

"She works over at Hudson's with me. Although she can't show up on time to save her life, so I have no idea why he keeps her around." Kinsley sneers, with her hand on her hip, earning her a laugh from Ellie.

Damn, I would give anything to hear that sound again.

"Is that right, you're working over at Hudson's?" I ask,

raising my brow with a knowing smirk on my face. So much for her not knowing where she was headed. I won't hide the fact it makes me happy knowing she has been living here this whole time.

"That's what I said, Reid. You gonna let her go sometime soon?" Kinsley jests, referring to Ellie's hand still wrapped around mine.

"Yeah, that's how I met Kins, well, through Hudson," she replies sweetly. I don't miss the familiar way she refers to Kinsley and Keith. "How is it you two know each other?" Ellie asks, pointing between us.

"Oh, Callum and I go wayyy back. I knew him when he was just a wild child, and well, before he turned into such a ladies' man. He was always easy on the eyes, though, weren't ya?" Kinsley laughs, throwing her arm around my neck and smacking a quick kiss on my cheek.

Thomas Rhett starts singing about dying a happy man as Wes comes up behind Kinsley, wrapping his arms around her waist.

"Baby, why you kissin' on my friend?" he teases, with his head on her shoulder throwing me a look. Raising my free hand, I shake my head, but he knows better than to think anything is between us.

"Come dance with me," Wes says, grabbing Kinsley's hand, leading her out to the dance floor. Kinsley looks back to where Ellie and I are left standing, her hand still in mine and a huge smile on her face.

Wes and I have been friends since second grade when he and his mother moved to Arbor Creek. The two of us grew up with Kinsley and our friends, Halle Keegan and Kyle Brannon. Kins and Wes were always crushin' on each other, but it wasn't until we were in high school when Wes worked up the courage to ask her on a date. Kinsley may have made him work for it, but we all knew it was inevitable. They are perfect for each other and have been together ever since.

"Hey, Ellie, you should dance with Callum. He's more than easy on the eyes. He's a great dancer," Kinsley shouts over the music, looking at me with a devious smile on her face as Ellie's head snaps up staring at me. I catch Kins throw a wink over her shoulder just as Wes quickly pulls her into his arms, causing her to unleash a fit of giggles.

Looking down at Ellie, I raise my eyebrow to her in question. "Well, you heard the woman. Can I push you around the dance floor sweetheart? I mean, I'm sure you're just begging to be wrapped up in these arms again."

"You know, for a second I was thinking about it, but I believe I'd like to get something to drink now instead," she retorts, turning as if she's going to head to the bar, using that sass she likes to throw around like a shield of protection.

"I'm just messin' with ya," I breathe out a laugh, pulling her back to me. "C'mon, baby, let's dance."

I don't give her a chance to second guess it as I use our connection to pull her closer, leading her out onto the dance floor, keeping my other hand pressed against her lower back. Turning so she is facing me, I draw her closer until she's pressed against my front, wrapping her arms around my neck.

Leaning down, I can't help but let my nose run along the side of her jaw, taking a second to appreciate the sweet scent of Ellie. She smells so much better than I remembered, like flowers and sunshine.

"I have to say, seeing you here has to be the best part of my day," I whisper against her ear. I don't miss the sudden inhale of breath or the way her eyes dilate when she leans back to look up at me as our bodies begin to sway to the music.

"You plantin' roots here in Arbor Creek or still not sure where you're headed?"

"I guess I don't know what the future holds. For now, I'm content with where I am."

I've thought about this girl more times than I can count since that day at the bus station. The fact that she is standing here before me with this sweet smile on her face, wrapped in my arms once again, has me sending up a silent prayer of thanks.

We dance for a couple more songs and not once does Ellie move to add some distance between us. At least, not until we're interrupted.

"Mind if I cut in?"

I grit my teeth in frustration, knowing right away who it is based on her voice. It's like nails on a chalkboard for me. Looking up, immediately my eyes connect with Madison. I should've known she would turn up here tonight, showing again how thirsty she can be for male attention.

"Of course," Ellie says, taking a step back.

"Not this time, Madison," I spit, annoyance clear in my tone as I pull Ellie closer. She should've known I am not interested.

"What, no hug or anything? I haven't seen you in months." Shooting her a look, I silently tell her to stop this conversation before it goes any further. The smug smile on her face says it all. She knows exactly what she's doing, and my reaction is exactly what she was hoping for.

The last time we saw each other was when she last visited her parents in town, almost nine months ago. I'm not proud to say it, but we hooked up in the back of my pick-up truck. We haven't been together for a few years, but while we were off finding ourselves, she always seemed to find her way back into my bed.

That's all it was, though, just sex.

"Callum, it's okay. Go ahead and dance with your friend." Ellie smiles, looking up at me beneath her long eyelashes. "I'm going to head up, get a drink, and chat with Kinsley."

Stepping back, she breaks the connection, and immediately my body feels the loss. A look of hurt crosses over Ellie's face but is quickly replaced with a reassuring smile, as she sashays over to the bar where Kinsley is seated.

Turning to Madison, I shake my head in frustration as she holds out her hand. Pressing herself in close, Madison comes just below my chin. Looking over her, my eyes connect with Ellie's. I wink at her, and she shakes her head, turning her attention back to Kinsley.

"I've missed you, Callum. When are we going to get together and catch up?" Madison whines. Good God, I don't remember the sound of her voice being this annoying.

Keeping my right hand clasped with her left, I wrap my arm around Madison's waist, making sure to keep enough space between us. We move along to the beat of the music, swaying in a circle. Throughout the song, Madison continues to try and persuade me into coming home with her tonight.

"Callum, don't you remember when we used to dance like this on the bed of your pick-up truck down by the pond?" Madison inquires, tilting her head back to look up at me.

"Yeah, Mad, I do, but those days are over now. They're in the past," I say with conviction.

Keeping my face angled down toward her shoulder, I use

only my eyes to seek out Ellie from across the crowded bar. Once again, our eyes connect before contact is broken as I watch her slide down from her seat and walk over to the bar to order a drink. A feeling of worry takes root in the pit of my stomach as I see someone slide in next to her at the bar. Quickly, I recognize the person next to her, as anger sets it.

"Damn it," I mutter to myself. "I'm sorry, Mad, but I gotta go."

Jeff Sahls.

Jeff and I have a rather lengthy history, going back to our high school days where we fought over the same girl. Madison.

Frustrated with the course the night has taken, I keep my distance, making my way over to the table where Wes and Brannon are seated, all while focusing my eyes directly on her. Although Ellie has her body angled away from me, I can see her face from where I'm standing. The soft smile she has on display for him has me kicking myself for letting her get away from me tonight, even for a minute.

After ordering a beer from one of the waitresses, I chug most of it and slam it down on the table.

"Whoa, Reid, you alright?" Brannon asks, but I don't even respond as my eyes fall back on Ellie. She is laughing at something Jeff said as he moves in closer to her ear. I clench my jaw to stop from yelling at him from across the bar, causing a scene. This girl has been on my mind for the past three months, and the second I find her again, she is off talking to the one person I hate more than anyone else in this world.

I can't say or do anything though, because as much as I feel connected to Ellie, she isn't mine.

"You could get up and go talk to her, ya know?" Kinsley

says, drawing my attention away from Ellie. "Listen, I don't know her whole story, but from what I've gathered, she's been dealt a shitty hand. She's a good person."

I know she is just looking out for Ellie, and I'm relieved. Ellie deserves to have people on her side, taking care of her, even if she may not want to accept it.

"You don't have to tell me what I already know," I say as I slide off my barstool and saunter over to where Ellie is seated at the bar.

"Excuse me, Ellie. Can I talk to you for a minute?" I ask, leaning in close to her ear. The music is loud, giving me an excuse for the closeness. A spark of electricity just from having her near jolts right through me, and I can't help but smile when I hear the hitch in her breath. She hasn't been able to hide her reaction to me.

Nodding her head, she turns around on her barstool as she places her hand in mine. She picks up her drink, which looks like lemonade, and carries it with her. I want to turn around and give cocksucker the finger, but Ellie deserves better than that. As I lead her away from the bar, I don't even bother to see if she says goodbye.

Moving so we are alone off to the side of the bar, I turn and pull her close to me again. I just need to feel her body pressed against mine. I don't know if what I saw was hurt, but I need to make everything right with her.

"I'm sorry," I say, not wasting a second of time. "She is just an old friend." Placing my hand on her hip, drawing her closer, needing to feel her body heat against mine.

"Callum, you have nothing to be sorry for. You don't have to explain yourself to me. You can dance with whomever you want." Sam Hunt starts to play, and I use the opportunity to have her body molded against mine.

"You may not think so, baby, but you need to know that you're the only one I want to be dancing with tonight. Dance with me," I ask, taking her drink from her hand, setting it on the table next to us. Looking up at me, the look that passes over her face softens, and I know I broke through to her.

Wrapping my arms around her as she slides her arms to my neck once again, I tighten my hold and pull her in. Pressing her closer to my front, my lips tracing the line up her neck to her ear, I sing along to the lyrics of the song while dancing slowly.

"Callum," she sighs.

Placing a soft kiss on her collarbone, I can hear her breath get caught in her throat.

"Ellie," I whisper back along her ear, running my hands along her lower back, enjoying the feel of her body shivering beneath my fingertips.

Keeping her forehead against my neck, I can feel her heavy breathing against my jaw. The rise and fall of her chest confirms she is feeling the pull between us, too.

It isn't until the song changes and she leans back, that it hits me where we are. Somehow, I found a way to get lost in her.

"Um… I think I'm going to step outside for a minute. Get some fresh air; it's warm in here," she says, looking around the room for the exit.

"Of course, let me walk you. I need to use the restroom, but I'll meet you outside." More like I need to take care of this growing problem. A problem that she undoubtedly felt when I had her pressed against me like she was a second skin.

I follow her toward the back of the bar; there's an urgency in her step. It isn't until she slips outside that I realize for the second time tonight I've made the mistake of letting her get away from me.

Six

Ellie

MAKING A MOVE TOWARD THE BACK OF THE BAR, I rush to escape the moment. I've never felt the way I just did, the way I still do. Being close to someone has never made me feel the way I felt wrapped in his arms. My nerve endings feel fried. I can feel him everywhere; every inch of my body is alive under his touch, like a zap of electricity coursing through me.

Stepping outside, I inhale a deep breath of fresh air, letting the cool night breeze wash over me. Leaning up against the side of the bar, I close my eyes and take a minute to clear my head.

I can't deny this feeling or attraction to him. The only other time I felt like this with someone was when we ran into each other that day at the bus station. I couldn't even help but feel jealous watching him dance with his friend. It was totally unlike me, yet I used the opportunity to distract myself from those jealous pangs by making conversation with the guy at the bar.

He started off as a complete gentleman, but when he wrapped his arms around me, panic set in. Before I knew it, Callum was there to save me.

Just like the day at the bus station.

"Looks like we have similar taste in men." The raspy voice sounds like nails on a chalkboard, drawing my attention to the woman standing before me. It takes me a second to recognize her under the dim lights, but I know who she is. Madison, I think her name is? She raises her lip, sneering, as her eyes rake over my body with a look of distaste.

Who the hell does this chick think she is?

"Excuse me," I spout, before I silently chastise myself. Normally, I'm very aware of what is going on around me. I feel like Callum has taken over my every thought since the day that I met him. I can't believe I've allowed him to let my walls down.

My thoughts are instantly diverted, taking a deep breath as the scent of clover cigarettes fill the air around me. It's like all my thoughts escape me, ending the conversation. Looking around, I see several groups of people huddled together. Some of them smoking, but the strong scent wraps around me like a vise threatening to choke me. I feel like I can't escape it. I need to escape it.

Running down the side of the building, I'm relieved when I see a cab parked along the curb. This is the last place I should be. I need to remember what I'm doing and why I'm in Arbor Creek in the first place. I needed to get away from my past, and at the first look of his gorgeous blue eyes, he was able to distract me.

Without thinking, I quickly open the back door of the cab and rattle off my address, thanking the driver for a ride. The drive home is quiet, once again I'm thankful for the silence. I can't help but feel guilty for leaving without saying goodbye. I don't want Kinsley to worry about me. I'm fine, though; I can take care of myself.

I feel like I'm trying to convince myself of that more than anyone.

When I wake up the next morning, I stay in bed longer than I normally do, especially on a work day. I didn't sleep well last night; I tossed and turned battling my thoughts. I kept replaying the night, not believing I have lived for three months in Arbor Creek without knowing Callum was this close to me.

So much for living in a small town.

I keep thinking about the look in his eyes when he saw me and how my body responded to his hands on my hips once again. The way my breath caught as he ran his nose down my neck. Getting lost in my thoughts, my fingertips draw the path Callum made, replaying his whispered lyrics in my ear for only me to hear. Just the memory of him has a jolt of lust running through my bloodstream.

Even with the weight of the world on me, I still feel high on him.

Thinking back to the way I left, just tucked tail and ran, leaves me with a ball of guilt sitting in the pit of my stomach. Kinsley has been such a good friend to me since I moved here, and I feel terrible that I just walked out without even saying goodbye. Remembering Kinsley would be working with Halle at the salon today, preparing for their grand opening on Monday, I decide to stop by to see her on my way to work.

Dragging my ass out of bed, I hop into the shower to clean and get myself ready. Opting to wear my hair up in a top bun, I leave a few tendrils of hair down around my face. Keeping it light on the make-up, I stick to my basic khaki shorts and a pale pink button-up shirt.

Arriving at the salon an hour later, I can hear the music playing through the open window. A bell chimes when I walk through the side door. I can't help but smile at how far it's come since the first time I was here. The walls of the salon are brick with two large mirrors taking over the length of the wall. The room has a rustic farmhouse feel to it with black iron accents. It's cozy and warm.

"Ells, hey! Gimme just a second," she yells, peeking her head out from the back room. Walking around the salon, I look at all the photos adorning the walls. The sound of muffled grunts behind me have me spinning on my heel to see Kinsley carrying two large boxes in her arms.

Quickly rushing over to help her, I take one of the boxes as she mumbles out "thanks". Following behind her, we walk up to the front near the shelves, depositing the boxes against the wall.

Dusting off her hands on her pants, she turns with her hands on her hips throwing me a glare. I knew this was coming, good thing I prepared for it.

"What?" I throw back, putting my hand on my hip, tossing her a smug smile in greeting.

"You care to share where you took off to last night like the devil was hot on your heels?" she retorts, heavy on the sass.

I knew the way I left last night without even saying goodbye wasn't going to sit well with her.

Avoiding eye contact I look away, clear my throat, and it comes out sounding more like a cough. This was going to be harder than expected.

"That's actually why I was stopping by. I went outside for some fresh air, started feeling a little light-headed, and I needed to get out of there."

It wasn't like I was lying to her.

Looking up at her, Kinsley raises her eyebrow and narrows her eyes at me questioning. I know she isn't buying what I'm trying to sell. Shaking her head at me, she straps on her sarcastic smile as she crosses her arms. "You haven't quite convinced me yet. Keep going." Nodding her head and waving me to continue.

I want to groan, but it's no use. Instead, I decide to stick with honesty being the best policy.

"Listen, it was shitty of me not to say goodbye before I left last night. The last thing I wanted was to worry you or dip out like a jerk. I just needed to get out of there." I look up meeting her eyes, letting her see the truth in my words. "I want you to know how proud of you I am."

Letting out a deep sigh, she walks over tossing her arms around my neck. "You're lucky I love you and that I know people," she mumbles, squeezing me. The movement takes me off guard, delaying my reaction before I raise my arms circling her waist.

"What in the hell is going on here?" Halle shouts, causing my heart to drop into my stomach, scaring the hell out of me.

"Seriously?" I mumble, but I can't help but laugh as I take a step back from Kinsley. Looking over at Halle, she has her hands full with a tray of coffee and a to-go bag tucked under her arm.

"Well, look who it is," Halle retorts. "I thought for sure after you went missing that you and Callum ran off together. He looked sexy, all rugged in those denim jeans. No one would've blamed you if you did." Halle is a lot like Kinsley in that she has no problem telling you what's on her mind. The difference between the two of them is Halle is unapologetic in her honesty and lacks a filter.

Case in point.

"I agree, you two hit it off pretty quick. You looked cozy over there in the corner last night. Care to share with us how that happened?"

"Nothing happened. Callum asked me to dance so we danced." I sigh, all while feeling the heat rise beneath my skin. Even the thought of Callum last night brings me back to how I felt at that moment and my heart starts to pound.

"Are you kidding? You were dancing so close to each other I wouldn't be surprised if you got pregnant. So, what, you went home after that? I bet your hand hurt after that workout." Halle calls over her shoulder, making her way to her station. She sets the coffee on the counter before sitting in her chair, spinning around to face us.

"Anyway, after you left he seemed concerned about you making it home safely. He never outright said it, he just kept reiterating that he knew you could take care of yourself. Any idea why he would ask me why you still don't have a phone?"

I can feel Kinsley's eyes burning into the side of my face waiting for my response. Crossing my arms around my middle, I clutch my right hand around the pendant of my necklace, replaying the conversation I had with Callum at the bus station.

"I've taken care of myself for most of my life and have gotten along just fine without a phone. No one gives a shit where I'm going, much less how to get ahold of me when I get there."

"He called Kolton from the bar and asked him to drive by your house to check on you. We knew you made it home because your lights were on."

There are so many questions I can hear in her voice, questions I'm not prepared to answer, mostly because I feel terrible for how I've treated him. Ever since the first day I met Callum he has looked out for me, shown more concern for me than anyone other than my father and Grams have.

I've done nothing but thrown his kindness back in his face.

Looking up, I meet Kinsley's eyes, and I know she can see it there plain as day on my face. She knows from what little I've told her about my past and the reason why I came to Arbor Creek that I can't do it.

I can't open up to him, let him in.

"Well, at least one of us got some action last night." Halle smiles as she takes a drink of her coffee, and I'm grateful for the change in conversation. "You'll never guess who I went home with."

"Who?"

"The Uber driver. Fuck, I can't remember his name. The one from Canada."

Kinsley doesn't appear to be the least bit shocked as she turns back to the stack of boxes, unloading them. "Casey! Halle, his name is Casey." The words sound like she is annoyed, but her tone implies this is not something she is surprised by.

"Ahh yes, Casey! Anyway, he picked me up from Brod's

last night and gave me a ride." She smiles, picking up on the double meaning as she opens the wrapper to her sandwich and takes a bite all while she continues to spin in her chair. I can't begin to understand how she can twirl around while eating, the thought making me nauseous.

"He was sweet, though, even knowing I kept calling him Canada. I was drunk so I don't remember much else."

"You know, he could be potential dating material if I didn't wake up this morning utterly annoyed with Pop Tart crumbles all over my bed. The asshole ate Pop Tarts in my bed! Who the hell does that? Let me just say, there is nothing sexy about waking up to jelly crumbs stuck to the side of your face."

"Good grief, I can't handle you today," Kinsley says as she bends down and picks up several bottles of shampoo in her hands, continuing to line them up on the shelf. "Wes is having a bonfire tonight, which means several of his guy friends will be there. Maybe you'll find one there who won't leave Pop Tart crumbs in bed."

Loading up several bottles into her arms again, Kinsley turns back around facing me. The smug look on her face says it all.

"Oh, and Ellie, after last night I'm expecting you to be there, too. It's an end of the summer thing; we've been doing it for years. Before you think about blowing it off, just know that I've been asked to make sure you'll be there."

Callum.

Seven

Callum

STANDING IN THE SHOWER, I LEAN MY HEAD BACK AND let the water beat down on my face and shoulders hoping to ease the stress of the day. So much has happened today and the fact that I got shit for sleep last night isn't helping anything. I spent most of the night tossing and turning; it was like my mind was on repeat, thoughts of Ellie running through my head.

Thinking about how she reacted when she saw me; the look of shock on her face as the blush spread across her cheeks. The subtle rise and fall of her chest as her body responded to mine said more than words ever could.

I couldn't shake the fact she had taken off last night, vanished without a single word.

After we couldn't find Ellie, I was pissed thinking maybe she took off with the douche bag from the bar. He was nowhere in sight, and I couldn't fathom the thought of her being around that motherfucker. Kinsley kept reassuring me the bar just wasn't Ellie's scene. Calling up Kolton, I asked him to do a quick drive by her house.

The fifteen minutes that followed felt like the longest of my life until his text came through confirming she was home. I ended up drinking another beer just to calm my nerves, and then I called it an early night.

Worrying about Ellie wasn't even the tip of the iceberg today. Randy got a phone call advising we lost one of our big contracts; one we had been counting on. I'm sure you can imagine why I am looking forward to the bonfire at Wes's house tonight. I just want to chill by the fire with my friends and drink a couple of beers.

I hope that Ellie shows up with Kinsley. I want another chance to see her, talk to her, and if I'm lucky, to have her wrapped in my arms once again.

Turning off the water, I quickly grab the towel from the rack and dry myself off. After I throw on some clothes, I shove my wallet in my pocket just as my cell phone starts to ring. Not even bothering to check the caller ID, I hastily swipe the screen to answer it.

"Reid."

"About time you learned to answer your phone." If the words didn't give me a clue, I would know who it was just by the cocky, pissed off tone in his voice.

"I don't have time for this right now, Mason. What the hell do you want?" He's the last person I want to talk to after the day I've had.

"You going to keep avoiding me forever? Doesn't it get old after a while, running from all your problems?"

I would tolerate it if I knew he was just giving me a hard time, but he's not.

"Just cut to the chase, what the hell do you want?" I yell, the anger rolling off me in waves as I clench my fist around my phone.

"You know it's been two years since you've talked to Dad. I've tried to stay out of your problems but the way you spoke to him when you were here was bullshit, man. It's fucking disrespectful."

Are you kidding me? He wants to act like our father's a saint when in fact he's the farthest thing from it.

"I'm not the one with problems. He is! He has a fucking problem with drinking too much and putting his hands on women, specifically our mother. Now THAT is disrespectful, Mason! The only thing I want to know is why you don't see his behavior as being an issue?" I can feel my chest heave, struggling to breathe through the adrenaline coursing through me. I could use a couple of rounds with the punching bag right now.

"Dude, he has paid the price for that. How long are you going to rake him over the coals and crucify him for it? Maybe if you had stopped acting like an asshole and listened to what he had to say when he tried talking to you, you'd feel differently."

"That's what you're not understanding, Mason. I don't give a fuck what he has to say anymore, the same goes for you. I'm done with this conversation."

Ending the call, I start pacing the living room before taking a seat, elbows on my knees massaging my temples in an attempt to calm the anger running rampant through me. I did tell my father he was a piece of shit back when I was in

Chicago, and I don't feel bad about it.

Not for a single second.

Mason defending him just goes to show he doesn't understand the depth of his issues I witnessed growing up.

Once my heart rate is back to normal, I pick up my keys and do not waste any time heading over to Wes's house. Stepping on the floorboard, I climb into my pick-up and turn up the music to drown out my thoughts. Pulling into Wes's driveway a few minutes later, I'm not surprised to see the property lined with cars and people milling around. Wes has always had a summer wrap-up party; our friends would come out to grill, shoot off fireworks, and just have fun.

Wes bought a couple of acres of his own after he graduated from college around the same time that he opened his Motorsports shop in town. He spends a lot of his time fixing up dirt bikes and ATVs and has made quite a name for himself in the motocross circuits.

Wes's tan brick house sits about a half mile from the road, overlooking Arbor Creek. The wooden porch wraps around the front of the house to the side patio where the bonfire is going on.

Parking my truck, I saunter toward the front of the house, grabbing a beer and greeting several of my friends along the way. My eyes roam over the crowd in hopes of spotting Ellie, but she's nowhere in sight. Kinsley promised she would try to convince her to come. I just hope she's able to pull through for me.

Taking a long swig of my beer, I feel a hard slap on my back, causing me to cough.

"What's up, bro?" I turn to see Brannon standing next to me looking proud with a shit-eating grin. The asshole knows what he did so I return the smack on his shoulder in greeting.

"Not much, fucker."

Just like Wes, Kyle Brannon and I grew up in the same neighborhood. Even through my parents' divorce, my mom remarrying, and us moving around, we still always kept in touch. Brannon knows everything that went down with my family, and he's always been a damn good friend to me.

We shoot the shit near the fire, the heat providing warmth from the cool night breeze. Relaxation starts to settle in as we talk about the work I'm putting into my dirt bike and the parts I just ordered.

I can feel Ellie's presence before I ever see her. The connection between us hits every one of my senses, as if my body is on high alert and can feel her near. I continue to nod along as Brannon tells me about the quad he is thinking about buying as I let my eyes search through the throng of people for her.

When I finally spot her, it takes everything in me not to end the conversation with Brannon and rush to where she's standing. The pull she has on me is irrefutable. My eyes follow her, taking in her cut off shorts and sweater down to those long bare legs as she makes her way over to Kinsley and Halle standing in a circle with their friends.

Brannon senses the change in my focus as he looks over at me, tracking my eyes to where Ellie's standing.

"What's goin' on with you and that girl, bro?" That caught my attention.

"Who, Ellie?" I say, cutting my eyes back to Brannon. "Nothin', man, she's just a friend of Kinsley's."

"If that's what you say," he says, chuckling and shaking his head. "It didn't look like it last night. I thought I'd have to pull you off Sahls after I saw the look in your eyes as you watched her talk to him."

Apparently, he doesn't miss much. Just a friend of Kinsley's, my ass.

"Well, I'll let you get to it," Brannon says, nodding his head toward where Ellie is standing looking at me. Our eyes make contact as she flashes me a small smile, tucking a small piece of hair behind her ear. Taking her cue, I mutter to Brannon I'll catch up with him later and wander over to Ellie.

The sleeve of her sweater has fallen off her shoulder, leaving her smooth tan skin glowing from the light of the fire. Her right arm is wrapped around her stomach and her left is clutching a necklace. As soon as I approach her, Ellie looks up and immediately our eyes lock on each other as I flash her a small smile.

Kinsley and Halle both greet me with a hug. I recognize one of the girls in the group, Kelly, and her eyes light up when she sees me.

"Callum, it's great to see you. You look great!" Kelly says with a mischievous smile on her face, opening her arms to me for a hug following Kins's lead.

Not wanting to be rude, I return the hug in greeting. Kelly is a sweet girl; we had a night together back in college, nothing serious. She was left stranded at a football game so I offered to give her a ride home where we ended the night with a kiss. The look on her face tells me she is looking for a repeat.

"Hey, Kelly, it's good to see you too!" Looking over the top of her head, my eyes find Ellie once again. Only this time she's looking everywhere but at me, clearly uncomfortable.

Clearing my throat, I back up from Kelly as I move to stand closer to Ellie.

"How are you, Ellie?" I ask, running my thumb along the skin on her shoulder. I can't help but want to reach out and touch her. "It's great to see you."

"I'm good, thank you! It's good to see you again, too." The emotion I saw on her face is gone, the woman standing before me looking closed off as I've learned she will be when she's upset. It doesn't escape me that she doesn't ask how I am as well.

"I'm going to get some more," Ellie says, holding her cup up just as she excuses herself. Kinsley encourages her to help herself, and Ellie turns on her heel, heading over to where the keg is located.

"I'll join you, I need another one myself," I say, drinking down what is left in my cup. Picking up the pace, I fall into step with Ellie as she walks with purpose toward the patio on the side of the house. There is an urgency in her step, proving she is doing it to separate herself from me.

"Hey there, sweetheart, where's the fire? You alright?" I yell over the groups of people, jogging behind her to catch up.

"I'm fine, Callum. Why wouldn't I be?" The words come out sternly as she stops, turning and looking at me. The way she crosses her arms and the glare she throws my way confirm it's me that's the problem.

There she is with that word again. *Fine*. She's always fine.

"I'm sure you're fine. Hell, you do a fantastic job of making it clear just how capable you are of taking care of yourself. I can't help but point out that you don't sound very fine."

We are standing off to the side of Wes's house, away from everyone. I'm grateful for that fact because I have no desire to draw attention to us.

"Listen, I don't need you to be my keeper. Contrary to what you may believe, I don't need you to look after me constantly. Now if you don't mind, I'd like to get my drink and enjoy the evening with my friends."

Holding my hands up, I take two steps back from her, putting a little distance between us.

"I was just asking if you were alright after you stormed away from me. I was wrong. Clearly, you are *fine*. I'll let you get back to it. Have a good night, Ellie."

I don't hide my disappointment as I shoulder past her, walking toward the coolers. I barely make it three steps when her soft hand wraps around my forearm stopping me.

"Callum, wait. I'm sorry." The words flow out of her mouth in a rush.

Turning my head, I look down at her hand wrapped around my arm.

"Why?" I ask. The campfire casts a glow on her face and adds a spark to her eye, feeling like a punch in the chest.

I can tell she doesn't know how to respond. There is so much I want to know behind that question. Why is she sorry? Why does she push me away?

"I shouldn't have gotten upset with you, not like that. I'm not used to people caring about me or being friends with guys. Kinsley is the first friend I've had in a long time."

"Oh, so we're friends now?" I jest. Rolling her eyes, she moves to pull her hand back when I clasp my hand over hers, using it to pull her closer as I turn so she's standing in front of me.

"I find it hard to believe that you didn't have people who cared about you before you moved here. Don't get me wrong; you work hard to be strong and keep people at a distance. What I can't understand is why?"

She takes a second to think about my words, using her

other hand to clutch the pendant of her necklace. I'm starting to notice this is something she does when she's nervous. I don't know why but she seems like she holds herself back.

"I moved in with my grandmother when I was going into high school. She was the only person I had. She took care of me until it became the time where she needed me to take care of her."

Running her tongue along her lower lip, she lets out a soft exhale, hesitating. I feel like my heart is in my throat just waiting for the words that come next. I desperately don't want to upset her further, for her to push me away.

"There is nothing lonelier than having everyone you've ever loved leave you. I've learned that people are going to go at some point; I can't stop them. I'm not going to let anyone hurt me anymore."

I know how she feels to be disappointed by the people who are supposed to be there for you. I'm sure the question is evident on my face, but she doesn't say anything more, giving little away. The sound of music playing in the background captures my attention as the song changes. At that moment, all I want to do is to wrap Ellie in my arms.

"Dance with me," I say. It's a question but comes out as a statement. She seems to understand because she just nods her head. Grabbing her hand, I pull her closer to me so we are near the side of the house behind one of the trees. If I didn't know better, I'd think she needs to feel this as much as I do as she leans in close, wrapping her arms around my waist and pressing her cheek over my heart.

Angling my forehead down to where her neck and shoulder meet, I inhale her sweet floral scent. Swaying along to the music, I press her closer, relishing the feel of her body against mine.

"I could spend the rest of the night with you just like this," I whisper in her ear.

Drawing my nose along her sun kissed skin, I place a soft kiss on her collarbone and again beneath her ear. My hands run along her lower back, beneath the thick sweater that is draped down toward her elbows.

Her breathing starts to pick up, feeling the rise and fall of her chest pressed against mine. My heart beats rapidly as my thoughts have gotten away from me, thinking about what it would feel like to have her in my arms for one night.

Taking a deep lungful of breath, I lift my head from her shoulder and use my hand to tilt her chin up until her eyes meet mine. I want to see her see my face, to believe my words, when she hears what I say.

"You're beautiful, Ellie. I'm a lucky man to have you here in my arms. I have thought of you several times since that day at the bus station, about the way you felt pressed against me and what it would be like to kiss those lips. I wonder if they're as soft as they look."

Her gaze drifts between my eyes to my mouth. I see a look of desire on her face as she lifts her head up to me and runs her palm over my chest. If I'm not mistaken, I think she wants it, too.

"Is that what you want, baby? You want me to kiss you?"

The subtle nod of her head has me growing hard in my pants.

With my hand still pressed beneath her chin, I use my thumb to trace the line of her jaw down along the curve of her mouth. Letting out a slow exhale, she wraps her hand around my wrist and whispers, "Kiss me."

I leave her no time to second guess or over think this moment. Once her lips connect with mine, I know I'm fucked. The strangled moan she unleashes from somewhere deep confirms it, just before she opens up to me.

Adrenaline courses through me as all my blood runs south to my cock, pressed firmly against her stomach. I know she feels it, too, as she rocks against me as if seeking her own release. I'm consumed by Ellie.

Breaking through my thoughts and the euphoria of the moment, I look down at her as she works to regain her breath. Her eyes are glossed over with desire, and her lips are stained red from being thoroughly worked over. She looks sated and happy. I could live the rest of my days putting that look on her face and be a happy fucking man.

That thought should scare me, but for some reason, it doesn't. Instead, without thinking I say, "Go out with me."

She smiles softly as she looks back up at me, then back down at my lips as she nods her head and whispers, "Okay."

Ellie

The quiet sound of the bedroom door clicking shut causes me to jolt awake. I know he is here before I even open my eyes by the sound of his harsh breathing. I always sleep on my side, facing the door, for fear that once the quiet stillness of the night approaches he will come into my room. My hands start to tremble as my heart pounds out of my chest.

The front porch light is on, casting a muted glow through

the window. Sliding my hands between my thighs, I will myself to stay silent as my eyes adjust to the darkness. My body struggles not to shake for fear of what's to come.

He stumbles toward me, sliding the covers over and moves to sit next to me.

"My beautiful, sweet girl," he rasps, lifting the blanket draped over my legs. My body jolts when I feel his hand run up my leg toward my boxer shorts.

I squeeze my eyes shut as I struggle to hold in the tears filling my eyes but it's no use. Choking on a sob, I succumb to what is coming. I want to scream and fight him off, but even drunk, I'm no match for his strength.

"Shh, don't cry. I promise I won't hurt you. I just want to make you feel good."

Keeping my eyes closed, I push down the bile that rises in my throat as I cover my mouth. I don't know how much time passes, but it feels like it drags on for hours. I don't open my eyes as I silently tell myself over and over it's only a dream.

This cannot be happening to me.

That was the night my innocence was stolen, crushing my heart and stealing my soul with it.

Shooting up out of bed, I take a deep breath as I take in my surroundings. I am momentarily disconcerted, and it takes me a minute to realize where I am. I move the pillows so I'm pressed against the wall, facing the door with my right hand pressed against my chest trying to calm my racing heart.

"Inhale. Exhale," I say out loud, attempting to reassure myself I'm not in that house. In that room.

I'm safe.

The smell of smoke lingers on my skin as memories from last night flit through my mind. A time that should fill me with warmth and happiness is just one of many that have been tainted by him. I hadn't experienced a nightmare in months, not since before I moved to Arbor Creek. This place was untouched by my past until tonight. The only way I can rid myself of the nightmares that plague me is to get the smell of smoke off my skin and scrubbed from my mind.

Pulling back the blankets, I swing my legs over and step out of bed. Padding to the bathroom, I turn on the light and quickly undress. Once I'm naked, I stand stoically in front of the mirror.

There is nothing beautiful about what I see. I feel ugly and dirty.

Tears fill my eyes, but I don't move to wipe them, leaving them streaming down my face.

I know I agreed to go out on a date with Callum, and with all my heart, I want to be able to follow through with it, but I can't now. The past always has a way of catching up with you, and as much as I wanted this to be a fresh start, I need to remember that. The thought of not feeling his arms around me or how my heart races when he is near creates another wave of emotion as I choke out a sob.

Turning, I open the shower curtain and step into the bathtub. I adjust the temperature until it's so hot that it's nearly unbearable. Letting the water cascade over my face, I wash away the evidence of my heartbreak along with my hopes for the future.

I stand in the shower until the water turns cold and I force myself to get out. Once I've dried off and in a nightshirt,

I waste no time in ripping the sheets from my bed needing to rid the smell from my room.

I know I'll have to break it to Callum that I'm not going on a date with him. I just don't know how I'll find it in my heart to go through with it. A selfish part of me doesn't want to give him up. The logical part of me says no attachments to Arbor Creek, remembering threats made by *him* promising to collect what's his.

Curling up on the couch, the tears fall hard, leaving my eyes feeling heavy and tired. I fall asleep clutching my blanket to my chest, wishing away the way things had to be.

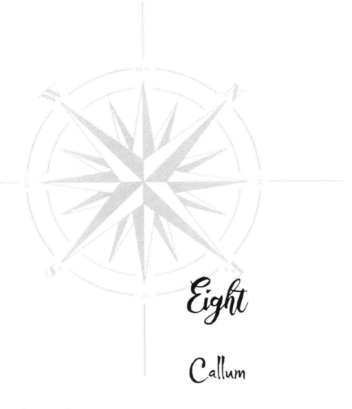

Eight

Callum

THE MUSIC BLARES THROUGH THE SPEAKERS OF THE gym, thumping a steady beat, drowning out my thoughts and the sound of my gloved fist hitting the heavy bag. Sweat trickles down my face and back, my breath comes out in pants as I unleash the pent-up frustration. The burn in my muscles is a welcomed pain.

Jab, jab, cross.

I have been coming to Grind's Gym since I was a teenager. After all the changes following my parents' separation, moving and my mother getting remarried, I was starting to act out. From fights at school to walking out of class to even staying out at night to avoid going home. Randy didn't let that shit slide though, at least not if I wanted to stay under his roof.

If it was a choice between staying there or moving in with my father, I think the answer was obvious. Randy saw what

I needed was a way to release the anger I had built up in me, which led him to introducing me to Grind's. Boxing gave me an opportunity to let out some aggression and clear my head, which is what I need right now.

With each blow, I feel the weight of the last five days lessen.

I haven't seen or spoken to Ellie since the night of the bonfire, but it's not without a lack of trying. When I got home, I once again couldn't sleep as thoughts of Ellie consumed me. When I woke up the next morning, I knew I couldn't waste another minute. She promised me a date, and I was using that reason as an opportunity to go see her.

What I didn't expect was for everything to change between us so quickly.

I hear the steps creak as I take them two at a time. With a bouquet of flowers in one hand, I use the other hand to knock on the door. The wind blows around me, causing the wind chimes to cling together as they move in the breeze. Ellie doesn't own a car, so it's hard to know for certain if she's home, but the bike I've seen her riding around town is leaning against the side of the house.

Turning to look at the window from the open porch, I can see the sheer white curtains blowing in the warm air with the television playing in the background. The faint sound of footsteps brings a smile to my face at the thought of seeing Ellie. I can only imagine how beautiful she looks fresh-faced in the morning. Seeing a figure moving through the glass window of the entryway, I decided to knock again telling myself that maybe she didn't hear me the first time.

"Ellie, it's Callum. Are you home?" I ask, knowing someone is here.

I don't know what it is at this moment, maybe it's the way my voice sounds through my ears, but I know something isn't right. A feeling of unease settles in my stomach.

Taking a step back, I turn to bend down and look in the window and see Ellie perched on the couch with her arms wrapped around her knees. Her head is burrowed in her arms as her small body shakes as the sobs rack through her body.

"Ellie, it's me. Are you okay?" I can hear her cries, but she doesn't move to look up or to open the door.

For whatever reason, I can't help but feel that no matter what I do, if I push her too hard or not enough, she is going to walk away from me either way. I know if I get in my truck and drive away, there is no telling if I will see Ellie again.

That fear has been weighing on my mind.

I've spent my whole life pushing people down a path, hoping that they will see the light on their own. In the end, all I've ever experienced was the disappointment as they chose a different course. I couldn't convince my Dad to stay with us, to be a better husband or father, and I couldn't convince Madison to choose me. At least, not while I still wanted her.

I'm not about to beg someone to stay, to be with me.

Turning away from the window, I lean against the side of the house as I rub my hand along my chest, trying to dull the ache from the weight pressing down on me. Every time people have left, they have taken a part of me with them. Sooner or later, there is going to be nothing left for anyone to take.

Leaning down, I set the flowers on the rocking chair on the porch. Turning back, I give Ellie one last chance to come to me. To open the door and let me in.

Brick by brick she continues to build the wall up around her heart.

Backing out of the driveway that morning, I fought against the urge to throw the truck in park and run back up to the door. To push her, to demand she tell me what is going on.

She wanted to be left alone, for whatever reason, so I gave her what she wanted.

I was so confident after the night of the bonfire that her walls were starting to come down, but I was wrong.

I stopped into Hudson's earlier this week to pick up a few things. They were things I needed, but it was an excuse to try and see her. I told myself maybe if she saw me, looked me in the eyes, maybe she would just tell me what was going on.

I still can't get over the look of sadness on her face. I didn't miss the way she looked at me as if she was cataloging everything at that moment. I couldn't ignore the niggling fear she was going to run - not just from me, but from Arbor Creek.

I know the feeling all too well of watching people walk away from you.

As soon as she saw me approaching her, she once again made a break for it. She took another piece of me when she did and only added to the heavy weight on my heart in the process. I have driven past her house every night since, finding comfort in seeing her lights on. I tell myself it's my way of checking whether she made it home safely. In all reality, I know I'm just checking to make sure she hasn't left town. Besides working and fixing my bike, I've been spending a whole hell of a lot more time at the gym.

Jab, jab, hook.

Jab, jab, cross.

I don't know how much time passes, feeling lost and zoned, out when I hear someone clearing their throat behind me, breaking me from my trance.

"What's up, bro?" Turning, I see Brannon and Wes standing behind me. A baseball cap pulled down low on Brannon's head and their gym bags slung over their shoulders. By the looks of their street clothes, they must've just gotten here.

"You alright?" Wes asks, his brows furrowing, taking in the sweat pouring from my face.

"I'm good," I say, and for a second I'm reminded of Ellie and her use of the words "I'm fine." If there is one thing my mother ever taught me, it's when a woman says she's fine, you can bet your ass she's the exact opposite.

That shit is like a trap.

Unstrapping my gloves, I pull them off one by one as I lean down to pick up my water bottle off the floor. Taking a quick drink, I pour some over my head, using it to cool my overheated skin.

"You sure, man? You didn't look alright the way you were going to town on that bag. This have to do with your brother?" Brannon asks. He grew up with both of us; it's not surprising that even though Mason's in Chicago, they would keep in touch.

"Fuck no, dude. I don't know what he told you, but he's the furthest thing from my mind right now." I can't help but let the frustration seep into my tone. Yeah, I'm still pissed about the bullshit that happened, but I'm not even giving it a second of my time anymore.

"Whoa. It's all good," Brannon says, holding up his hands, sensing my anger. "Does this have something to do with you and that girl?" He asks, changing the subject.

Wes starts coughing behind me as I turn to see him gesturing for Brannon to cut off the conversation there. I haven't had the chance to talk to either of them about what's going on with Ellie, but what is there to tell now? Apparently, Wes knows more about it than I do.

"You got something to say? Why don't you just tell me," I grunt. The frustration is back, causing my shoulders to tense.

What is it about this girl that has me wound so tight?

"Chill, man," Wes reassures me calmly. "Kins was just telling me about their girls' night they have planned for tonight. She just mentioned Ellie had been down lately, and she's worried she may be dippin' out of town."

Wait, so Ellie is thinking about leaving? I mean, I had a feeling it was coming. Heck, I expected it after our conversations, but hearing Kinsley share the same fears puts me on edge.

FUCK!

Balling my hands into fists, I turn and walk away needing a minute to collect my thoughts. I want so badly to just walk out of this gym, to find Ellie and talk to her. Bending down near my gym bag, I pull out my cell phone, quickly unlock it, and pull up my message history with Kinsley.

Callum: You think she'll leave?

Kinsley hasn't asked me much about our relationship. After that night at the bar, she could tell I was upset after Ellie had bailed. The words of anger when I first thought maybe Ellie left with that asshole. She didn't question it, though. The look in her eye when she saw my reaction, she knew it was more.

My phone vibrates in my hand as I look down at her message.

Kins: I don't think she wants to, but I believe there's more to it. I don't know.

Kins: We have plans tonight, and I'm hoping she'll talk to me. You know I'll do my best to convince her to stay. She's one of my best friends. I don't want her to go either.

Wes claps me on the back as I turn to face him, "I haven't talked to her since the bonfire at your house, man. Hell, you knew more than I did."

"It'll be alright, bro. You need to get your mind off everything. Let's go out for beers tomorrow night and watch the fights. Champs at 8?"

Like any good friend, they know exactly what I need. Tossing my phone in the pocket of my gym bag, I bend down to throw my gloves in before zipping it up.

"Count me in! I'm going to hit the showers quick before I head to work. I'll see ya tomorrow night at Champs," I say, sliding the strap of the bag over my shoulder as I turn toward the locker room.

Ellie

"I'm so glad we decided to stay in and do a girls' night," Kinsley shouts from the kitchen. I just heard her mumble an "oh shit" as pots and pans clanked together. I'm beginning to wonder if I should be concerned by the amount of noise coming from in there. If it weren't for the fact that she keeps yelling to me, carrying on a conversation, I'd be more worried. It sounds like she is close to bringing down the house all while making a bowl of popcorn.

"I am, too. I needed this!" I sigh, calling back to her, rubbing my hand over my chest trying to lessen the pain. Looking over at the beautiful flowers sitting in the vase on the end table, I feel the weight press down thinking about when Callum showed up at my house the other day.

I wasn't prepared to see him, to explain the reasons why I couldn't go on a date with him. I know he would want to know why, and he deserves that explanation. I just needed more time, but at this point it almost feels like I'm taking more time to convince myself why this is the right decision.

Kinsley has been worried about me this week; she called me out at work for pulling back lately. She is friends with Callum, so I am sure she knows something is going on. After the third attempt of her trying to make plans to get together, I couldn't blow her off. I wouldn't doubt for a second that she'd just show up at my door if I kept putting her off. Knowing her, she'd somehow find a way to get a key from Hudson, so it really was no use.

It's been five days since I last saw Callum. My resistance is starting to wear thin, and I can feel myself giving in. I haven't been able to stop thinking about him.

"I needed this and THIS!" she says, holding up a full glass of wine, raising her brows suggestively. "Are you sure you don't want to try some? It's delicious, and it helps me relax, which you clearly need." Kinsley takes a big drink, before raising the glass as if toasting for a special occasion.

"I am okay. I think I'll pass but thank you."

I can't help but laugh at Kinsley's choice of wine glass.

Before she came over, I warned her I didn't own any wine glasses. Flashing her hand to me, she reassured me she had it covered. I certainly didn't expect her to show up with a glass so big she could probably pour the entire bottle into it.

Now that I think about it, I'm sure it's why she bought it.

Pressing play on the movie, Kinsley hands me the bowl of popcorn as I fold my legs underneath me, settling into my spot on the couch. When we were deciding on a movie, I made Kinsley promise it would be a comedy. More than anything, I needed something funny to loosen me up and help keep my mind off Callum.

Just thinking about him makes my heart ache a little bit more. I haven't said the words out loud, mostly because I'm not ready to fully admit it, but I know I miss him. The way his body felt pressed against mine when he kissed me. I've never felt anything like it.

Shaking myself from my thoughts, I look up to find Kinsley watching me. It wouldn't take a genius to figure it out where my thoughts escaped to. Giving me a small, sad smile to match my own, she settles into her spot as I place the popcorn on the cushion between us.

"I can't believe you've never drank wine!" Kinsley sighs, sounding almost exasperated.

"You'd be amazed then. There are a lot of things I haven't done." I laugh. If only she knew half of what I've been through, maybe she would understand.

"Like what?" she asks, looking at me. "You are one of my closest friends, Ellie. I feel so comfortable when I'm around you. I know I can tell you anything and you will never judge me, never tell a soul. I wish you knew that it's the same on my end. You know you can talk to me, right?"

Nodding my head, I let my eyes meet hers again before turning my attention back to the movie to distract me.

"I've never had a boyfriend. At least not in the real sense of one." The look of surprise on Kinsley's face proves she never expected to hear that.

"Before your eyes fall out of your head and roll across the floor, I should clarify I have had sex. I'm not that innocent." I laugh, knowing exactly where her mind is going. Despite all the shit I've been through, I'm not so fucked in the head to where I can't stand a man's touch. In fact, I think in a way after high school, I found myself craving it for all the wrong reasons.

During college, I met a guy while I was working at the coffee shop down the street from Grams. Cameron was a nice guy, handsome in a boyish sort of way. He didn't ask questions or push me to talk. At the time, I was looking for something to fill the pang of loneliness I was feeling. Grams's health had started to deteriorate, and I was struggling to come to terms with the fact that sooner than later, I would be alone in the world.

I wanted to feel like for once in my life I wasn't as broken as I felt. Cameron gave me something no one else in my life had given me.

Intimacy.

As quickly as it started, it was over with. Cameron broke the news a couple of weeks later he was moving back home at the end of the semester. He tried to hang out a couple of times after that, but what was the point? It's not as if I loved him, I'm not that naive. I just couldn't help realizing once again, someone else I had allowed myself to get close to had chosen to walk away.

"I've never had a friendship like the one I have with you." I look up at Kinsley, and I can see the emotion pass over her face hearing the words. "Although, I don't think there are many people like you in this world," I say, laughing as I run my finger over the top of my nails to detract from what I know I'm going to say next.

"I've never felt the way I do about Callum," I admit. The words come out so fast it's as if I want to spit them out before I can stop myself. "It terrifies me."

The tears well up in my eyes, the truth behind the proclamation hitting me.

"Oh, honey," Kinsley says, setting her glass and the bowl of popcorn down on the coffee table. She slides down the couch, wrapping her arms around me. As soon as her arms are around me, I rest my head against her shoulder and let the tears stream down my face.

"I know Callum feels the same way about you, babe. Wes told me he was a mess the last time he saw him. He really is a good guy, and you can trust him. I know it may not be easy but you can. I hope you know how much we all care about you. Callum, Grandpa, Halle, hell, even Kolton. He can be a little bit of a jerk sometimes, but in some messed up way he wouldn't act that way if he didn't. You aren't alone, Ellie. You have people here who love you."

Leaning back, I look at Kinsley and I can see the emotion on her face. "Don't cry or you'll have me in tears. We are too pretty for that." She smiles, running her thumbs under my eyes, wiping away the tears.

"I think I do," I say, answering her earlier question. "That's why I'm scared. I am just afraid if I let myself care about people - you, Callum, anyone - that it could all be taken away from me." Kinsley's hand is still pressed to my shoulder, rubbing it reassuringly, urging me on.

Letting out a deep breath, I work up the courage to tell her everything.

"Alcohol symbolizes everything in my life that has gone wrong from day one. It's why I don't drink. My father had just graduated from the Police Academy when he and my mom found out they were pregnant with me. My dad told her he wanted to take care of her, of us, and not even two months later, they were married."

"He loved her more than anything. There are little things about him I remember. Like how he would always dance with us in the kitchen or twirl her hair while she curled up into his side on the couch. It was two days after my ninth birthday when a drunk driver killed him. He had left work early because I had gotten sick and was in a rush to get home. The driver had crossed the median and hit him head-on when he was driving home from his shift. My mom was never the same after his death. It's ironic you know, that alcohol played a role in my father's death, and it's the same reason why I haven't spoken to her in almost eight years."

I can see the confusion on Kinsley's face as if she is trying to piece together where I'm going with this. I don't think she can because no sane person could make up this level of screwed up.

"I have almost begun to forget what she was like before the alcohol. In the back of my mind, I would tell myself she was hurt, heartbroken, and that she was using it to numb the pain. It was like she was a different person, though. Eventually, she started dating, bringing around a new guy in what felt like every couple of weeks. Most of her boyfriends weren't too bad;

I mean they left me alone, and that's all I could ask for. She had started drinking after he passed, but it wasn't until she began dating Royal that it escalated. The drinking, the fighting. It was all just a recipe for disaster really."

I don't know if Kinsley is expecting what's next, and I don't want to see the look of disgust or pity on her face. It's the same look that led me to leave Garwood and the whispers of the past I carried with me.

"First it started out as groping over my clothes, either when my mom was passed out or when she went to the store. When she lost her job, she was home more, and I think he felt like it was harder for him to be alone with me. He started coming into my room in the middle of the night. There were times where I would wake up to him touching me, and then there were times where I knew he came in and I never even woke up," I say. The tears are back, flowing freely down my face. Wrapping my hand around my necklace, I close my eyes just as the sob escapes me.

"Jesus," Kinsley whispers, wrapping her arms around me once again. "I'm so sorry, Ellie. I had no idea you had been carrying all of this with you." Her voice quivers as if she is fighting off tears of her own.

It hasn't been a secret, what happened to me, for a long time. That's what happens when you live in a small town. Secrets don't last long. Kinsley is the only person I've trusted opening myself up to besides Grams.

"It continued to happen for about two years before I worked up the courage to tell Grams. At first, I started going over to her house more often, just to get away from him. One day, I walked to her house after school and asked if I could stay at her house for the night. I remember the look on her face; I hadn't spent the night at her house since I was little. I just knew I couldn't do it; I couldn't go back there. So, I told her everything."

"He always told me no one would believe me and that my mother would leave, choose him. After so long, I believed him. Come to think of it, he wasn't lying. She blamed me for everything. She said I was lying about the abuse and said it was my fault my dad had been driving on that road when he was hit."

I can hear the hitch in her voice hearing the rest of it, although she tries to cover it up and be strong for me. As much as I've always hated the way people have shown pity over me, I know with Kinsley it's different. The emotions she's feeling come from a place of sadness for me, and I feel it as she envelops me in her arms.

"Ellie, you are one of the strongest people I've ever known. I hope you know none of this is your fault, none of it! I'm so sorry for everything you've been through, for what you've had to deal with on your own. Not anymore, though," she says, the words hold so much emotion and conviction as tears well up in her eyes. I can feel the power behind them. "I meant what I said earlier. We all love you and are here for you. This is your home now. You are not alone. Not anymore."

Nodding my head, I give her a sad smile as her arms wrap around me once again. I let the feel of her words and the warmth of her hug soak in, and for the first time in a long time, I let myself believe them.

Nine

Callum

PULLING MY TRUCK INTO THE PARKING SPACE AT Champions, I shift it into park and quickly check my phone. I don't know why I bother at this point. Ellie doesn't even have a phone, which leaves little opportunity to contact me. I guess I just hoped after leaving the flowers at her door, she would find a way to reach out.

Waking up this morning, the frustration I had been feeling was gone and all I was left with was sadness and longing. I crave the way she looked at me the night of the bonfire. Her eyes full of desire lit a spark in me; it shined bright as if I saw every thought and emotion pass over her face. Having her body molded so perfectly against mine felt as if she was made for me. I ache for her, to feel her sweet lips against mine.

I know I sound like a pussy but damn. This girl has fucked with my head.

It's time to move on, Callum.

The urge to throw back a couple of beers is strong. On top of everything going on with Ellie, the stress at work also has the tension running high. We've had another possible job come through, which we desperately need. If we get it, it could be one of the biggest jobs we've taken on since I started working alongside Randy. Over the last few days, I've done nothing but focus on finalizing the bid proposal. Now it's just the waiting game, leaving me with even more bullshit weighing on my mind.

Sliding out of my truck, I slip my phone in my pocket as I slam the door shut behind me. I can feel the sweat forming as I move toward the front of the Sports Bar. While it's a bit of a drive, especially when we want to have a few beers, the atmosphere is perfect for watching a game or the fights with the guys.

"Hey there," the hostess drawls, smiling sweetly up at me. The bright green eyes peering up at me combined with the long golden blond hair that falls down her back immediately remind me of Ellie.

"Just you?" she asks, looking over my shoulder checking to see if I'm alone. I don't miss the hopeful look that passes over her face when she finds I am.

Not even allowing my mind to entertain any thoughts of hooking up with her, I search out my friends in the crowded bar.

"I'm meeting some buddies here to catch the fights," I say, pointing toward the back corner where they are sitting looking over at me. Brannon is waving his hands in the air like he's an Aircraft Marshall, while Wes, Levi, and Spencer shake their heads at his antics. I make my way through the packed bar stopping to get a beer on the way. By the looks of the empty beer bottles sitting near the middle of the table with half eaten wings, I'd say I'm a little late to the party.

"There he is! I thought we'd be at least three beers in before Callum decided to finish styling his hair and show up," Levi chides.

Flipping him off, I pull out my chair, taking a long pull from my beer, feeling the tension in my shoulders ease. Wes and Spencer are discussing a dirt bike Wes is going to look at tomorrow as we wait for the fights to start.

"I meant to tell you, I should be getting a shipment in early next week. The part you ordered is supposed to be with it. I'll bring it to your house after work," Wes offers. He has been helping me with rebuilding the engine on my bike.

Looking over his shoulder, I notice Kinsley approaching with a finger over her mouth, signaling for me to be quiet. As soon as she is standing behind Wes, she leans forward, wrapping her arms around his neck. I can't help but laugh as his eyes widen in surprise. He moves to turn just as Kinsley leans in close whispering something in his ear. Grabbing her arms, he turns, pulling her into his lap. Whatever was said was meant only for his ears.

While Wes was always a wild one growing up, taking risks for the thrill of the adrenaline rush, Kinsley always seemed to keep him grounded and level-headed. While she has put up with a lot from him, their relationship has seen its fair share of ups and downs; I can't help but envy the love they have for each other.

Leaving them to their moment, I turn my attention to the TV when Halle approaches with a beer in her hand.

"Alright, boys," Halle says, setting her beer down on the

table, clapping her hands together as if she is stepping up to the plate ready to lay down a challenge. "Who has placed their bets? I want in on this," she declares.

"You're going down, firecracker," I say, smirking at her. "I hope you brought a box of tissues with you; this may not end well."

"Don't you wish, Callum!" Halle says, smiling as she rounds the set of tables to where I'm seated. She has a little sway in her hips that has me shaking my head, leaning back crossing my arms.

"Hey, sugar," she says sweetly, leaning down to give me a hug and places a kiss on my cheek.

"Hey, sweetheart, what are you girls up to? Causing trouble, I see," I say, shaking my head at her grin.

"I'm here to get my money from you handsome gentlemen and scoping out the guys here. These fights bring out the alpha in you men," she replies, tapping her finger against her chin as she looks around the room, surveying all the possibilities.

"If you're trying to find yourself a man, darlin', I have all the man you need right here," Spencer says, grabbing his junk as he starts making a thrusting movement, raising his eyebrows suggestively.

Halle moves to stand behind him, patting Spencer on his chest and laughs. "We both know you wouldn't know what to do with me, honey, or that. Good try, though."

Taking a drink from my beer, I slam the bottle down on the table trying not to choke. Damn it, woman.

"See, look what you did. Even your friend here can't believe the shit you're spewing. You alright, Callum?" Halle asks, rubbing her hand over my shoulder like she's concerned for my well-being. Coughing again, I try to clear my throat forcing a breath. It doesn't help because just as I look up, my whole body tenses at just the sight of her standing there in front of me.

She looks beautiful, and it's as if the wind is knocked right out of me. Her hair is curled in soft waves pulled up in a high ponytail that drapes over her shoulder, and she is dressed in a light green t-shirt, bringing out her eyes.

Her skin and features are soft, but if I weren't paying close attention, I would've missed it. The hint of sadness I saw the other day at Hudson's is still there beneath the surface. Once again, she has me questioning how I could consider giving up on her so easily.

Sliding into the seat directly across from me, she doesn't make eye contact, instead focuses intently on the screen mounted above me. The strap of her handbag is draped across her chest, and her knuckles are turning white as she wraps her hand around it tightly.

My mouth feels dry just seeing her sitting before me. Taking a long swig from my beer, I slam the bottle down and continue to focus my stare on Ellie. I feel like I've thought about this moment all week, what I would do if I saw her again. What I would say if I had the chance to talk to her. Now that she is sitting in front of me, I just let my gaze drift over her, taking her in. She looks as breathtaking as I remembered her to be.

"I don't think I'll be staying here all night. I have a sex date with Canada," Halle says, nonchalantly, breaking through my thoughts. Ellie, still focusing on the TV, bites her lip to hide her laughter but it doesn't work. The sound hits me right in the chest as I fight back a grin of my own.

"The hell did you just say?" Levi laughs, the movement

causing his whole body to shake. I swear to God this woman.

"Casey," Kinsley says, turning away from Wes. "How many times do I have to tell you his name is Casey!" Turning her attention back to Brannon and Levi, she continues. "Just ignore her. She gets off on calling him that like she is making some sort of oath of allegiance to his cock."

Brannon and Levi both try to disguise their look of shock, choking out a laugh, as Halle rolls her eyes. Her phone beeps with an incoming text, drawing her attention away from the conversation to the messages on her screen.

Drinking back the rest of my beer, I push my chair back from the table heading toward the bar to order a second one, asking the group if I can get them anything. Brannon and Levi shake their head no, Kinsley and Wes are in their own little world as Halle is still focusing on her phone, furiously typing out a response. Ellie, however, continues to look everywhere but at me.

"You want something to drink, sweetheart?" I ask as Ellie pushes her chair back from the table as well, standing up.

"No, it's okay. Thank you, though, I just need to use the restroom." She flashes me a small smile.

I nod as I turn away from her, making my way over to the bar. I can't help the feeling of frustration and disappointment. Since I met Ellie, she has kept me at arm's length at almost every turn. Reminding myself of what I was saying when I first got here, that it's time for me to let it go and move on. I just wish I knew what changed and why.

Paying for my beer, I quickly deposit it on the table with the guys before making my way over to the bathroom. I know the only way I can talk to Ellie is if I'm able to catch her alone. I just need to know what I did to change her mind so quickly.

Walking down the narrow hallway leading toward the restrooms, I lean against the wall and decide to wait her out. She could refuse to talk to me, but on the off chance she will stay and give me some answers, I'm willing to take the risk and try.

It isn't long before the bathroom door swings open and she walks out. She doesn't see me standing here, as I grab her by the waist and usher her into the corner away from anyone passing by. The lights are dim, but I'm still able to make out her face.

"Jesus, Callum, you scared me." She grumbles, placing her right hand against her chest as she struggles to breathe.

"Sorry, sweetheart, I didn't mean to catch you off guard."

Like a magnet, I feel like I'm pulled to her. Having her near me in such small quarters, I can feel the electricity between us. The current is so strong and from the look in her eyes, I know she feels it, too.

My right hand is still on her hip as I draw her closer to me. I know I shouldn't, but this may be my only opportunity to get her in a quiet place where she can't run. I just need a minute of her time, a chance to talk to her.

"I am sorry," I say, letting out a deep sigh. Looking up at the ceiling, I struggle to collect my thoughts before I look back down meeting her eyes. "I just wanted to talk to you; I needed to make sure you were okay. I have been trying to get in touch with you, but it seems like any time I get a chance, you avoid me."

Placing my left hand on the side of her face and neck, I move my thumb below her chin, angling her face back up to meet mine.

"Ellie, will you talk to me? Will you tell me what changed after the bonfire?" I ask, searching her eyes for a sign of the answers I know I may never get. The look of sadness is still there even though she tries to hide it. Rubbing my thumb along her cheek, I take in the feel of her soft skin beneath mine and the steady pulse of her heartbeat. Having her this close to me again has my heart beating out of control just waiting for her to respond.

"It's just… I just can't, Callum. I'm sorry, I just can't," she whispers. Moving my hands away from her, I take a step back giving her space. The loss of the connection is like a shock to my system, and as soon as it breaks, I feel empty, like something is missing.

"You can't what? Huh, what can't you do?" I say, running my hand through my hair, pulling on the ends in frustration.

"You can't talk to me? You can't see me now?"

My tone is harsh; the frustration is evident in my voice. The look of hurt on her face confirms that she didn't expect this kind of response from me. What did she expect? I've tried talking to her several times over the past week and what do I get?

Nothing! She gives me absolutely nothing.

"I just didn't come here expecting this. I didn't expect to ever meet you, to run into you at the bus station, or see you again in the bar. I didn't expect for this to happen when I moved here. I can't get involved with anyone, Callum." The way she says it, there is a hint of frustration, but it's not directed toward me. It's almost as if she is frustrated with herself.

"I didn't expect for this to happen either, Ellie," I say, taking a step toward her again. I don't move to touch her, only feeling the closeness from her proximity.

"What do you keep running from?" I whisper. Looking up at me, she meets my eyes, and I can see it all laid out in front of me. The question wasn't intended as the past but rather the connection that we have between us. However, seeing the look in her eyes now, I know there is more there. Since meeting her, I've picked up bits and pieces of something that she keeps buried so deep.

"Do you trust me?" I ask, staring into her eyes. I wait for her response, searching her eyes for what I see when she finally answers the question.

"More than I probably should," she responds so quietly that if I hadn't been standing this close to her, I probably would've missed it over the loud noise coming from down the hall.

She must read the question on my face as my eyebrows bunch together trying to piece together what she means. Reaching up between us, her hand wraps around the pendant of her necklace while her other wraps around her middle.

"I have a lot of scars that you can't see. Ugly scars," she whispers, pausing for a second, her lips parted slightly. "Ugly scars, Callum. I'm scared if you ever saw them, you'd never look at me the same way again. I don't think I could bear for you to look at me differently than you do now." She looks lost as tears fill her eyes.

Closing the distance between us, I move my arm, so it's once again positioned at her hip, drawing her to me. Placing my other hand against the wall just near her head, leaving a little room between us, she comes to me easily without any argument, grabbing onto the bottom of my t-shirt holding me to her.

Moving my hand to frame her face, pushing away the pieces of hair, I slowly rub my thumb along her cheekbone, wiping away an escaped tear sliding down her face. I hate seeing her like this. I can't help the heavy weight of her words bearing down on me.

"Ellie, there is nothing you could tell me that could change the way I see you." My finger continues to stroke along her soft skin. "I want you to show me every part of you that you don't love. Every scar, every bruise, every tear. When you're done, baby, I'm going to show you all the ways life tried to break you down but never won."

She doesn't respond to me, only nods her head acknowledging she heard me. Moving my right hand, so they are both framing her face, I brush the hair back from her face. My thumb traces along her bottom lip, tugging it free from where she's biting down nervously on it.

Even in the dimly lit hallway, I can see and feel her body, the warmth of her skin beneath the palms of my hands. The deep inhale of breath tells it all, I know she's affected by this connection just as much as I am. I'm right here with her as my breath comes out in thick pants at the emotions coursing through me.

Looking up from her mouth, I meet her eyes, and I see it. Her walls are coming down again as she lets me back in. I know it's going to take more than just words to get through to her. I'm going to have to prove to her how I feel about her and only time can do that. I am going to be here to prove to her I'm not going anywhere and that I mean what I said.

"I'm going to kiss you now," I whisper, slowly bringing her mouth to mine.

She is hesitant at first, but it doesn't take long before she opens herself up to me, my tongue eagerly seeking hers out. A moan escapes me from somewhere deep within my chest, and I hear Ellie whimper as she uses the front of my shirt to pull me closer to her. Pressing my forehead to hers, I meet her eyes as we both struggle to breathe. It's like all the oxygen escaped me the second my lips found hers.

"I am not going anywhere, Ellie. You may not believe it now but I'll prove it to you."

Ten

Ellie

THE NEXT DAY, CALLUM STOPPED BY HUDSON'S AFTER he got off work to say hey. I'm confident Callum would look sexy in anything he wears, but just seeing him standing there in a plaid button-up shirt with his sleeves rolled up below his elbows had me nearly drooling.

Arm porn.

I've never been one to admire a man's forearms, but damn. The way his muscles flexed as he moved had me staring. I had to remind myself that not only were we in public, but I was at my job no less.

The smartass he is, he knew what he was doing.

"You can't look at me like that right now. Not unless you want me to come over this counter and do something about it." The harsh whisper was quiet enough so only I heard him, but it was laced with so much promise. If I had been anywhere else, I

wouldn't have done a damn thing to stop him.

That wasn't the only time he's stopped by to see me. Last night after I got home from having dinner with Kinsley, he stopped by my house. I could tell he was tired, but the smile on his face when I opened the door had a warm feeling coursing through me.

He didn't stay long, just said he wanted to see me and asked if he could still take me out on our date. Not letting myself second guess it again, I told him "yes" and he promised to pick me up later this afternoon. My mind trails back to what he said before he left.

"Don't wear clothes you don't want to get ruined," he murmured. The way his gravelly voice came out was like a direct line to my nervous system.

My breath caught in my throat as thoughts of what he had planned raced through my mind. Seeking some relief, I rubbed my thighs together needing the friction. Growling, he closed the distance between us.

Wrapping his hands around my waist, he pulled me close to him until I was flush against his chest. Taking a deep inhale of breath, I looked up to meet his eyes as desire flowed through me, grabbing onto his strong forearms to hold me still.

My eyelids were heavy, the need burning through me was too much. The feel of my nipples pressed against Callum's chest had me struggling to find a breath. I could feel his arousal pressed against my stomach which had me squeezing my legs together, seeking relief of my own.

Leaning down, he brushed the hair away from my face as he whispered in my ear.

"I want nothing more than to touch you, to alleviate the burn I know you feel baby." He groaned, leaning back to meet

my stare. "It's not because I don't want to, because it's killing me not to touch you. I just want to be real clear with what you want because once I'm finally inside you, I'm never letting you go."

I struggle to keep myself busy for most of the day. I run through possible outfits to wear. Callum said not to wear anything I wouldn't want to get ruined. Still, I want to look good when I see him, which makes it difficult considering I don't have much of a wardrobe selection.

Taking a quick shower, I freshen up and pull my hair into a messy bun. I know how much Callum likes kissing along my neckline, and I don't want anything to obstruct his access to me.

It's a few minutes after three o'clock when I hear his pickup truck pull into my driveway. After doing a quick check in the mirror, I open the door to greet Callum.

Once again, there are no words to explain how handsome he looks dressed casually in a black t-shirt, jeans, and his Chucks. Taking a minute, I let my eyes wander over his body. Admiring the way his hair is pulled back beneath his backward baseball cap, how the cotton showcases his incredible chest, and his muscular arms fill out the sleeves as my eyes roam back up to meet his stare.

His eyes are bright with amusement, appreciating how I just blatantly checked him out. He doesn't even try to hide his smile.

"You ready, sweetheart, or do you need a minute for a second look?" He chuckles.

Smart ass.

"I mean, you won't see me objecting," I retort, raising my eyebrow as I flash him a smirk of my own. I can tell by the smile on his face he is enjoying our banter just as much as I am.

"As much as I'd love to see that delectable look of desire on your face again, baby, I have plans for you. C'mon!" he says, holding his hand out, ushering me onto the porch as he takes the keys from my hand.

After he safely locks up the house, he takes my hand again and leads me out to his truck. Helping me into the passenger seat, he leans over and secures the seat belt.

After double checking that I'm safely buckled in, he leans back to meet my eyes again. Searching my face, I wait for him to say whatever he so clearly wants to say. My eyes trace along his sharp jaw down to his lips as I peer back up to him, hoping he feels this pull between us and will finally put me out of my misery.

"There will be plenty of that later. Just you fucking wait," he says as if reading my mind, grunting as he steps back down to the ground and slams the passenger door shut. Letting out a heavy sigh, I follow him as he walks around to the driver's side and quickly climbs into his seat.

Leaning over, he turns on the radio as he backs out of the driveway. It doesn't take me long to realize we're heading out of town. The excitement sets in, wondering where he could be taking me.

"You going to tell me where we're going or what our plans are when we get there?" I ask, looking over at him.

For a minute, I think he is ignoring me until he looks over at me. He smiles smugly, and I know without a doubt it's his way of telling me, "not a chance."

The song changes to a tune that I know so I turn it up and settle back into the seat with a huff, hearing him chuckle to himself. The lyrics of the song are about a girl teasing a man by making him want her and it spurs something inside me.

Turning my head to Callum, I let my eyes roam over the side of his face, down his chest to the slight bulge in his pants. Seeing how his body reacts to me has me fighting my own arousal. Making the path back up to his face, I can see his jaw clench, resisting the urge to look at me, his eyes focusing hard on the road.

The tension in the cab of the truck has quickly changed. The air charged with the connection between us strong, it's pulling us together. Resting my elbow on the center console, I lean in closer so we are touching, causing Callum's arm to tense as I use my index finger of my right hand to trace along the inside of his forearm.

That sexy fucking arm.

Leaning in closely, I release a slow breath along his jaw until my mouth is just next to his ear.

"You look so sexy driving this truck, Callum," I whisper softly as I run my tongue along the shell of his ear, nipping softly on his ear lobe. It's an action so very unlike me, but I can't hide the way he makes me feel.

Slowly blinking his eyes, I watch for a second as he closes them just before he forces them open as if forgetting where he was. Smothering a smile, I remove my arm from around his, leaning back against my seat.

Grunting to himself, he quickly moves his right hand down to his lap, working to conceal his reaction to me, grumbling, "Just you wait, sweetheart, I'll get you back for that. Just wait!"

Callum

I swear this woman is going to be the death of me. The way she ran her tongue along my ear had me struggling against pulling this truck off to the side of the road and pull her and her smartass mouth into my lap.

Picturing her straddling me, rubbing her warm heat against my aching cock while covering her mouth with mine floods my mind. It took all my inner strength to avoid closing my eyes right then and letting the thoughts evoking me take over. Everything about this woman consumes me.

Moving my hand to where Ellie is sitting, I trail my fingers down the inside of her arm, over her wrist, sliding my hand into hers. Lifting her hand to my mouth, I kiss along her knuckles, running the top of her hand against my lips before setting our joined hands in my lap.

A few minutes later, we approach the gravel road leading us toward our destination. I know Ellie has no idea where we are going, and I can see her staring at me once again, waiting for me to give something away. I could tell by what she was wearing when I picked her up she wasn't expecting this.

Growing up in a small town doesn't offer a lot of options when you're a teenage boy without looking for trouble. Wes's love of adrenaline and anything fast had us spending a lot of our time here. The Big Dirty is a 500-acre off-road park full of 4x4 trails and two motocross tracks. The trails range from beginners to extreme riding.

As soon as we pull into the entrance of The Big Dirty, I can only imagine what she is probably thinking while reading the sign. Looking over at her, I try to gauge her reaction, but nothing could've prepared me for what I found.

"Is this what I think it is?" she asks, with a mix of surprise and excitement.

You can hear engines revving in the distance through the windows. Spotting Wes parked off to the side, I drive down to the gravel parking area and pull into a spot next to his truck and trailer.

"And Kinsley is coming with us? That little brat! I saw her earlier today, and she said nothing about this!"

"Yeah, baby, I asked her to keep quiet about it so I could surprise you," I say with a hint of a smile. "Stay right there," I say as I slide out of my truck, hurrying around to the passenger side.

Opening the door, I step up onto the running board and lean over Ellie.

I'm a few inches from her face as I slide my hand up her thigh toward where the seat belt buckles her in, looking her directly in the eye.

"Thank you for bringing me today. I've never done anything like this before," Ellie whispers. There is a joyfulness in her tone that has the sides of my mouth turning up.

"You don't have to thank me, sweetheart. I'll do just about anything to put a smile like the one you're wearin' on your face." I grin, leaning forward to press my lips against her forehead.

Grabbing her hand, I help her climb down out of the truck.

I hear the shriek of excitement from behind me, turning to see Kinsley dressed in a black tank top and jeans with her hair pulled high on top of her head.

"You're here!" she shouts, jumping up and down, clapping

her hands.

"Of course I am," Ellie says, shaking her head as she crosses her arms. She doesn't like being kept in the dark, but I know she's excited just the same. "I told you I was going out with Callum when we were together earlier today."

Letting go of Ellie's hand, I leave her and Kinsley to chat as I head over to where Wes is unloading the two four-wheelers. I own one of my own but knowing I wanted to surprise Ellie; he offered to load up both of his.

"What's up, bro? Here, let me help with that," I say, unbuckling the straps securing the four-wheelers to the trailer. We work together to remove the belts, backing the ATVs down the ramp.

Grabbing two helmets from the back of the trailer, I head over to where Ellie and Kinsley are perched on the tailgate of my pick-up. Their legs swing as they lean close to each other, laughing. It makes me happy to know Ellie has someone like Kinsley in Arbor Creek looking out for her. Even when Ellie and I weren't talking, Kinsley would often send me texts filling me in on how my girl was doing.

My girl.

When Kinsley sees me approaching, I can hear her shush Ellie as she whispers not to tell me. Raising my eyebrow to Ellie in question, she bites down her lip to cover the small smile that appears on her face, shaking her head saying she's not telling a soul.

Standing in front of Ellie, she opens her legs so I can move between them. Setting my helmet on the truck bed next to her, I grab hers in both of my hands turning it so it's facing her.

"Ready, sweetheart?"

Her small smile turns into a full-on grin as she nods her head impatiently. Brushing back the pieces of hair blowing across Ellie's face, I lean forward to press a soft kiss against her mouth. I can hear Kinsley mumble about us getting a room as Ellie leans back, letting me slide the helmet on. Lifting her head, I raise the face shield up so I can see her eyes.

"You good, baby?" I ask.

"Yep!" she declares, giving me two thumbs up.

Kinsley hops down from the tailgate and heads over to where Wes is getting his gear together. Helping Ellie slide down, I grab my helmet and lead her to where the four-wheelers are parked.

Wes has two custom built Polaris Sportsman quads. One of them he had built as an upgrade to the one his uncle bought him growing up. They're nearly identical. He favors his first one more for sentimental reasons.

Stepping on the footrest, I swing my right leg over, taking a seat. Looking over at Ellie, I can tell she is anxious as her hands are twisted together in front of her.

"Don't be nervous, baby. I wouldn't let anything happen to you," I reassure her. I know she can hear me as she nods her head.

Pulling the helmet over my head, I put the key in and turn over the ignition. The roar of the engine vibrating beneath me has always had a calming effect on me. Riding is something I've enjoyed doing since I was young and now sharing this with Ellie, I can feel the excitement pumping through me.

Holding my hand out to Ellie, she places her palm tentatively in mine. Even with the vibrations below me, I can feel her hand shaking with nerves. Placing her left foot next to mine, she swings her right leg over positioning herself behind me.

Once she is seated, I grab the outside of her thighs and pull her closer so her legs are fitted to me like a second skin. Taking her hands from resting on her knees, I wrap them around my middle so she's holding onto me. She could also hold onto the metal bars on the back, but I'm not going to mention that.

I want her close to me.

"You ready, baby?" I shout over the sound of the engine.

Giving me another thumbs-up, I turn my head back to where Wes and Kinsley are loaded up and starting his engine. With a nod of my head, I rev the engine and venture out toward the trails. Having been out here hundreds of times, Wes and I have the paths memorized like the back of our hands.

It's another warm day in Arbor Creek with the sun shining down on us. The breeze feels good against my skin. Making our way toward the back of the park, we follow behind Wes and Kinsley through the trails. It rained most of the night and early into this morning, making the park extra muddy.

I can't wait to see how sexy Ellie looks covered in mud.

Knowing Ellie isn't expecting this, she is going to be shocked when we hit some of the puddles, covering her with muddy water. Going up the first hill, I speed up and rev the engine. Mud and dirt fly over us as Ellie lets out a shriek followed by a laugh.

"Oh my gosh, Callum!" she yells, laughing. "This is so much fun!"

There is an exuberance in her tone and I can't help but grin at how happy and carefree she sounds. Wanting to hear more of Ellie's infectious laugh, I rev up the engine and shout back, "You better hold on real tight, baby. We're only getting started."

The next hour is spent riding the trails. I've become addicted to Ellie's laughter and I promise myself to spend all my days working to hear that very sound. With one hand on the gear shift, I run the other over Ellie's hand wrapped around my waist.

I don't care that we are both caked in mud right now. I love having her close.

After her antics in the truck and having her body wrapped around mine, I should've known better than to think she wouldn't try it again. As if it isn't hard enough to focus, I can't ignore the feel of her soft breasts pressed against my back. The water from the puddles causes my shirt to cling to me like a second skin. Ellie's hand runs along my chest as the muscles in my stomach clench.

Not wasting any time, I pull off into an alcove on the side of the trails and park where no one could see if they're driving past. Turning off the engine, I slide my helmet off and hang it from the handlebar as Ellie does the same.

"Come here, baby," I grunt, unwrapping her hands from around my waist and helping her move to step off the side of the four-wheeler. Sliding back further on the seat, I pat my lap inviting her to sit as I raise my eyebrows suggestively. She returns the smile that has nearly taken over my face before looking around checking if anyone can see us, but I don't even give her a chance to overthink it.

"No one will see us out here, I promise."

Her eyes light with desire, and I'd be damned if I'd let someone get a glimpse of her like this. Ellie steps up onto the footrest and slides her leg over, positioning herself facing me on my lap. Running my hands up her thighs towards her ass, I pull her closer to me once again so there isn't even an inch separating us.

"Hi," she whispers, as her warm heat connects with my straining cock.

"Is this what you wanted earlier, baby?" I ask, hoping like hell I didn't misread her cues. Looking me dead in the eye, I can see everything in the depths of her glittering green eyes. She runs her gaze over every inch of my face before landing on my mouth.

"Kiss me, Ellie," I say, needing to taste her. Running her hands through my hair, she pulls on the strands, causing my head to tip back.

"You know I don't like being told what to do, Callum."

There she is, that fiery, passionate woman she likes to keep hidden. With my hands pressed against her ass, I grind my cock up, letting her feel me rub against her as her eyes start to close with the weight of her desire.

"Ellie, you may not think it now, but when we're like this, when you're in my arms and you have that sexy as fuck look in your eye, you are mine." I can feel her body tremble against me as she fights against her reaction to my words. "So, when I tell you to kiss me, I want you to give me those lips, baby," I command.

As soon as I say the words, her lips connect with mine in a punishing kiss. Weaving her fingers through my hair, she tugs on the ends as I let out a deep moan. Opening my mouth, I feel her tongue connect with mine as I run my hands up her back, sliding under her wet t-shirt feeling her soft skin beneath my hands.

It's as if the sound of my moan spurs her on as she forces

her aching core down, grinding on top of my dick, her breath coming out in heavy pants. Keeping my forehead pressed against hers, I break the kiss and force air into my lungs.

"I can feel your heat through the denim of your jeans, sweetheart. If you keep rubbing against me like this, I am going to lose all control and end up taking you right here." I groan, running my palm over her rib, grabbing a handful of her breast. Her nipples pebble beneath the cotton of her t-shirt as I run my thumb back and forth over her tightened peak, letting out a strangled moan.

"That feels good, Callum. Please," she breathes heavily, throwing her head back in pleasure. "Please keep touching me. Don't stop."

It's as if she's lost all her inhibitions and is driven purely by the need racing through her bloodstream. Hearing her take control of her pleasure, telling me what she wants, is the sexiest thing I've ever seen. My cock is straining against the zipper of my pants. As much as I want to take this further, to give into the arousal, I know she deserves better than this. I want our first time to be special.

That doesn't mean I can't give Ellie a taste of what we could be together.

Sliding my hand back down between us, I run my hand beneath the fabric of her shirt lifting it up to expose the black lace of her bra. I can see her rosy nipple straining against the fabric as Ellie leans back, bracing her hand on the handlebars, offering herself to me.

"God damn, Ellie. Look at you!" I groan, leaning forward to wrap my lips around her puckered flesh as Ellie unleashes a series of curse words.

The shy and tentative woman she was before is gone.

Tangling her fingers back through my hair, she presses my face into her chest as she says my name over and over in a chant.

"Callum, I think. Oh, fuck," she moans, "I think I'm going to come. Please, I need to come."

My fucking pleasure.

She continues to grind against me seeking her own release as I use my teeth, biting softly against her tender flesh. The unexpected pain sends her catapulting over the edge as her body trembles against mine. I can feel her arm start to give out as I wrap my arms around her. With my head tilted back, she leans forward and presses a deep kiss against my lips while she continues to ride out the high.

I know without a shred of doubt that I'm lost in Ellie. Now that I've gotten a taste of her, I won't ever be able to let her go.

Mine.

Eleven

Ellie

"**L**ET'S HEAR IT FOR THE BOY, LET'S GIVE THE BOY A hand." I sing along to the "Footloose" CD blaring from the speaker in the kitchen. The smell of the sugar cookies baking wafts through the air as I clean up the chaos that I've created. Cookie dough sticks to the counter and the inside of the mixing bowl. Scraping what is left onto a spoon, I take a heaping bite, smiling as I continue to dance.

Callum is coming over today and I decided I wanted to do something nice for him. In fact, he should be here any minute.

Piling the spoon and utensils into the mixing bowl, I dump them into the sink. While the cookies bake and the dishes are soaking, I move my hips along to the beat of the music, sweeping up the mess I've made on the floor. Things have been so busy lately that finding days to get things done around the house have been few and far between.

The song changes to "Footloose," bringing back a flood of memories from my childhood of my mom and dad dancing together in the kitchen. I remembered when they would hold me in both of their arms as they danced around the small dining room. The smile on my mom's face would be so big and bright, it nearly split her face in half.

I shuffle my feet on the floor, singing along to the lyrics. Letting the beat flow through my body, I rotate my hips imitating moves I've watched on "Dancing with the Stars." With an extra bounce in my step, I slide my foot across the linoleum floor. The movement takes me by surprise as my feet slip out from under me. Sticking my hand out, I try to brace for my fall. The sound of skin smacking fills the air as I land hard on my side, cracking my head again the cupboard in the process.

Sitting up, I groan through the sharp pain pounding through my skull leaving me dizzy. Wrapping my fingers around my left wrist, I apply pressure in hopes to dull the ache. That's how Callum finds me as he makes his way around the corner and into the kitchen. I hadn't heard him walk through the door over all the commotion.

"Ellie, what happened?" Callum shouts over the music, rushing to me as he bends down next to where I'm sitting. Even over the loud music, I can still catch the panic in his voice.

"It's okay, I'm fine," I say, opening my eyes to look up at him. I wince from the brightness of the lights shining above, forcing my eyes closed again as I rub my fingers over my forehead.

"That didn't sound like everything is fine. I walked inside because when I knocked, instead of hearing you respond, I heard what sounded like a slamming." Callum is upset, causing his nostrils to flare and his jaw to tick. If I had to guess, it's over my lack of concern of me sitting on the floor in pain.

"I was dancing and fell. I uhhh—" I grunt, shifting my left hand to the floor. Releasing the pressure on my wrist causes a throbbing pain to shoot up my forearm. The pulsating in my wrist matches the pounding in my head.

"I landed funny on my wrist, hitting my head against the cabinet in the process."

Making a move to stand up, I set my non-injured hand on the floor only to land in something wet.

"What the hell," I mumble to myself, holding up my palm as I survey the floor. "Something must've spilled." I can hear the confusion in my voice as I look around for what it could be.

"C'mere," Callum says. "Let's get you up off the floor first. I'm more worried about you and that pretty head." Leaning over, he slides his arms underneath my legs just below my knees, wrapping his other arm around my lower back. My arms curl around his neck as he lifts me up, moving effortlessly to set me on the counter.

It briefly crosses my mind how messy it still is with cookie dough caked on top of it, but my worry doesn't last long when the incessant pain in my eyes forces my eyes closed once again. Resting my forehead against Callum's shoulder, I let out a quiet groan.

"I know, baby," Callum says, "I'm going to check you out."

Once he has me seated and is sure that I'm not going to move or injure myself further, he takes a step back to survey the damage. Crouching in front of the sink, he opens the cabinet as he shuffles the cleaning products I have stored out of the way.

"Uh, Ellie, it looks like your sink is leaking."

"Are you serious?"

"Yeah, it looks like the water is coming out from this pipe down here. Has it done that before?" Callum asks, looking up to me with questioning eyes.

Without thinking, I shake my head no. As my vision gets a little fuzzy, I rub my fingers across my forehead.

"When I first moved in, Hudson came by and said he needed to fix the sink but I haven't had any problems," I mumble, rubbing my hand against my forehead trying to ease some of the tension.

"Just a second, sweetheart. Let me get this turned off," he says.

He jumps up quick and disappears down the hall, only to return with two big bath towels from the hallway closet. Once he has them spread out on the floor, he is back standing in front of me.

"How you feelin', sweetheart?" he asks, brushing the hair back from my face.

"Like I just about put my head through the cabinet door," I whine. "And I can hardly move my wrist."

Callum grabs my right hand, running his fingers over the swollen skin. It's growing more and more stiff as the seconds tick by. Even through the pain, his touch still causes electricity to course through my body. I can't help the groan that escapes, which comes out sounding more like a moan. I can hear Callum's sudden inhale at the sound.

The song changes and the music continues to drone on. When they sing, "C'mon, baby, make it hurt so good," Callum lets out a deep laugh.

Struggling to hold back a smile, I glance up at him. A

look of concern is on his face, and if I'm not mistaken, a hint of desire is hidden under there, too.

"Footloose," I say, explaining the reason for the music.

Callum shakes his head at me as he leans over to turn down the music.

"Just a little too footloose, I'd say." He snickers. "Thankfully, I don't think it's broken, just a sprain I'm sure. I'm more concerned about your head. I think we should go get you checked out."

"Whoa there, I don't think that's necessary. I'm a klutz, I fall all the time. You'd think you would know this by now," I joke, referring to the time we met when I so gracefully fell into his arms, hoping to reassure him.

"Can't we just go lay down for a little bit? That sounds like a lot more fun. I'm sure we'd both feel better about this after a nap." Looking up at him beneath my lashes, I hope to convince him while trying to hide my nervousness at the thought of going to the hospital.

It's not like I've been forthcoming about who I truly am, at least not to everyone in Arbor Creek. Hudson promised to keep my secret and all the bills under his name, understanding why I didn't want a trace leading to where I am.

When I left Garwood, I did more than say goodbye to my home. I also said goodbye to Ellie Hayes, the real me.

"Ellie, could you imagine if I hadn't shown up here just now? You don't even have a cell phone. What could you possibly do in that situation to call me, Kinsley, or Hudson?" The tone of his voice changes just thinking of something happening and not having a way to reach out for help.

"Oh, please!" I scoff, not wanting to do this with him right now. "You know how I feel about cell phones. It's not like phones have been around since the beginning of time." I admonish, crossing my arms over my chest, being mindful of my injured wrist, holding my ground.

"See, that's the thing. I don't want you to have to do this on your own anymore. I want you to let me in. I haven't had a chance to talk to you about it, but if we get this job I'll have to go out of town in a week and I'll be gone for five days. What am I supposed to do then?" he asks, his voice laced with both determination and exasperation as he rubs his palms up and down my thighs.

As hard as it is for me to admit it, he is right about the first part. I can feel my resolve chipping away just a little bit more, thinking about how much I want to continue opening up to Callum. Knowing he is going to be gone for almost week only makes it more difficult to say no to him.

I run my palms over the top of Callum's hands, ignoring the stiff pain in my wrist as I peer up at him.

"I'm sorry, I know you want to take care of me. What you need to understand is it's hard for me to let go. I've been doing this on my own for so long. Just thinking about you being away for that long with no contact," I admit, letting out a sigh. "It's hard to even think about."

Moving to stand between my legs, he runs his hand along my cheek, brushing his thumb down my jaw. The pounding in my head hasn't lessened but I don't say anything, fearing that he would move away from me. Instead, I just close my eyes and soak in the warmth of his skin against mine.

"Good, I'm glad, sweetheart, because none of this was up for negotiation anyway. I'm taking you to the hospital to get checked out whether you like it or not. Then tomorrow, after I get off work, I'm taking you to get a cell phone."

Opening my eyes, I find his staring back at me. I can see the intensity in his gaze as he waits for me to respond, to challenge him. There are so many things I want to say, just on the tip of my tongue. Before I get a chance to say them, he's there pressing his soft lips against mine, taking all the fight I had left right out of me.

Callum

It took some coaxing but I convinced Ellie to go to the hospital to get her head and wrist examined, especially after I told her we would have to make a trip to Everton, which is where the nearest hospital is located. When she asked if she could wear my sunglasses inside, I realized she was with me in the decision to come here to ensure everything was okay.

They had us fill out some registration paperwork when we got here. Since Ellie doesn't have insurance and I was the reason for dragging her here, I gave them my credit card not wanting her to have to worry about the bill. I could tell it made her uncomfortable, but she realized quickly that it wasn't something I was going to give in on.

Now here we sit in the waiting room with her forehead pressed against my neck. We've been sitting here for a little over forty minutes now, the wait to see a doctor on the weekend is taking longer than either of us would like.

"Ellie Ryan," a woman in a nursing uniform announces cheerfully.

"Come on, sweetheart, let's get this over with. Then we

can get you back home to rest," I urge, standing up and turning to help Ellie do the same.

"That's us," I say with a small wave to the nurse. The smile on her face matches the sound of her voice, but I don't miss the way her eyes rake over me.

Wrapping my arm around Ellie's shoulder, I kiss the top of her head and usher her along behind the nurse, down the hallway toward the examination rooms. Helping her get seated on the bed, I run my hand along her back.

The nurse takes a seat on the chair and looks up at us, "So, I understand you had a fall, hitting your head and injuring your wrist. Is that right?" she asks, letting her eyes linger on me.

Ellie nods her head, dropping her hands into her lap as she lifts her head. "Yeah, I was doing the dishes in the kitchen. While I let the dishes soak, I was dancing." Ellie laughs. "Apparently, the sink had started to leak without me knowing. I slipped and fell, trying to catch myself in the process. I landed on my wrist and ended up hitting my head on the cabinet door."

The nurse grits her teeth sympathetically as if picturing the whole thing going down. "I understand, I hope you're okay." She continues to ask Ellie more questions about the symptoms she is experiencing while going through the routine of checking her blood pressure, pulse, temperature, and heart rate.

"I will let Dr. Sahls know. He should be back here in just a few minutes," she says with a warm smile as she finishes typing up her notes on her tablet, before making her way toward the door.

It takes a minute for me to register the name before it

clicks into place.

Dr. Sahls... Jeff Sahls.

"I'm sorry, Sahls?" I ask, cutting her off. Are you fucking kidding me? I knew he was a doctor, but I've never given a shit to pay attention about the details. "Don't you have someone else she can see?"

She must sense my anger as she holds up her hand defensively as if she is silently asking me to calm down. Ellie wraps her hand around my forearm, pulling me back to her.

"Callum, what's wrong with the doctor?" I look down at where Ellie's hand is on my arm, turning my head back to her seeing the concern on her face before turning back to the nurse.

"I'll be damned if I will have that asshole anywhere near my girl. So, you'll have to find someone else," I demand, not taking any other option.

I look up at the nurse to find her eyes nearly bugging out of her head. She probably thinks I'm going to lose my mind. I certainly don't want them to throw my ass out of here. It's not her fault I hate that sorry son of a bitch.

Letting out a deep sigh, I will myself to calm down and try this again.

"Listen, I'm sorry. I just don't like him nor do I want him around. Alright? Is there anyone else you could have look her over?" I ask, my patience wearing thin. If I wasn't so worried about Ellie and making sure she was okay, I would wrap her in my arms and walk her straight out of this fucking hospital.

"I'm sorry, sir. We are a small hospital, and he is the only doctor on call. If you want her to be seen here today, it must be by Dr. Sahls," she says apologetically.

"Alright, alright!" I say, holding up my hands, taking a

step back to sit on the chair next to Ellie. I'm not leaving this room but if I don't get my anger under control, I may not have a choice.

"I'll let the doctor know you're ready. He should be back in just a few minutes," she murmurs, forcing a smile as she opens the door exiting the room.

"What the hell was that about?" Ellie asks as soon as the door closes, anger and concern laced through her soft tone. She clearly didn't like how I reacted, but this is the first time she's seen this side of me.

The side that would love nothing more than to knock that fucker out.

Looking up, her eyebrows are bunched together as her fingers are wrapped around her injured wrist tightly. Seeing her in pain brings it all crashing down around me, remembering why we are here in the first place.

"It's nothing, baby. I'm sorry," I say, standing and moving close to her. Running my fingers over her wrist, I try to steer the conversation away from what happened, not wanting to start an argument.

"How does it feel?" She moves her fingers away so I can inspect her wrist. It's swollen and clearly sore, but hasn't changed colors, which I take as a good sign.

"It's sore, but I'm fine."

Looking up at her, I run my hand along her cheek. I know she is worried about why I blew up and was so upset. Brushing Ellie's hair back, I press my lips against her forehead as I lean back, searching her eyes for the way to explain it to her. She deserves an explanation as to why I reacted the way I did.

The sound of knocking, followed by the door opening has

us both turning our heads as Jeff walks in.

"Knock, knock. Ellie, how ya doin'?" he says, a smug grin taking over his face, at least until he sees me standing here next to her. Clearly the nurse didn't give him a heads up because he looks a little taken off, but recovers quickly. His eyes roam over to me, taking in my hand still resting along the side of Ellie's face.

I can't hide the shit-eating grin taking over my face as I move to stand next to Ellie, running my hand along her back. I'm guessing Ellie has an idea of why I was pissed off as her back tenses, recognizing him as the guy from the bar.

The guy she was talking to in an attempt to ignore me, only pissing me off.

Yeah, baby, he isn't coming anywhere near you now.

"I'm okay," she says, her voice is low and hesitant.

"I hear you had a fall, we will get you checked out," he says, turning his attention to me. "Callum," he greets, tipping his head and narrowing his eyes, acknowledging me. There is a challenging look in his eye, that has me moving my neck to the side, loosening up, as if encouraging him to test me.

With a smirk on his face, he turns back to Ellie asking her what happened. Standing here with my arms crossed, I hear her replay what happened leading up to her fall. When she gets to the part of the story where she explains that I came in, I want to flash a smug-as-fuck grin right back at him.

"Well, I'm glad you came in to get checked out. It's better to be safe," he says, looking at her with a smile. "First, let me check out your head, I just want to rule out a possible concussion. How are you feeling? Anything abnormal since you bumped your head?" he asks, moving to stand in front of Ellie.

"No, just a headache. At first, I thought my skull was

splitting in half. Now it just feels like a throbbing pain," she grumbles as I run my hand up her back, doing my best to comfort her.

Nodding his head in understanding, "What about sensitivity to light and sound, as well as any nausea?" he questions.

"I'm not feeling nauseous, but the sunlight and sound definitely doesn't help with the headache," she tells him, as he holds up a light to check her pupils. His closeness to Ellie, even though I know he is just checking her over, has me riding on the edge.

"It looks like your pupils are responding so that's a good sign. It doesn't appear to be a concussion although you do have some of the symptoms," he says, looking at both of us. "I would recommend getting some rest and taking it easy for the next couple of days, okay?"

Ellie nods her head in understanding.

"Now let me check out your wrist."

Ellie holds out her hand to him as Jeff wraps his fingers around her wrist. Watching him feel along her soft skin has me wound tight. The tension in this room is so thick you could cut it with a knife. Ellie must sense how I feel, as she peers up at me. Careful of the tenderness on her head, I lean in close and press a small kiss to the side of her head.

I can see the subtle tic of Jeff's jaw as he continues to run his fingers along Ellie's wrist.

"I don't think it is broken but definitely appears to be a sprain. I think some rest and taking it easy will do you a lot of good. Icing it will help reduce some of the swelling you're seeing," he says as he continues to run over a series of instructions.

"I'll write down my number in case anything comes up or if your symptoms change." As soon as the words leave his mouth, I can't control the growl that emanates from deep in my chest. The nerve of this prick.

"That won't be necessary," I say, interrupting him. "Thanks for your concern but I'll make sure she is well taken care of."

Stepping in front of Ellie, I cross my arms blocking him from her. I know it's a move that's likely going to piss her off, but I don't care.

"Callum, are you fucking kidding?" she retorts. Ahh, there's my girl. "I'll take care of myself, thank you very much."

Turning and looking at Ellie, I lock my jaw not wanting to do this with her right now either. Ellie slides down from the table, turning to look at Jeff.

"Thank you for your help. If that's all, I think I'll be going now," she announces, taking the discharge papers from his hand. Without even looking to see if I'm behind her, she opens the door and makes her way out of the room and down the hall. It isn't until we are outside in the parking lot that she finally acknowledges me behind her.

"I can't fucking believe you," she mumbles under her breath, knowing I'm right behind her and can hear her. Reaching my hand out in front of her, I grab the handle of my pick-up truck, stopping her from opening it.

I know she doesn't feel well and I don't want to fight with her right now, but we need to put this to rest.

"You can be pissed off all you want, sweetheart, but it's the truth. We can talk about this later, once you are feeling better," I say, stepping in front of her. Grabbing the keys out of my pocket, I click the unlock button and open the door, holding out a hand to help her in.

With her arms crossed, she props her hip out in defiance.

"The way you behaved back there was uncalled for. He

was being respectful and you were practically pissing on me, marking your territory. How many times do I have to tell you I can take care of myself?" she chides, ignoring my offered hand and climbs up on the foot step seating herself.

I swear this woman can push my ever-loving buttons sometimes.

Stepping up on the footrest, I grab the seat belt and move to buckle her in as she holds up her hand halting my movement.

"I can do that too you know. I'm not going anywhere," she affirms, rolling her eyes as she takes the strap out of my hand.

Once the buckle clicks in place, I lean back looking over her face.

"I think you like it when I'm chasing after you, sweetheart. Just so you know, I wasn't marking my territory back there. I was just clearing something up for him. I'm yours and you're mine, which means I will do whatever I need to do to take care of you.

"By the looks of it, you could use a reminder, too. So, let me remind you, Ellie Ryan. You're mine, which means this sass, that smile, that laugh I fucking love so much, the place on your neck I want to kiss every second of every day, that's mine. You can push me away, but you need to remember, I'm not going anywhere."

Leaning forward, I press a small kiss on her forehead, against her cheek, and ending with a kiss on my favorite spot where her neck and shoulder meet. I don't miss the way her breath catches as her chest heaves, struggling to catch a breath.

"You're mine, Ellie," I whisper in her ear before I step down, closing the door behind me.

Twelve

Ellie

AFTER SLEEPING OFF THE HEADACHE FROM YESTER-day, I wake up the next morning feeling well rested. It's a perfect day to be outside so I make it a point to do just that. I spend most of the morning, and if I'm honest, the early afternoon, too, sitting on the rocking chair on my front porch reading a book. It's something I've gotten in the habit of doing when I have a lot on my mind and with Callum coming around more, saying I have a lot on my mind is an understatement.

On the way home from the hospital last night, he brought up the subject of me not having a cell phone again. As he has mentioned a couple of times, he is concerned about me not being able to reach someone, especially knowing I am walking around town, even sometimes after dark. When that didn't seem to work, he used the fact he would be heading out of town for almost a week for work.

Not having a way to talk to him for a week seemed like forever.

Realizing it was a battle I wasn't going to win, I told him I would get a phone but only under one condition - it must be a prepaid phone. I sold it as I didn't want him to be bothered by adding me to his account. I didn't tell him the truth, that the thought of having my name on something, a way to tie me back to Arbor Creek, scared me.

I earned a grunt, but in the end, he was getting what he wanted, so he agreed. Callum promised he would stop by and take me into town to get it squared away when he got off work tonight. He can be a little overprotective, okay well maybe a lot protective, but I know he means well.

It's early afternoon when I finally realize the time and force myself to get up and do something with my day. I still have plenty of homemade cookies left over after all the baking I did yesterday. With not much to do, I decide to put together a plate of goodies and head down the road to the Hudson's.

Hudson and his wife, June, are two people in Arbor Creek I've gotten to know quite well. A couple of months after I moved here, Hudson invited me over to his house one Sunday afternoon for their family lunch. Kinsley was standing next to me as we were locking up after work the night before.

"If you thought the banana bread was good, you don't want to miss out on Nana's peach cobbler."

Ms. June is quite possibly one of the best bakers in the state of Iowa. The first day I met her, I shared with her how one of my favorite memories growing up was spending time in the kitchen with both my father and Grams. Ever since then, she's been sending me home with recipes or leftovers after family dinner. Sometimes, she'll even send me a treat with Hudson on days she knows I'll be working at the store. It seems only right that I stop by and bring her some of the homemade cookies she had given me the recipe for.

We spend most of the early afternoon sitting in her kitchen. She told me about memories of Kinsley and Kolton growing up, how she and Hudson met and what led them to building their house here. The land was originally owned by Hudson's parents. After they both had passed, his mother left the property, including the house I was staying in, to him.

I couldn't help but think about my Grams sitting at her dining room table, listening to all the stories she told me. It reminded me of the times she would tell me about my father and his two brothers growing up.

Checking the time, I knew I was cutting it close. If I didn't leave soon, I wouldn't have much time to get ready before Callum arrived. With a hug and a wave goodbye, I headed back to my house. Deciding to take the quick route, I cut across the property through the trees that separated our houses, offering some seclusion from the rest of the Hudson Ranch.

Walking along the trees near the back side of my house, I bend down picking up a large tree branch that appears to have fallen after the last thunderstorm, being mindful of my injured wrist. What I see on the ground before me has me halting firmly in place, feeling as if the wind was knocked right out of me. Dropping the branch on the ground, I take a step back and focus on what I'm seeing.

Sitting on the ground near my bedroom window is a tree stump. A ceramic pot appears to have tipped over, littering the ground with cigarette butts. Immediately, my thoughts are brought back to him as memories plague me. Pressing my hand against my throat, I feel as though I'm suffocating as my vision starts to fade and the tears start to form in my eyes.

You're going to regret this one day.

Rubbing my palms over my eyes, I wipe away the tears staining my eyes and mixing with the sweat on my face.

"You're okay, Ellie, he's not here. You're okay," I reassure myself out loud, forcing air into my lungs.

"He's not here," I repeat over and over.

Not bothering to move the branch, I race to the front of the house and up the porch steps, slamming the front door shut behind me. Locking it behind me, I slide down the front of the wooden door. As soon as my butt hits the floor, all my emotions escape me. The tears flowing down my face are for the scared, broken girl who is still locked up inside because of him.

I cry because, even though he is locked up in prison, he still has a hold on me.

I don't know how long I stay here before I convince myself to get up. It won't be long before Callum is here, and I know if he were to show up with me like this, he'd be worried. My thoughts continue to replay what I've seen, over and over like a photo reel. My mind is swirling, but I keep coming back to the thought that it's not possible.

He is still locked up for what he did for another two years.

My heart beats out of control, thinking of him being released and finding me here in Arbor Creek. The sudden realization I may have to leave Callum, Kinsley, Hudson, Halle… hell, even Kolton, and the guys, breaks my heart. I feel like I have a family here and it would kill me to have to leave them behind.

Thinking of Kinsley and her family has a thought clicking

WHERE I FOUND YOU

into my head. Since I've moved here, Kolton often helps Hudson out doing yard work on the property. Resigning myself to the fact no one from back home knows where I am, I let myself consider the cigarette butts were left there by Kolton. He was just here last week mowing the lawn. The property is so big. I know he occasionally takes a break, heck there are times he'll come inside for a glass of lemonade.

The grandfather clock in the living room dings, breaking through my reverie and drawing my attention to the time. It's a little after four o'clock which means I don't have long before Callum will be here. Turning around, I look in the mirror in the entry way, and for a moment, I just stare at my reflection.

I make a promise to myself that as of today, I will no longer be the scared little girl he once brought out in me. I don't have to hide anymore; I have people here who care about me. Starting today, I'm going to take back my happiness.

I'm ready to live my life for me.

I feel a lot better after I get out of the shower, washing away all the tears focusing on the hope of what the future could bring. I have been standing in front of the closet for a solid ten minutes with a towel wrapped around me when I hear Callum's truck pull into the driveway. Looking down, the feeling of panic take over when I realize how little I have done with myself only to freeze at the sound of him knocking on the front door.

"Shit. Shit. Shit." I swear to myself as I tighten the towel wrapped around my body.

I do a quick double check in the mirror, confirming all

the important parts are covered as the sound of Callum shouting my name spurs me forward. I know he will be concerned if I don't answer the door after the accident I had yesterday.

"I'm coming!" I shout as my bare feet pad down the hall.

Unlocking both the deadbolt and lock, I swing open the door before wrapping my arms around my chest, suddenly feeling self-conscious, wanting to make sure the towel stays secure.

A look of concern is written all over Callum's face as he stares at the locks before drawing his attention back to me. I can feel the heat of his stare as his eyes draw a line from my feet up to my face, causing my body to tremble from the desire I see shining back at me.

As if he doesn't already look sexy as it is, I just can't seem to get enough of him in his work clothes. The way his button up shirt and worn denim blue jeans fit him so perfectly, as if they were made for him alone. Something about the thought of him working outside with sweat dripping from his brow down the column of his neck has me wanting to run my tongue along the same path.

Drawing myself out of my musings, I tighten my hold again as my chest begins to rise and fall in time with my breathing. The look on Callum's face tells me he is just as affected as I am by my current state.

"Hi," I say, not knowing what to say, feeling embarrassed by my lack of clothes and perusal of him. "Umm… I'm running a little behind; I got back from visiting with Ms. June a bit late. I had lost track of time," I ramble on.

Looking me over again, I can hear him whisper to himself about "being right on time," and I can't help the smile that takes over my face.

"If you can just give me a few minutes to get changed and do something with my hair, I'll be ready," I say, turning toward the hallway while waiting for his response. He doesn't say anything, only nods his head as I rush down the hall, leaving only the sound of his growl behind me.

Quickly shutting the door, I grab a cotton t-shirt and my favorite jeans from my closet, tossing them on the bed next to the bra and underwear I had pulled out earlier. Once I'm dressed, I towel dry some of the excess water from my hair. Running my fingers through my damp hair, I quickly braid the strands in a fishtail. Keeping it simple, I swipe some mascara on my eyelashes before I hurry to join Callum.

"All ready?" he asks, standing up in front of me.

Nodding my head, I'm not able to resist the urge to touch him as I run over his forearms, before wrapping them around his neck drawing him into a hug. I let myself enjoy the way he sighs or how he lightly brushes his lips against the soft skin on my neck.

"I'm ready," I declare, tilting my head back.

Leaning down, Callum presses a soft kiss against my lips. I don't even recognize the strangled moan that comes from me as I pull him closer to me, seeking comfort in his arms as I open my mouth to deepen the kiss.

When my tongue connects with his, Callum unleashes a deep groan as he slides his hands over my ass drawing me closer to him. I can feel his arousal against my stomach as our tongues continue to duel with each other.

Ever since the day we went mudding, we've been riding this line, but it hasn't quite crossed over to more. We are playing with fire. It's dangerous, I know, but I can't find it in me to stop.

He continues to run his hands over my ass, drawing them up underneath my shirt, along my lower back, tightening his arms around me. Leaning back, he breaks the connection as he presses his forehead against mine. We both struggle to force air into our lungs. He never ceases to take it right out of me.

"Give me a minute, and I'll be ready, too," he whispers. Looking up into his crystal blue eyes, I nod my head knowing exactly what he means. I purse my lips together, trying to hide the smile that breaks out across my face.

I think it's safe to say he is feeling this, too.

Callum

Leaning forward, I pick up the remote from the coffee table and click off the TV. After Ellie and I had gone into the city earlier tonight, we rented a movie from Redbox and grabbed some take-out from a little Chinese restaurant. There are limited options in Arbor Creek. Knowing I would be going out of town next weekend, I wanted to make use of spending time with her.

I could tell she was tired on our way back, the way she covered her mouth to stifle her yawns. The sun had started to set on our drive home, only adding to her tired state. It wasn't even twenty minutes into the movie when she curled up on her side, laying her head across my lap. She took her hair down from that bun thing she does, leaving it fanned out across my lap. Her face is soft and peaceful as she sleeps.

A soft vibration from my pocket distracts me from Ellie's

beautiful face. Slowly sliding my hand down beneath the pillow, I slip my phone out to check the notifications and find two missed text messages from my father. We haven't spoken since I left Chicago.

Steven Reid: Callum, will you call me soon?

Rubbing a hand over my face, I take a deep breath and lean back against the plush cushion of the couch. I don't know how I could ever move past how my father would lash out when he was drinking or the way he would treat my mother. Then having him tell me he wanted nothing to do with me after choosing not to follow in his footsteps solidified how I felt. What makes it even more difficult is knowing that even today, my mother still doesn't say a bad word against him.

"I know your father loved me, Callum. He had a bit of a temper when he drank but, beneath it all, he is a good man. He loved you and your brother more than anything."

The stress I feel over the whole situation is like a fresh wound. I know talking to him will reopen the wound I've been working to heal. It doesn't surprise me that, as the calls and texts from Mason stop, they're now picking up from Steven.

I tell myself I will deal with him at some point, but not tonight. Checking the time, I see it's a little after eleven p.m. before I slide my phone back into my pocket. The fact that he is even bothering to text me this late tells me he hasn't bothered to put down the bottle.

Positioning my arms beneath the pillow, I move to slide out from where I'm seated under Ellie. I briefly consider leaving her to sleep on the couch, like she often does, covering her up with a blanket. Knowing how tired she has been, I decide against it.

Bending down, I pick her up and carry her down the hall. As soon as she is in my arms, she instinctively wraps her arms around my neck and mumbles my name softly.

Once I lay her down on her bed, her eyes snap open, bright with panic and fear.

"Hey, hey. It's okay," I say reassuringly. "It's me, you fell asleep watching the movie, and I wanted to bring you to bed before I took off." Sitting on the edge of the bed, I lean down and brush the hair away from her face. Looking up at me, she flashes a tired smile as she leans her face into my palm.

I think too long about the worry in her eyes before she realized it was me, leaving me with a knot forming and taking root deep within my stomach. Thinking about where this intense fear could stem from, considering someone would so much as harm a hair on her head, fills me with a level of anger I haven't felt in a long time. I know without a shadow of a doubt that I would do anything to protect her.

"Thank you," she whispers softly. My eyebrows bunch together, forming a deep V, the question evident on my face. What could she possibly be thanking me for?

"Thank you for continuing to show me, in even little ways, that I can trust you. I know I pushed you away in the beginning out of fear. Thank you for not giving up on me."

She says the last part as a whisper.

I think she knows how I feel about her. Hell, I do my best to make sure I do more than just tell her. I want to show her through my actions.

"When I bumped into you that day at the bus station, I don't know if I could ever describe the way I felt. I was captivated by you. I spent the entire ride wanting to be close to you, trying to figure out a way to talk to you after you and your sexy ass stormed off," I confess, laughing. Fighting back a smile, I continue, "I could sense you had a wall up, a big wall. I know what it's like to have people in your life you trust walk away. I can promise you, Ellie, I'm not going anywhere. I'm going to be here, every day, reminding you why I'm not giving up on you," I say confidently. I have never said anything and meant it more than I do in this moment.

Tears fill her eyes as she takes in the words I've poured out to her, wanting her to understand the gravity of my feelings. The emotions that, while I am still working to understand fully, feel so strong and real.

"Will you stay with me?" Ellie's words come out in a whisper with a hint of vulnerability there.

Standing up, I plant both of my hands on either side of her hips and swing my leg over to the opposite side, climbing over her. Once I am lying on the bed, she moves her head to my shoulder, turning so she is curled into my side.

"You can go to sleep now, baby. I promise I'll still be here when you wake up," I reassure her, pulling her hand up to my mouth, pressing a soft kiss against her palm before resting it against my heart. She doesn't say anything as she lets out a soft sigh of contentment, closing her eyes.

Moving my hand to brush her hair away from her face, I get lost in how peaceful she looks like this. Hearing her breathing even out as sleep pulls her under, I run my lips on her temple and take a deep breath, letting the scent of Ellie wash over me.

Even in the quiet stillness of the room, I feel the fears I've tried to keep tamped down push their way up to the surface. I know it's no coincidence that these feelings reveal themselves after hearing from my father.

When you've had people disappoint you countless times, you can't help but expect for it to happen again. Focusing on the feelings and emotions I have for Ellie, I've fought against the fear that she can do to me what has happened so many times. What if she wakes up one day and decides Arbor Creek isn't where she wants to be?

The feelings I have for her grow stronger every day. The way she makes my heart race when she's near feels a lot like love. It's more powerful than anything I've ever felt.

It's foreign, but it feels so right all at the same time.

I think that's why I find myself fighting against her when she pushes me away. I know what it's like to have someone turn their back on you and give up so easily. All I've ever wanted was for someone to fight for me.

I do for Ellie what I wish would've been done for me all along.

I fight for her, while in the back of my mind I fear maybe, eventually, I could push her too much, to where she would walk away.

It scares the hell out of me. To want something but knowing that the more you give to them, the more you have to lose if they walk away. Or maybe I'm just scared of losing her because for as short of time as I've known Ellie, she has come to mean more to me than I ever thought possible.

Letting that realization wash over me, I close my eyes and let sleep pull me under, like the waves of reality crashing over me.

Thirteen

Ellie

Age 13

A LOT HAS HAPPENED SINCE I TOLD GRAMS ABOUT THE abuse. *As if my heart wasn't already breaking into pieces, I was shattered watching the way she sobbed after I told her everything.*

She promised me that day I would never have to go back there, and I was so grateful to hear those words.

Everything after that was a blur. Grams reported the abuse to the police department, and I was forced to sit behind some glass window, retelling them everything. Living through abuse has a way of breaking you down, crushing your soul through the weight of the burdens you carry until you're left with a shell of who you once were.

I quickly learned that the threats he made if I broke my silence were nothing more than promises of what was to come.

Walking out of the interview room, hearing my mother's cries, I knew she was just another person in my life to betray me, leaving me behind.

"YOU'RE A FUCKING LIAR, ELLIE. YOU TELL THEM THE TRUTH; YOU TELL THEM WHAT YOU SAID IS NOT TRUE," my mother wailed, throwing herself onto the floor.

It had taken three police detectives to restrain her, carrying her out of the room. I will never forget the words she yelled back at me as I watched her go.

"I can't believe you're doing this to me. You've taken everything away from me, Ellie. Tell them the truth!"

Staring down at my homework, I lazily draw circles along the side of the paper before lightly filling them in. Since it was almost the end of the school year, the principal and my teachers agreed to let me finish my assignments from home. Today was the first day I made it out of bed before one o'clock. I caught the way Grams looked at me, her eyes full of worry. I didn't want to upset her any more than she already has been, so I made a promise to myself I would get up early and focus on my school work. I'm smart enough to know I don't need or want to go back to my school, so I'll do whatever is needed to prevent that.

Grams left a short time ago to pick up the fixings from the store to make dinner. I heard her on the phone earlier this morning with her doctor. She wouldn't tell me, but I know the doctor is concerned about her blood pressure. He had called in a prescription for her to pick up while she was out.

As if on cue, the phone rings from where it hangs on the wall, drawing my attention away from the constant thoughts swirling in my mind. Pushing my chair from the dining room table, the chair scrapes across the floor as I stand up, making my way over to the phone. Pressing the receiver against my ear, I answer with a "hello" as I wrap my fingers around the tangled cord. I hear the phone clicking as I hold the phone in front of my face, wondering if the call disconnected.

"Hello, are you there?" I ask again as an uneasy feeling settles in my stomach.

"I was wondering if you were going to answer." I would know that gravelly voice anywhere as my hands tighten in a fist around the cord. My heart starts to pick up pace as the panic fills me. I don't think I could speak, even if I wanted to.

"What, don't tell me you thought that just because your Grams isn't home and you have me locked away that I wouldn't reach out to you."

How could he possibly know I'm at home alone right now? Covering my hand over my mouth, I fight back the strangled sob that threatens to let loose.

The detectives promised me that once I told them what happened, he would be put in jail where he couldn't hurt me again. The fear that he could've somehow got out has me sliding down the wall hiding beneath the counter of the breakfast bar.

"I'm going to have to make this quick; I gotta get back. I am upset with you for what you've done, Ellie. You've caused a lot of trouble for me, but I want you to know I forgive you. Once I get out of here, I'll come find you, and we can be together."

Bile rises in my throat as the strangled sob is unleashed. "Bye, sweet girl," he says before I hear the phone clicking once again.

Dropping the phone on the floor next to me, I pull my knees up to my chest as I wrap my arms around them tight, burying my face into the crease of my arms. I knew that free-dom from him was only temporary. I knew he meant what he said. That although he was going away for now, he would eventually be released.

A day would come when I would regret this decision. I just hoped I was far away from here when it came.

Jolting awake, the panic starts to set in as my eyes adjust to the darkness. The light from the bathroom is on with the door open just a little, casting a soft glow in the room. Feeling the weight of an arm draped across my hip and the warmth at my back, I turn my face to the side and see the light shining on the side of Callum's face.

All the tension I felt when I woke up leaves me in relief as I take in the stubble lining Callum's jaw down to his long lashes resting on his cheekbones. Just knowing he stayed with me is just another way he continues to show me he wants to be here with me.

Being mindful not to wake him, I attempt to slide out from beneath his hand draped across my side, needing to use the restroom and get a drink of water.

I just need to wrap my head around everything.

I should have known better than to think I could slip out unnoticed as his hand flexes around my hip, halting my movement.

"Hey, baby," Callum whispers, his words coming out more of a mumble. "You're awake." He smiles, as he covers his mouth to hide his yawn. I can't help but return his smile, just taking in the sleepy look on his face.

"I am, just having a hard time sleeping. When I woke up, I guess I wasn't expecting you'd still be here," I confess, looking down at his toned chest to avoid his eyes, rubbing my hand up the arm draped across my hip.

Seriously. These arms.

"You asked me to stay. If you give me the chance to be near you, I'm going to take it. I'm not going anywhere," he affirms, sliding his hand up the side of my body until he reaches my face. His open palm spans the side of my face, brushing my hair back in the process.

Placing my hand over the top of his, I take a minute to just appreciate the feel of him here with me.

Leaning forward, Callum presses his forehead against mine. When our eyes meet, I don't miss the look on his face. I can see it in his stare, something more there.

"Hey, is everything okay?" I ask as my brows furrow. "You look like something is bothering you, like your mind is somewhere else." Immediately, I want to be concerned; everything was fine when we got back to my house earlier. I don't know what could have changed in such a short time.

Callum rolls over, leaning back against the pillow and breaking our connection as he rubs his hand over his face. Turning over on my side, I move and lay my head on his shoulder resting my hand against his chest, feeling the steady beat of his heart beneath my palm.

Wrapping his hand around mine, he breaks the silence. "My father texted me earlier after you fell asleep. I haven't heard from him since I was in Chicago, and let's just say it didn't go over well." The words come out with a hint of sadness, and if I'm not mistaken, a tinge of anger.

"Do you want to talk about it?"

Staring up at the ceiling, the seconds tick by and after a while I think he is going to ignore my question and let it go.

"He has had an alcohol problem for as long as I remember. When he would drink, he often put his hands on my mom. More times than I can count, I would wake up hearing him yell as he smacked her around."

The anger I heard in his voice earlier is wrapped around every word he has spoken.

"I remember the last fight they had before my mom finally left him. He had stumbled through the door late at night. I don't know what time it was, but I know it had to have been late because even my mother had gone to bed. He had the nerve to get mad at her, to put his hands on her because she put the leftovers from dinner in the fridge. That asshole made her get out of bed to heat up his food, and when it wasn't hot enough for him, he slapped her across the face, splitting her lip in half.

"Growing up, he always wanted me to become a lawyer and follow in his footsteps. I didn't though. I'm not... I'm not like him." The last four words come out full of so much emotion. I can hear the uncertainty in his voice as if for a minute, he feared he could ever be like his father. "I don't want anything to do with him. I don't want to be like him. Why doesn't he get it?" he asks, looking me in the eye.

I can't help but think of how much both of our lives have been altered at the hands of people who brought us into this world. By people who are supposed to care for us.

"We aren't them, Callum," I say, angling my head up to look at him. His eyes are still focused intently at the fan circling above us. Moving my hand to the side of his face, I turn his head until his eyes are once again back on mine.

"You are not like your father, Callum Reid."

Nodding his head, he leans forward and presses a kiss against my lips. They are soft, but commanding. I can feel the emotion waging war beneath the surface. I don't let him pull back, instead urging him on, moving my hand into his hair, deepening the kiss. I can feel his mouth open as his tongue seeks entrance, and I open up to him.

It's as if everything goes right out the window and it's only the two of us here in this bed. Callum lets out a growl from somewhere deep in his chest, and the sound reverberates through me, followed by the feeling of warmth rushing through my bloodstream.

Rolling over onto my back, I pull Callum's body with me to avoid breaking our connection. As his tongue continues to duel with mine, I run my hand through the short hair at the base of his neck. Pulling back, he severs the connection but never breaks eye contact with me. He melts my insides with the words that come out of his mouth next.

"I would be a lucky fucking man to wake up next to you every day, Ellie. I want you to know that I won't ever stop showing you how happy you make me. I'll prove to you every day that being by your side is right where I want to be," he says, leaning down, placing a soft kiss on my lips, moving his way toward his favorite spot on my neck and ending just above my heart.

Callum is still laying on top of the blankets, the sheet adding a layer of separation between us. Pulling them back, he slides beneath them and resumes his position above me. He doesn't move closer, instead looking down at me as if he is silently asking for permission.

"I need to feel you," he says, the words filled with so much need. "I could start a fire with the way my body burns for you."

When his eyes meet mine again, I can see the desire in their fiery depths. Never taking my eyes off his, I run my fingers along his hip toward the waistband of his jeans. I can see the effect the movement has on him as his nostrils flare and his chest heaves as he struggles to control himself. I don't hide the way my mouth turns up, enjoying the way he responds to my touch.

Lifting the hem of his shirt, my fingers continue their path as they curl around his waist, pulling him forward pressing him against me. The move catches him off guard as his eyes light up with surprise, followed by a low moan as his body connects with mine positioning him between my legs. I can feel his arousal pressed against me as I let out a shuddering breath.

"Mmm, now that's better," I hum, moving my hand up his stomach, over his chest, wrapping it around the back of his neck. Pulling him closer to me, I press my lips against his in a searing kiss felt through every fiber of my body as Callum lets out a deep groan. As if he is unable to control himself, he rubs his cock against me, causing my body to jolt as pinpricks spread across my skin.

"FUCK! Ellie, baby, you feel so good. So fucking good," he moans, continuing to rock back and forth. The sound of his dirty words whispered in my ear and the feel of him rubbing against my swollen clit has me fighting for more as I run my hands down his back to his ass pressing him against me.

"I need more, Callum. I need you to give me more!" More of him, more friction, more of his lips pressed against mine. I need so much more and fear I will never get enough.

My legs tighten around his hips as if silently begging him to put me out of my misery.

Like a bullet shot out of a gun, he springs into action, leaning back pulling his t-shirt over his head, tossing it to the floor.

"Lift your arms," he whispers, grabbing the hem of my shirt, doing the same to mine just before he adds it to the pile. This is different than the time I was with Cameron on the couch in his living room with only the television offering any lights in the pitch-black room.

Having my body laid out here for Callum and the vulnerability of the way his stare burns a path over my skin has me wrapping my arms around my chest, covering myself.

"Please don't cover yourself up, baby. You have no idea, no fucking idea what you do to me."

Sliding off the bed, Callum stands before me not breaking our eye contact as he unbuttons his pants, shoving them down his legs along with his underwear. Bending down, he picks up his wallet and tosses a condom next to me on the bed. Kicking his pants to the side with the rest of our clothes, he tosses his wallet onto the pile. I watch as he widens his stance, wrapping his hand around his aching cock as he continues to work himself over with a clenched fist.

Words escape me as my tongue darts out to wet my dry lips.

Holy shit.

"Don't you see what you do to me? I fucking ache for you." He groans, grabbing my face in a kiss so passionate I can feel it clear down to my toes. It starts out as a spark, which leads to a slow burn. If this is the fire he was talking about, I hope we burn this whole house down.

Callum

I feel like at any second I'm going to explode, ending this before we ever have a chance to get started. Her lips are so soft and commanding as if she is begging me silently to give her more. Keeping my hand wrapped tight around my cock, I squeeze the tip to hold off my impending release.

That is until I feel Ellie's small and tentative hand wrap around mine, forcing my mouth away from hers as I let out a deep groan.

Her soft skin on my sensitive head has me biting the inside of my cheek as I struggle to keep all the blood from racing south.

"Callum," Ellie whispers encouragingly, begging me to open my eyes. I can't help but take in the way her hand wraps around me, her eyes bright with desire. Rubbing her thumb over the head of my cock, she swipes the drop of pre-cum before lifting her finger to her mouth.

"Holy fuck," I grunt, forcing a step back as I watch her mouth tighten around her finger. This isn't how I wanted our first time to go. I wanted to take my time with her, draw this out, and make her feel good.

"Give me a second, baby," I beg, squeezing my eyes shut, trying to fill my mind with anything other than what I just saw.

"No. You don't want me to cover up or hide from you, well I don't want you distancing yourself from me. I need to see you, feel you, kiss you."

Opening my eyes, I let them fall on her and rake them over her creamy smooth skin. Her hair is a mess, falling down her back in waves. Moving her hands so they are no longer covering her chest, she leans back on both of her palms. The move causes her chest to stick out further, forcing my attention to her beautiful breasts on display for me and only me.

Throwing the covers still wrapped around her torso to the side, removing every layer between us, I crawl onto the bed.

"Lay back, Ellie." Her body trembles before doing what I ask.

Running my hand along the inside of her leg, I kiss a slow path up her stomach until I'm positioned above her chest. Using my tongue, I circle her stiff peak before trailing kisses up her neck to my favorite spot.

"I've thought about what it would be like to be with you a thousand times, to watch you fall apart beneath me." Leaning back, I look into Ellie's eyes, needing her to see and hear the sincerity in my words. "I want you to know how much it means to me, for you to give yourself over to me," I say, leaning down to press a soft kiss against her lips.

Opening her mouth up to me, I find her tongue seeking entrance as I run my hand up the side of her face. "I'm yours, Callum. I want to be yours in every way," she whispers. The words are nearly my undoing.

Sliding my hand down her stomach, I dip my finger in her warm heat, finding her wet and ready. Pulling out my finger, I add a second, hearing her soft moans.

"I can't wait anymore, Ellie. I'm sorry, I promise next time I'll take my time, but I need to feel you." My voice rough. I'm wound so tight, I feel like at any minute I could break into a thousand pieces.

Grabbing the condom off the bed, I quickly tear it open and roll it down my length. Rubbing the head of my cock along

Ellie's wet pussy, I press a hard kiss against her lips. Sliding the tip inside her, I let out a deep breath forcing air into my lungs. I can't take my eyes off her as I pull out, before pushing my way in once again.

Dropping down to my elbows, I lean in closer as my hips thrust slow and steady.

"I want you to feel me, Ellie. Feel how your body comes alive beneath me. I don't want you to ever forget all the ways I can love you."

I can feel her body melt below me. She wraps her arms around my lower back as she digs her fingers into my ass. Raising her hips toward me, she urges me on.

Growling, my hips move faster as she clenches around my dick. She's coming and it's so tight, I nearly can't breathe.

"I'm going to come," I moan.

I can hear her whimper as she spreads her legs wider. Burying my face into her neck, I slam into her once, twice before following her over the edge.

All the emotions coursing through my body leave me feeling raw and exposed. What I didn't expect is the love I feel for her to surge through me.

Everything in my life leading up to this point has taken another piece of me. Breaking it off, bit by bit. In this moment, I know Ellie is helping mend the pieces of my broken heart. Together, she will make me whole again.

Fourteen

Ellie

I'M JUST WALKING OUT OF MY BEDROOM WHEN I HEAR knocking on the front door. Padding down the hallway, I flip the lock and swing the big wooden door open. I can't help the smile that takes over my face when I see the one greeting me.

"Morning, Ells!" Hudson says, his voice warm yet husky, holding up a bucket in his hand filled with what appears to be several tools.

Hudson reminds me of a big teddy bear, and he has a heart of gold to match. The day I found the ad on Craigslist and I called him from the phone outside the library, I hadn't told him a lot about me except I was moving out of Garwood to start over fresh. I will never forget the concern he had in his voice as he told me to be safe and even offered to give me the job at Hudson's to help get me on my feet.

After getting to know him, he's become more of a father figure to me. I feel safe with him around, and I know he is looking out for me. He doesn't know the details of my past, well at least I haven't told him. He still knows me as Ellie Hayes, and with that tidbit of information, it wouldn't be hard to dig up the past I've worked hard to keep buried.

"Good morning to you," I say, smiling back at him. Stepping to the side, I wave a hand in front of me ushering him inside.

"You feeling better after your fall? June told me you injured it slipping on the water coming from under the sink. Does it still hurt?"

"Thankfully, my head felt a lot better after I got a good night's sleep. My wrist is still a little sore, mostly when I try to bend it too much. I'm doing alright now though. Would you like something to drink? I have water, lemonade, or sweet tea. I just made the sweet tea yesterday, so it's fresh," I say as I walk over to the refrigerator.

"I'd love some sweet tea. Thank you, Ells!" He smiles as he bends down on his knees on the kitchen floor, looking up at me. "I'm glad to hear you're feeling better, too. Callum seemed to be anxious when he called me up yesterday," he says, moving things around underneath the sink.

"You talked to Callum about the sink?" I ask. I'm sure Hudson can hear the question in my voice. Growing up with Kinsley, I don't doubt Hudson got to know Callum well. Why am I not surprised he reached out to him after the trip to the hospital?

"He called to ask if he should hire someone to fix it. I'm going to see if I can figure out what's wrong with it. If not, I'll have someone come by the soonest I can to get it fixed," he reassures me, leaning underneath the sink, getting to work.

Taking the sweet tea out of the fridge, I pour two glasses, leaving one sitting on the counter near him. Heading over to the table, I sit down deciding to look through a magazine I picked up at Hudson's last night during my shift while keeping him company in case he needs anything.

Turning the page, I see an ad where the model is standing in the middle of a forest, reminding me of what I found outside the house. The anxiety and fear I felt seeing the pile of cigarette butts is once again back. Callum had taken my mind off it to the point where I had forgotten it until now.

"I didn't get a chance to tell Kolton thank you when he was over here last week. I think the mulch he put down around the trees and in the flower bed looks a lot better. Did he mention anything to you about the pot that must've tipped over behind the house?" I ask, the words coming out sounding more worried than I intended them to.

Hudson stops what he is doing, leaning back on his haunches before shooting me a questioning stare. "Didn't Kinsley give you the message?" His eyes are burrowed in confusion as if he's trying to piece together what I'm saying.

"About the pot spilling? Oh, it's not a big deal." I wave my hand at him, feeling relieved I was worried for nothing. Looking back down at the magazine, I flip to the next page. There is some gossip article about the recent Bachelorette couple splitting up. Do the people on those shows think their relationships are going to last? Seriously.

"Sorry, Ellie. I thought Kinsley had told you when you went to lunch the other day. She had stopped by before she was meeting up with you." Hudson stops, continuing to look confused. "Kolton wasn't able to stop by and do the lawn care last week. He had a test to take at school, so I came over and got the yard taken care of. Although I don't know anything about a pot spilling." He looks at me, searching my face as he waits for me to respond.

My hand stills as I'm turning the page, as my heart starts to pick up its pace. I tell myself there is nothing to fear. It's not at all what you assume it to be. He is behind bars right now; there is no way it's related.

My phone buzzes from where it sits on the dining room table. The sound and the vibration against the wood distracts me. Mumbling an apology to Hudson to give me a minute, I pick up my phone as a text message from Callum appears.

Callum: I can't stop thinking about last night.

My body hums as I feel my face heat up thinking back to how amazing Callum was last night. It's as if all the air has been sucked right out of me thinking about how good he made my body feel.

Callum: or this morning either ;)

I can't help the goofy grin that takes over my face. Once again, it's like all my fears are knocked right out of me. The sounds of Hudson resume as he works away not paying any attention to me.

Raking my teeth over my bottom lip, I focus my attention back on Callum as I quickly type out a response. While it has taken me awhile getting used to having a phone, it's days like this when he is at work I'm glad to have this connection to him.

Me: I can't either. I wish you were here.

Hitting the lock button, I look back over to Hudson bringing me back to the present. Callum is good at drowning out the world around me.

"Sorry," I mumble, "Back to what I was saying. There was a flower pot out back and it looks like it had been spilled over outside of my bedroom. It was full of cigarette butts." Letting out a slow breath, I take a second to prepare myself for my next question as I wrap my hand around my necklace. "Do you know who those are from? Besides Callum and Kinsley, you and Kolton are the only ones who are ever here."

I feel like I'm holding my breath waiting for him to respond. Leaning back on his knees again, I can see the look of concern on his face. He must sense my fear, the way I clutch onto my necklace when I'm nervous is a dead giveaway.

"Ellie, no one should be here unless you want them to be. I'll take care of it out back before I take off. I want you to know you can call me if you need anything, ya hear?" He grunts, making it clear he's serious. "If something's wrong like your sink or somethin's got you uneasy, you tell me. I don't live far, and I can be over here in two minutes if I need to be. Plus, I know both Callum and Kinsley wouldn't like it much knowin' you're worried."

Raising his eyebrow at me, he's calling me out, and I nod my head letting him know I hear him. He isn't wrong; I'm good at keeping people at arm's length.

"You got the day off today, why doncha head into town and see what Kins is up to?" he says, turning away and getting back to work under the sink.

"That sounds like a good idea." The stress I hadn't realized had been weighing me down lessened some just hearing him reassure me of the people I have in my life that I can trust.

Deciding to stop by the library to return my book I finished yesterday, I shoot off a text to Kinsley, asking if she'd be interested in grabbing lunch. Just as I snag my books and purse after saying goodbye to Hudson, a text comes through from Kins saying she's wrapping up with a client and will be waiting.

After the last twenty-four hours, I really could use some time with my friend. I'm glad to have one to turn to.

I have so much on my mind the entire bike ride into town. Between the news from Hudson, Callum texting me, and my constant thoughts of last night, I've been on a rollercoaster.

To think it's only been two weeks since the night at Champions, so much has happened. I can't help but feel like last night changed everything between us. The way it felt to have him wrapped in my arms, to give myself to him. I've never felt more cherished and safe in my life. I want to open up to him about my past, but I'm scared of exposing the wounds of my past.

He has the power to destroy me, and that's what scares me the most.

If I'm honest, I'm terrified of how he would react. The uneasiness of him looking at me differently than he does now scares me. If I think too long about it, the fear of never finding this again with someone else has me wanting to wrap my arms around him.

He has the power to crush my already broken heart if he

were to walk away from me.

Leaning my bike against the side of the library building, I grab my purse from the front basket and drape it across my left shoulder as my phone starts to vibrate in my pocket.

Smiling to myself, I slide my phone out, finding a missed text from Callum. His job has kept him busy wrapping up the loose ends before he goes out of town on Sunday, so any opportunity to talk to him before he leaves makes me happy.

Callum: Staring at all these papers on my desk, I can't even concentrate. I miss you, sweetheart, and those lips.

My lips feel tingly just thinking about kissing Callum.

Feeling bold, I open the Camera app and scroll over to the video option. Turning the camera so it's facing me, I hold the phone out in front of me. Hitting the record button, I smile at the camera and tell Callum I miss him, too, before blowing him a kiss. Before I consider chickening out, I upload the video and quickly hit send.

Staring at the messages, I wait to see the bubble appear alerting me he's typing. Chewing on my lip, I count the seconds as they tick by waiting for him to finish typing until my phone vibrates again with his message.

Callum: Fuuuuck, you're beautiful.

"Ellie, is that you?" I hear, startling me. I can feel my face turn red as if I was caught doing something wrong. Not to mention, not many people know me in town.

Turning around, I recognize Jeff standing in front of me.

He looks handsome with a navy and orange plaid button up shirt, worn denim jeans, and brown Oxfords. His hair is styled so it's swept out of his face in a careless look. He has an easy smile and strikingly beautiful eyes.

"Jeff, hey! Nice to see you!" I say, remembering my manners but also not forgetting the way Callum reacted to seeing him at the hospital.

"It's great to see you, too. You look good," Jeff says, raking his eyes down my body briefly before bringing them back to meet mine. "How is your wrist?" he asks, seemingly interested.

"It's okay, still a little sore but feeling much better. Thank you," I say, ignoring his earlier comments. I feel awkward because both times I've been around him there was some nervous tension between him and Callum. I still don't know their history, but I can tell something is there boiling beneath the surface.

Jeff, being a complete gentleman, continues to ask questions about how things have been since the move and asks what I'm out doing. I humor him, but in the back of my mind, I know that this conversation would likely upset Callum, which I'm not interested in doing.

"Do you have any plans for this evening?" he hints, "I know this is short notice and all but I have tickets with a couple of friends to the Jason Aldean concert for this weekend up in Monroe. I have an extra one if you'd be interested?"

"I'm sorry, I have plans," I say, feeling uncomfortable. He must pick up my hint, nodding his head. "Thanks for the invite, though; it's kind of you to offer."

This is not something I'm used to doing, turning down a date. Where I am from, most people didn't even notice me.

Correction: Most people wanted to pretend I wasn't there.

"I should probably get going," I mumble, pointing behind me toward the library. "I have a lunch date after I get done with some errands."

"Yeah, sure no problem. It was great to see you." He smiles brightly, leaning in and kissing me on the cheek, his hand pressed against my lower back. I feel my body tense at the unexpected gesture. Reminding myself to breathe, I take a step back forcing a smile and leaving him with a wave.

Callum

Rubbing my fingers across my forehead, I massage it hoping the pressure alleviates the dull ache. I've been looking over these documents and contracts for an upcoming project, and things just aren't adding up. I'm sure if I took a break and closed up for the night, coming back to it fresh tomorrow will probably help, but I need to get this squared away. I have no desire to come into the office on a Saturday.

This project has been consuming my every minute this week.

The vibrating sound of my phone on my mahogany desk draws my attention away from the papers laid out in front of me. Reaching over, I pick up the phone hoping to see Ellie's name across my screen. We have plans for me to stop by to-night. Since I'm heading out of town on Sunday, I want to spend all the time I can with her.

I can't help the annoyance that seeps in seeing a missed text message from Madison. Ever since the night at Brodie's, I made it abundantly clear I was no longer interested. She didn't take it very well, but she hasn't been known to back down.

If she thinks I'm interested, she has another thing coming.

Mad: I didn't realize your friend was talking to Jeff as well?

What the fuck is she talking about? Tapping on the keyboard, I start to type out a response when a picture pops up on my screen. Double clicking on it, the image maximizes to the full screen, and my heart drops to my stomach as I curl my fist.

"What the fuck?" I shout.

The picture in front of me is a man leaning down in front of him to a petite blonde. The man has one of his hands pressed against her lower back and his head angled down toward her neck. Although I can only see Ellie from behind, I can tell it's her by the color of her hair and the shirt she is wearing. It's the same shirt she was wearing in the video she sent me earlier.

Growling in response to seeing another man with his arms wrapped around my girl, I stand up, pushing my chair against the wall, hitting it with a loud bang.

The throbbing pain in my head continues as I stand with my arms crossed in front of me, rubbing my head. Picturing Ellie with Jeff, thinking about him being on the receiving end of her sweetness, fills me with so much rage. Questions of when they were together and what they were doing consume me, and I know I need to leave. I need to go to her, talk to her, and get answers.

I'm not going to go through this again.

The knot in the pit of my stomach leaves me feeling

nauseating. Shuffling the papers on my desk together, I deposit them in my file cabinet and quickly lock up. As I walk out, I see the light in Randy's office is still on.

"Hey, I'm going to take off. I got some things to take care of. I'll be in at some point to wrap things up before I head out on Sunday," I say curtly.

Randy looks up at me from his desk. "Everything okay, son?" he asks, concern lining his brow.

"S'all good," I say, wanting to make it quick so I can leave.

"I could hear you yelling and banging around in there. Does it have to do with your brother?"

Ever since the argument with Mason, I've continued to answer questions from my mom and Randy. I know they are just worried, but at this point, there isn't much to say.

"No, just have some things to handle."

"Alright, son, you have a good night and drive careful," he says, nodding his head as I exit his office. Not wasting any time, I head out to the parking lot around the back where my pick-up is parked and pull the keys from my pocket. Pushing the button to unlock the door, I hear the beep of the alarm as the locks click.

Climbing in the cab, I throw my phone in the cup holder and lean back with my head against the headrest. I need to chill out before I talk to Ellie, knowing it would likely scare her or piss her off. I keep hoping I've misunderstood the picture Madison sent, but seeing his arms wrapped around her and his head near her neck has a weight settling on my chest nearly crushing me.

Picking up my phone, I shoot Wes a text asking him to meet me up at Brodie's when a text message from Ellie comes through.

Ellie: When will you be here? Miss you.

Hearing those words from Ellie has me rubbing my hand over my chest fighting off the tightness I feel. Wes responds back that he'll meet me there in ten minutes.

Me: I'm meeting up with Wes for a beer at Brodie's.

Staring back at the screen on my phone, I can see she read the message and the bubble appears alerting me that she is typing a response. I know she is probably wondering what is going on and I can't help but feel like I'm going out of my mind thinking the same thing.

Ellie: Oh. Okay.

I throw my phone over on the passenger seat away from me. I know I need to talk to Ellie about the text message. I'm taking my past with Jeff out on Ellie, but I can't help wanting to demand that she tell me what the hell this is about.

I just need to cool off before I go in heated and end up ruining things with her. A few minutes later I pull up in front of Brodie's next to Wes's motorcycle. It's a chilly night, and the sun is starting to set, but that has never stopped Wes from riding. These are the nights he enjoys the most.

Heading up to the bar, I take a seat next to Wes, clapping a hand on his back.

"What's up, bro?" The words coming out rougher than I intended. Sitting down, I see he took the liberty of ordering me a beer, which I'm grateful for.

"Hey, man, not much. Everything alright?" It's not unlike

me to call or text Wes on short notice and ask him if he's free to meet for a beer. I'm sure my less than chipper self tells him that something is off.

Pulling my phone out of my pocket, I pull up the text message from Mad and hand my phone over to him. "I was great up until I got this message about an hour ago."

Picking up the phone from the bar, he studies the message and picture. Handing it back to me, he looks up at me with the same anger in his eyes. He knows all about my history with Jeff.

"Is that who the fuck I think it is?" he spits out angrily, pointing at the blonde in the picture. Wes has been here for me through it all. Through all the bullshit with Madison and Jeff. This isn't the first time we've had a look of hatred in our eyes for him.

Nodding my head, I acknowledge his question. Rubbing my fingers across my forehead again, I wrap my fingers around the neck of the bottle and take a swig.

"She met him that night at Brodie's, and we ran into him again when we were up at the hospital," I say, pain and frustration lacing my voice.

"Have you asked her about it? Maybe it is all a misunderstanding," Wes questions. He knows as well as I do that having his arms wrapped around Kinsley would easily set him off, too. Mad is hardly a person to be trusted when it comes to being a trustworthy source of information.

"Nah, I haven't talked to her much except to tell her I was meeting you here. Although, I made it a point the day we were at the hospital I wanted him nowhere near her, which she was pissed about. I needed to chill before I approached the subject." Wes nods in agreement.

"I think you should talk to her. Ask her what's going on." Shaking my head, I look up at the TV screen mounted on the wall. "You're different with her, man. She's not Madison. Don't let her fuck this up for you, that's what she wants."

I hang around for a little while longer, shooting the shit. I tell Wes about the job coming up and how I'll be heading out of town on Sunday. We bullshit about how things are going with the bike rebuild and how things are going at the shop. Two beers and a little over an hour later, I'm ready to head out to see my girl.

Fifteen

Callum

WHEN I PULL UP THE GRAVEL OF HER DRIVE, THE light on her front porch is on, and I can see the soft glow of the lamp shining through the window. I picture her sitting on her couch with a book in her hand or curled up under her blanket.

Opening the screen door, I knock twice before taking a step back. I use it as separation from her because nothing is stopping me from taking her in my arms when she's standing before me. Through the window, I can see her eyes peer out at me with her hair piled high up on her head. She's wearing the glasses she normally wears for reading, so it looks like I was right.

The locks click and the old doorknob twists and creaks as she swings the door open. Her eyes are full of concern and worry. Her left arm is wrapped around her middle while her right hand tucks a piece of hair behind her ear. I can see the hesitancy in her movements, uncertain what's going on.

"Hi," she mumbles softly, looking up at me to meet my eyes. "Everything okay?"

"I'm hoping you can tell me," I say, jumping right into it. "Can I come in?"

She nods and steps back, motioning for me to enter. Sliding my shoes off, I follow her over to the couch to take a seat. It takes everything in me not to wrap her up in my arms and pull her to me. My need to feel her close is consuming me, but I know now more than ever that I need to address the elephant in the room.

"Have you been seeing anyone else?" I ask, needing to know the answer to my question. The anger in me from the picture bubbles out, giving an edge of irritation to my tone.

"What the hell do you mean?" she bites back harshly. There she is – my feisty girl.

She keeps so many things hidden from me, and I've given her space in letting our relationship progress naturally, not wanting to put pressure on her. I know there are parts of her she hasn't been ready to share with me yet. I understand and respect that. With everything going on, now the questions swirling around in my brain have me questioning so much.

Things I don't want to question. Not with her.

Putting both of my elbows on my knees, I fold my hands together and rest my chin against them in thought.

"What are we exactly?" I question, turning my head to look at her, searching her eyes for answers. "Who am I to you, Ellie? You know how I feel but you keep so much from me that sometimes I worry I don't even know who you are."

A wave of hurt flashes on her face as her hand wraps

around her necklace. She starts to rub her fist over her chest, as if my words are causing her physical pain which makes me feel like shit.

"Up until you showed up here and started spewing this bullshit at me, I thought we were together. After what happened last night, I sure as shit hoped we were. I don't have a label for it," she says, raising her voice. "I don't know what it is exactly. We've never discussed it. If I'm being honest with myself, the way you look at me and the way you make me feel does more to me than anything I've ever felt before. More than any label I could possibly put on it. I just knew I was yours, and I thought you were mine. However, now I'm questioning what the hell is going on," she says with a huff, sliding to the opposite end of the couch, putting space between us.

More space than I want between us right now.

All I can think about after hearing her out is the part about how the way I look at her and make her feel is more than any label she could come up with. Leaning back against the back of the couch, I open my arm in invitation. "Come here, baby," I say softly.

Her eyes roam over my face with a questioning glare. Her face softens as she slides closer to me. Shaking my head at her movements. "Not good enough, babe. I need to feel you."

Sliding back to give her room, I motion for her to climb over me straddling my lap. Swinging her leg over, she slides over onto my lap. Moving my hands up her thighs and over her hips, I drag her closer so she is pressed against me, leaving little space between us as I hear the subtle inhale of her breath.

Sliding my phone out of my pocket, I pull up my messages and click on the picture Madison sent me. Seeing the picture again has the anger bubbling along the surface, tempting me.

Turning the screen around to face Ellie, I study her reaction as I ask, "Care to tell me what this is about?"

A look of surprise passes over her face as she studies the picture. I can tell something is bothering her by the way she chews on her bottom lip, avoiding my stare.

"Is this what has you so upset?" Ellie asks, choosing to ignore my question. Leaning in closer wrapping her hands around my neck, she draws me in so my forehead is pressed to hers.

"It's not what it looks like, I swear," she whispers against my mouth. Letting a breath out I didn't realize I was holding, I nod my head. Leaning back a little to look me in the eyes, she keeps her hands wrapped around my neck.

"I ran into him outside of the library when I was heading over to Kinsley's salon to meet up with her for lunch. He saw me when I was locking my bike up and was saying hello. This was him saying goodbye," she explains, pointing towards the picture.

"I don't want him touching you or anywhere near you. You are mine, Ellie!" I growl in response.

Ellie moves to slide back, breaking the connection that we had. Her arms are crossed in front of her, and her face is straight with indignation. She exudes so much sass I nearly laugh. This is not up for negotiation. She is mine and I will not let anyone, especially Jeff Sahls, touch what belongs to me.

"You look real cute when you're mad, sweetheart. Any argument you have on this topic is pointless. It's a fucking fact, like the grass is green and the sky is blue. You are mine and I don't want anyone touchin' you, especially him!"

"Why did you get so upset the day we were at the hospital?" she asks, searching my face. I should've known sooner or later this conversation would come up again. I should've expected she would want to know our history, and that's not something I want to go into. The past, just like it is for her, is not something I want to explain or relive.

"I got upset at the hospital because Jeff has a history of going after what is not his to touch and what happens to be mine."

"Madison," she says, matter-of-factly. I only respond with a nod of the head. "That…" She pauses, as if she is searching her memory.

"That's why… it makes sense now," she says, pressing her fingers to her lips as if everything is coming back to her and the pieces are starting to fit together. "I saw Madison outside at the bar when I went out to take a breather. She approached me and made a comment about me having good taste in men. I didn't think too much into it at the time. I thought she was talking about you, but she wasn't. She was talking about Jeff, too."

Nodding my head, I look down to where my hands are holding her in place. I know it's time for me to tell her the rest of the story, seeing the questions in her eyes. Pulling her back against me, I begin.

"Madison and I started dating our sophomore year of high school. She was beautiful, outgoing, and full of life. It's what drew me into her. She and Kinsley hung out quite a bit so it was only natural we would run into each other. Not to mention, it's not like Arbor Creek is big to begin with. They were both in cheerleading together, and with us playing football, we were often at the same places, running in the same crowds, that sort of thing."

Letting out a deep breath, I don't even realize how much

this has been weighing on me.

"Jeff and I were buddies, I mean we played football together and ran around with the same group of people. There was a party one night, out on some land down by the woods. I didn't end up going. I messed up my back during a game so I was laid up, resting at home with muscle relaxers. Madison was there though, with her friends, and she hooked up with Jeff. The bigger problem was it didn't stop after the first night. Apparently, it happened a couple times and I had no idea. Kinsley heard about it from their other mutual friends and ended up breaking it to me."

"Oh, God, I'm so sorry, Callum." She sobs, pulling me into a hug. "I'm sorry," she whispers, laying her head on my shoulder.

"Madison and I were over after that. We saw each other over the years, but as far as a relationship goes we have been over for a long time. She just doesn't seem to get it through her head. She knew if I thought you were talking to him, I would cut you off. It's what she wanted."

Ellie moves to lean back, and for the first time since the day at the bus station, I see a glimpse of the broken woman she works to keep hidden away from me.

"That's what she wanted, she wanted you to believe that I was like her. That I would betray you, try to hurt you." Tears stream down her face but she doesn't move to wipe them away as she continues. "I wouldn't, Callum. I don't want to do anything to hurt you. Not ever." Hiccupping, she lets out a sigh.

Rubbing my thumbs underneath her eyes, I wipe away the moisture on her face.

"How can you be this beautiful even when you're crying?" I whisper, bringing her face closer, pressing her lips against mine. Running my tongue along the seam of her mouth, she opens for me.

Groaning against her mouth, I lean back and whisper, "Take your hair down."

Letting one of her hands go from the side of my neck, she untwists the hair tie, letting her soft hair fall down her back in waves. Wrapping my fingers in her hair, I draw her mouth against mine again and take her in another life altering kiss.

Her lips against mine is like a direct line to my cock. Need pulsating through me, I slide one of my hands down her shoulder over her arm to her hip and press her against me. Feeling how much my body needs her, Ellie begins to grind her hips against me. Her heat pressed against mine, creating a friction in my pants, has me fighting against my own arousal.

Keeping my forehead pressed against hers, I lean my mouth away from hers as I let out a moan. "Fuck, baby, you feel so good pressed against me."

This woman is a mixture of so many things. She is soft spoken, kind, and caring. Yet other times she is fiercely passionate, determined, and so stubborn. She is so many things I never knew I wanted yet, everything I've always needed. I can't imagine what my life would be like without her in it.

Taking my right hand, I frame it along the side of her face, pressing it against my palm. The light from the lamp on the end table casts a muted glow against the softness of her face. I search her gaze for any hesitation but there is none there. Instead, what I find is desire, pure and raw.

"Ellie, I have to tell you it's taking everything in me not to take you right here."

Before I know it, she leans back and all contact is gone. Standing before me, Ellie slides the soft cotton of her lounge pants down her slender legs until they are pooling at her feet. Crossing her arms over her chest, she grabs the hem of her shirt and whips it over her head adding her shirt to the pile. Standing in front of me, she looks like an angel in her bra and panties. Her long hair falls down her back with pieces framing her face, laying over the swell of her breasts.

"Fuuuuuck!" I groan.

"I want you to touch me," she commands.

Holding my hand out to her, Ellie resumes her position on my lap. Wrapping my arms around her lower back, I pull her until she is flush against my chest and her knees are pressed against my hip.

"Come here, baby," I say, using my right hand to frame her face, bringing her mouth back to mine.

As soon as our lips connect, it's like a match was lit in my bloodstream and everything is heading south to my cock. Letting out a deep moan, I hold her mouth to me, continuing the assault. Her tongue continues to duel with mine, giving to me as much as I give it back to her.

Ellie wraps her arms around my neck, pressing herself to me. Her body molded to mine, not knowing where I end and she begins. Looking for relief, she continues to grind herself against me, rubbing her pussy back and forth over my aching cock.

"Ellie, sweetheart, you can't do that or this is over before we've even had a chance to get started," I say, mumbling on a groan.

"Callum, I need you to touch me," she says, begging as I run my finger over the soft swell of her breast down her stomach. Her body trembles beneath my touch.

"You want me to rub this sweet pussy for you?" I groan.

I'm so fucking hard right now that my cock is two seconds away from busting through my pants.

Jesus fuck!

"Yes! Yes, please!" she says, continuing to rub her pussy against me.

"Lean back, baby," I command, sliding my hand down her stomach, moving her underwear to the side. When my finger finds its way home in her wet heat, I let out a strangled growl.

"Holy shit, baby, you're so fucking wet. Is this for me?" I ask, needing to hear her words.

"Yessss!" she says as I slowly slide my finger up, between her folds rubbing her clit. "Oh, God, don't stop," she moans.

"I couldn't stop even if I tried. I'm going to give this sweet pussy exactly what it wants." I groan, stroking her clit back and forth, moving lower entering one finger into her tight heat. Pulling back out, I add a second.

Dear God, what kind of sweet hell have I got myself into?

I continue to fuck her with my fingers while she rides my hand, rubbing her clit against my palm. It doesn't take long until I feel her body tense up, and I know she is close. Leaning in, I continue to fuck her with my fingers as I kiss down her jaw to my favorite place where the base of her neck meets her shoulder.

Kissing back up her neck, I whisper in her ear. "You look so sexy like this, Ellie. Using my hand to find your pleasure. Come all over my hand, baby. I want to taste you."

Just like that, she throws her head back and continues to grind against my hand, riding out her orgasm, taking every ounce of pleasure. The confidence she exudes is so fucking hot, it has me nearly turning her over and taking her on this couch.

Taking my hand out of her underwear, I move them back in place and immediately draw my fingers into my mouth to taste her sweet juices. She keeps her eyes fixed on mine as I do, letting out a moan. Pulling her closer, her lips meet with mine.

Leaning back, I whisper, "Baby, you taste better than anything I have ever dreamed of."

Ellie

With my legs draped across Callum's lap, I rest my head on his shoulder as I struggle to regain my breath. Lost in thought, my mind replays every moment with Callum as I run my index finger across the collar of his shirt.

Just thinking about what Callum has come to mean to me over the past few weeks fills my heart. The emotions have consumed me. I don't know if there are even words to express it. It's something I've never experienced before, a feeling so deep in my soul.

He broke down all the walls I had around my heart without me even noticing.

"Why so quiet, sweetheart?" Callum questions, turning his head toward mine, rubbing his lips against my forehead.

"I'm just thinking."

"About what?" he asks. The words come out mumbled with his mouth still pressed against my temple.

"About you, about life, how I ended up here," I say, absorbing the warm feeling flowing through me from his closeness.

Leaning away from me, Callum moves his hand beneath

my chin and lifts my eyes to meet his, searching. I can see the questions in his gaze as he looks for the answers hidden on mine. I know he is concerned, especially when he looks down at my hand to see it wrapped around my necklace.

I'm not sure if I'm ready to share everything about my past with him yet. Callum has shared his secrets and trusted me with his heart. He deserves to hear mine, to know about the scars that I keep buried deep.

My heart rate picks up at the thought of how he will feel about me when I'm exposed to him. It's more than just skin deep.

Could he ever love the person I am beneath it all?

"Whatever it is, you're nervous or you wouldn't be holding your necklace," he whispers, wrapping his hand around mine. Silently asking me to open up to him, to trust him.

It's the strength I need to tell him about my past.

"My dad was the greatest man I've ever known. He was brave, honorable, and kind. He would've really liked you. He taught me never to judge a book by its cover, rather to open the book and read it page by page. He believed you got to know people by what's written in their heart," I say, feeling his presence wrapped around me, just thinking about his memory.

"Growing up, we had an unspoken agreement every Sunday he would make us pancakes. He liked to make mine in the shape of Mickey Mouse topped with chocolate chips." I can't help the smile taking over my face. "We would dance around the kitchen with pancake batter splattered all over us, singing the lyrics to 'Ain't No Mountain High Enough' as they cooked away."

Remembering how happy my father was standing in the kitchen, the way his broad smile would light up the room.

"I knew something was wrong when I woke up that Sunday morning to find my dad wasn't there. Waking up, I ran into my parents' bedroom, only to find the blankets untouched." My mind drifts back to the soft cries I heard in the living room as my feet quietly padded down the hallway toward the living room. "I searched all over for him only to find my mom laying on the couch, curled in a ball, crying.

"I tried talking to her, but the second the words escaped my lips, her shrill wails shook her entire body. The pain in her cry terrified me, as I took off running towards the hallway. With my body pressed against the wall, I didn't know what to do, so I just stood there and watched her as tears streamed down my face."

I could still hear the harsh sobs overtake her body, the way her hands wrapped around her stomach as if she was trying to hold herself together but could barely contain it.

"A little while later, my Grams showed up and took me to the park. Looking back on it, I could see the grief written all over her face. I remember wanting to fight her on it, to beg her to stay with me while we waited for my dad to get home. She put on a brave face though, just like my dad would've."

I can feel the tears threatening to spill down my face as I quickly brush my finger under my eye. I know if I wasn't wrapped in Callum's arms, I wouldn't be able to get through this. Taking a deep breath, I force the words out as I continue. They don't even sound like me as I replay the day I found out my father had died.

They sound cold and detached.

"Everything changed after my father's death. I hardly even recognized the person my mother had become. She went from being someone who was nurturing and loving to someone who was angry and acted like I wasn't even there. She blamed me for what happened to my father. She would get so drunk sometimes, she couldn't even walk. She would try to crawl to her bedroom, only to pass out in the middle of the hallway. It got to the point where I practically lived in my bedroom just to escape her.

"As time went on, I started to forget who she was before my father died. In a way, I felt like the person she was before had died right along with him. When she wasn't drowning in vodka, she had a new boyfriend coming in and out of the house. They weren't all that bad. Honestly, most of them just ignored me and left me alone, which was fine because the older I got, the more I understood being left alone was a blessing."

I can feel the words getting stuck in my throat as Callum's entire body tenses, sensing where this conversation is going. I can't hold it back anymore. The tears stream down my face, the emotions speaking all the words I can't bring myself to say.

"I don't know how it was possible, but her drinking only got worse when Royal started to come around. There were times they would leave me home by myself until late at night, only to come home stumbling through the door. With my mom passed out, it gave him the opportunity to be alone with me."

Callum moves to wrap his hands around the side of my face, pushing my hair back with it as he tips my head up to look at him. I wasn't expecting to find what I see staring back at me as more tears fill my eyes, threatening to fall from his eyes.

"Please tell me you are not about to say what I think you're going to. *Please, Ellie.*" The words coming out of his mouth sound like a plea, my heart breaking with his.

"It first started out as little things, like touching me over the top of my clothes or making me sit on his lap. When he moved in though, it changed," I whisper, nearly choking on the words. "There was one night my mom had passed out early into the evening. They had been drinking heavily for most of the day. I was young, around twelve or so, when he played a trick on me mixing my glass of water with his vodka. I had never drank alcohol so I didn't know what to expect. It must not have taken much though. I remember waking up in the middle of the night feeling sick to my stomach, only to find him there.

"I don't remember anything, I don't know what happened. I just know that next morning when I woke up my underwear had been on inside out. I know he had touched me and I feel disgusting when I even think about it.

"After that night, I had a hard time sleeping. I would spend all night laying in my bed, watching the door as if I was waiting for him to walk through the door."

My breath is coming out in pants so strong, struggling to break through the rise and fall of my chest. Callum leans forward with his forehead against mine, as I feel his tears fall, mixing with mine.

I thought telling Callum had the possibility to break me, but what I didn't think of was how much this would break him in the process.

"I'm sorry," I say, the weight of these words settling on my chest. "I know what you must be thinking and I'm sorry."

Callum quickly pulls back, his eyes wide and wild. "You have nothing to be sorry for, do you hear me? Nothing!" The words come out of his mouth so quick, but firm. "I swear to God, Ellie. I will kill the motherfucker, I'll kill him." The words roll off his lips. Leaning back with his head against the couch cushion, Callum rubs his hands over his face wiping away his tears.

"He... he's in prison," I say, hoping to reassure him.

Moving to slide off his lap, Callum wraps his hand around my legs draped across his lap, halting me from moving. "Please don't move, I need to feel you next to me. I can't help but picture, I can't help-" he says, cutting himself off as he runs his hand back over his face, trying to stay calm.

"I feel like I'm picturing what happened to you, him hurting you and it's making me go out of my mind right now. I just need to feel you with me right now. I need to know you're here in my arms, that you're safe."

Callum is always so strong, especially for me, but I can't help but feel like he's getting lost in his head.

Moving my legs, I resume my position with my knees on either side of his hips. I need and want more than anything to feel him closer to me. Wrapping my arms around his neck, I lay my head against his shoulder, feathering kisses down his neck.

"Callum, I'm here. I know you'll always keep me safe," I whisper. "It's because of you that my heart is starting to feel whole once again."

"I wish I didn't have to leave so soon," he groans, wrapping his arms around me, holding me closer to him. "It's only four days, but I know it's going to feel like forever."

I haven't felt as close to someone as I do to Callum in a very long time. When I came to Arbor Creek, I was broken and lost. I can't help but feel like I've found all I had been looking for right here in Callum's arms and in his heart.

Sixteen

Callum

"ARE YOU FUCKING SHITTING ME?" I GRUNT, LEANing over the bed of the pick-up truck. Reading through the order of materials, I scan the invoice for the information I'm looking for but come up empty.

"Elliott, can you come here?" I shout over the sound of the guys unloading the materials while one of the trucks beep as it backs up. "I need you to get on the phone with Randy and find out how this could've gotten messed up. The order is correct so we need to figure out why we are missing half of the materials."

The stress of the day is weighing down on my shoulders as the sunshine hanging overhead beats down on me. We have been working on this job, remodeling one of our hospitals up north. It's a huge job for Whitt's. The time it would take to get an order in for the missing materials would likely push the plan back a week, extending my time.

"Sure thing, boss," Elliott says as I hand the invoice over to him.

Nodding my head, I look down at my phone to check the time. I silently groan when I see it's not even lunchtime. This is going to be one hell of a long day.

I'm ready to call it a day, head back to the hotel, and call Ellie. As much as it's been a pain in the ass being away from her, I've enjoyed spending every night with her sweet voice on the other end of my phone. I can't help but feel like the distance has brought us closer together. Clicking on my messages, I scroll through to Ellie's name, pulling up our conversation from yesterday.

Since the incident with Jeff, she has sent me pictures or videos of herself every day. Talking to her helped me get through being away, but seeing her beautiful face in the pictures she sends brings a grin to my face every damn time. Staring down at the last picture she sent me, she's standing in the backroom at Hudson's wearing a button up plaid shirt. Her hair is pulled up, away from her face, with a few strands left hanging down. Her lips shimmer from the stuff she likes to put on that smells like watermelon.

"Okay." I hear Elliott approaching as I close out of the message and turn toward him. "I just talked to Randy. I got good news and bad news. The good news is the order is in; it was just split into two separate shipments." He is hesitating in the rest of it so I know where this is going.

"What's the bad news?" I spit, cutting to the chase.

"The bad news is it won't be in until Friday," he says, inciting an immediate grumble from me as I know exactly what this will mean.

"I'm sorry, man. I need to get back, we have the rehearsal dinner. I was on the phone with Trisha for two hours last night because she was hysterical over everything. Being away is putting a lot of stress on her right now," he says, picking up on my frustration. It's not his fault, there's nothing he could've done to prevent it.

We were only supposed to be in town through Wednesday, heading home tomorrow morning. Elliott is getting married this weekend, and while it is important for me to have him here on this job, I know it's more important for him to get back home to his fiancée.

However, now I'm likely not going to get done at the job site until late on Friday. I could probably make the drive back to Arbor Creek, but after a long day at work and seven hours on the road, it'll make for a long fucking night.

"Not your fault, man, I'm happy for you and Trisha. I'm just glad I'll still be able to make it. I'm looking forward to getting back," I say, knowing he understands what I mean. I hate this living out of a hotel shit. Like me, he wants nothing more than to get back home to his girl.

"I feel ya, bro. You know I would stay back and cover for you if it were any other time," he says, holding out his hand to me.

"Of course, I do, man," I say, shaking his hand. "Thanks for checking into the order for me, glad it isn't going to set us back in our time line. We need this to run like a smooth fucking ship from here."

My phone vibrates in my hand. Glancing down, I hope it's Ellie with another picture of her. As if the news we just received wasn't bad enough, the notification popping up on my screen adds another layer of shit to the pile. Letting out a groan, I click on the message.

Steven Reid: I'll be in town a week from Saturday. I'd like it if we could meet for lunch.

I still haven't reached out to my father after the text I received at Ellie's the other night. The way I see it, what else is there to talk about? Not to mention, the asshole doesn't even ask if we can go to lunch, and instead just implies, like I would agree to his statement, makes me want to blow him off even more.

Not bothering to respond, I slide it back in my pocket and focus my attention on work. I've got a lot to finish up before I can leave the job site. The quicker I get it all squared away, the sooner I can head back to the hotel and talk to Ellie.

I pull up in front of the hotel a little while later. It's a little after dinner time, and the wind has started to pick up. It looks like there's a storm coming in. The warm breeze feels good against my face after the long day I've had. I'm ready to shower, call in room service, and spend the night talking to Ellie.

And I end up doing just that.

Pulling back the comforter on the bed, I take a second to situate the pillows against the headboard. Climbing under the sheets, I hit the call button as I use the remote to click through the channels trying to find something to watch.

"Hi," she answers. "I didn't think you were ever going to call."

"Hi, sweetheart. You sound like you were asleep."

It's still early but I know she just got off work not too long ago, texting me as soon as she got home. The silence on the other end of the line has me fearing she will want to call it an early night. After the shitty day I've had, the only way I want to end it is with the sound of her voice.

"I was just resting my eyes waiting for you to call. I'm awake now though," she murmurs, the raspy sound of her voice cracks as she clears her throat.

"How was your day?"

"Long! Kinsley drug me with her to go shopping in Everton and then I had to work. Shopping is not my favorite pastime, but thankfully Kinsley is like a pro. I was worn out when we were finished and was ready to go home. What about you?"

"Mine was long, too. We had an issue with an order which delayed the materials we needed to finish up the job. I won't be leaving to come back until Saturday morning. I'll be back just in time to pick you up for the wedding."

"Oh," she whispers. I can hear the sadness in her voice.

"I know, baby. I'm not too pleased about it either. A lot happened today and all I wanted to do is come back to the hotel room to talk to you."

"I could tell something was bothering you. Do you want to talk about it?"

"My father sent me a text again today." After our conversation before we left, I know Ellie understands my feelings why. Having someone betray you once, you don't want to let them get close enough again for fear that they'll do it again.

"I guess he's going to be in town next weekend and wants to do lunch. I just…" I start, running my hand through my damp hair, feeling frustrated. "I wish I knew what the hell he wanted, you know?"

"Well, what do you think it could be?"

"The thing is, with him, you never know. I haven't talked

to him in over two years. The way we had left things, I thought I had made it pretty clear how I felt about the situation."

"Have you considered perhaps maybe he wants to talk to you because he wants to apologize?" she says with a pause, letting the words sink in. "Do you think you would be able to forgive him?"

I've never thought about what it would take to forgive him. I've spent so much of my life being angry for everything he put us through. I never thought to think of it any other way.

"Steven Reid is too much of a prideful man. I doubt I'll ever see the day when he owns up to his mistakes, much less apologizes for them."

"I don't know how I would feel if my mom tried coming around again. I guess I'd probably feel the same way you do."

When Ellie told me the story about what happened to her, I couldn't suppress the anger I felt thinking about another man hurting someone I love. To hear about her Mom, the person who gave birth to her, who is supposed to love her and care for her, chose to walk away from her topped it all off.

Stopping myself from where my thoughts are drifting, I focus on Ellie and the dejected tone of her voice. I don't want to hang up the phone with this conversation on her mind, so I decide it's time to change the subject.

"I wish I was lying next to you. This bed is cold and hard, and the pillows don't smell nearly as good as you do," I say, rubbing my hand along my chest.

"I know. I can't wait until you're back home with me. Having you next to me sounds perfect." I close my eyes, taking in the sultry sound of her whispers floating through my ears.

"What are you wearing to bed?" I ask, the words coming out more like a grunt as my mind is replaying the way she fell apart for me when we were together on the couch. The visual of her head thrown back as pleasure coursed through her body is burned into my memory.

"I bet you'd like to know." She laughs. "I'm wearing the t-shirt you left here. It still smells like you."

"Mmm," I groan. "And…"

"And, what? That's it. What are you wearing?" she asks, quickly diverting the attention away from her and back to me.

"Fuuuuck," I say, sliding my hand down my chest and into the waistband of my boxer briefs. "Baby, that has to be the sweetest fucking picture," I groan, wrapping my hand around my hard length.

Closing my eyes, I imagine standing in front of Ellie as she lays on her bed in nothing but my t-shirt. Her hair splayed around her and her legs open before me with her hand sliding down her stomach, over her pelvis and between her legs. My cock is throbbing at the picture painted in my mind, begging for me to give it some relief.

"Tell me," she whispers with conviction.

"Tell you what, sweetheart? You want to hear what I'm thinking about or what I'm wearing?" I ask, referring to her earlier question.

"Both. Tell me both." She demands, the edge of need in her voice matching my own.

"Well, that kind of depends. My boxer briefs are about halfway down my legs with the direction this conversation is going."

Groaning, I jerk my hand up my cock feeling the rough skin of my palm over the sensitive tip of the head.

"The thought of you lying in front of me in nothing but my shirt has me so hard. I'm picturing you tracing your fingertip around your soft nipple, circling it as it tightens in arousal. The same hand then travels down your tight stomach over your pelvis between your smooth legs.

"If I was sitting in front of you, I would tell you to open your legs wide for me so I can see every fucking inch." I groan, forcing a deep breath into my lungs.

Hearing the hitch in her throat confirms she's right there with me. I don't stop.

"I would watch your fingers slide over your wet clit, rubbing circles over the tight bud, tracing your finger down your soft lips. Spreading your pussy for me to show me how wet you are."

I can hear Ellie breathing heavily through the line, her sharp inhales reveal she is just as effected by this as I am.

"I bet your pussy is wet for me, isn't it, sweetheart?"

"So wet." She sighs, "Keep going," she groans, urging me on as she's waiting for my instruction.

"If I were there, it would take everything in me not to crawl on the bed and put my face between those smooth legs. I would have you begging for it because when I'm finally between those legs, I will have you unraveling before me. I want you coming so hard your legs wrap around my head, holding me against you with need so deep."

"Yes, I'm close. Fuck, I'm so close." Grunting in response to her cries, I thrust my hips up and fight off the urge to come. I want to ride this out with her and lose myself the moment she comes in my ear.

"I want you to take two of your fingers, baby, and I want you to fuck that tight pussy."

"Your fingers feel so good, Callum. So so good! I'm about to come, tell me you're with me. I'm about to come." She cries again, begging me for release.

"I'm with you, baby. Come for me. Come all over my fingers, I want to feel it." I urge, stroking my cock with vigor. The roughness of my palm over the sensitive skin of the head feels so fucking good. I picture the soft skin of her hand squeezing me as I thrust upward again searching for release.

"I'm right there, right there, right there," she says, over and over. "Mmm," she moans into my ear. "I'm coming, I'm coming!" she repeats. The mantra playing over and over in my mind urging me forward with a force so strong I can hardly control it.

Following right behind her, I am catapulted forward as ribbons of cum shoot onto my chest. I can't contain the feeling or the release; it's as if it goes on and on forever. My oxygen leaves me in a quick breath, ragged as I struggle to calm my rapidly beating heart. That was unlike anything I've ever felt before.

"You awake over there, sweetheart?" I ask, hearing her sigh deeply.

"I'm here," she mewls lazily. "Sleepy."

"Get some sleep, baby. I'll call you in the morning," I whisper, not wanting to hang up, yet loving the sated sound to her voice, knowing I put it there.

"Night, Callum."

"Goodnight, sweetheart."

Ellie

The sound of gravel crunches beneath my feet as I walk down the driveway. The sun is peeking out just slightly over the clouds, leaving streaks of light shooting across the sky.

I stop at the end, opening the mailbox and grabbing the contents, quickly shuffling through them. When I moved to Arbor Creek, Hudson agreed to keep all the bills in his name and I would pay him monthly. Usually, I'm just stuck with left-over catalogs from when Kinsley lived here during college.

The sound of honking behind me causes me to jump, scaring the shit out of me as my heart hammers damn near out of my chest. Turning around, I see a smiling Kolton pulling up behind me. As he rolls down the window, I can hear his laughter floating through the air.

"You're even more of a jerk today, I see," I say, rolling my eyes at him over my shoulder. I swear sometimes he picks on me like he does Kinsley.

I don't tell him this because I know it would only encourage this behavior, but I enjoy it.

"Good morning to you, too, Ellie. What, did you forget to drink your coffee this morning?" he asks with his arm resting on his steering wheel while leaning over onto the driver's side door. The smug grin on his face has me fighting the urge to roll my eyes at him.

"I'm just here to take care of your yard," he says, pointing his thumb to the trailer behind his pick-up truck. Stepping off to the side, I sweep my hand in front of me, gesturing for him to enter as he revs the exhaust and pulls in.

What is it with these guys and their frickin' trucks?

It's been a long week with Callum out of town. I have one

more night of him being away, and I feel like I'm counting down the minutes until he'll be here.

He called me again last night when he was back in his hotel room, and we spent two hours talking. Going from being someone who hated the idea of carrying a phone, it's been easy for me having his voice on the other end of the line.

The night before he left, he mentioned his co-worker Elliott was getting married. We hadn't been introduced before, but Callum asked if I would attend the wedding with him as his date. It wasn't until last night that he mentioned that both his Mom and Randy would also be there.

The nerves have started to set in as butterflies take flight in my stomach. Up until this point we had only talked about his family, but now knowing I'm going to be meeting them, the idea of where this could be going with Callum hits home.

The more I thought about it, the more nervous I was about what they would think of me, about wanting to make a good impression. Before I was even out of bed this morning, I shot off a text to Kinsley with a plea for help, already feeling a little over my head. A minutes later she replied telling me not to worry and that she would be over this afternoon.

I knew she would have my back.

As if right on cue, the sound of honking behind me has me turning again. My heart, once again, hammering nearly right out of my chest when I see Kinsley's Jeep parked next to me. What in the hell is wrong with these two today?

The top was off, which is why I can see her arms sticking straight up in the air waving at me.

"Woohoo! Hey, girlfriend," Kinsley cheers.

Her exuberance once again has me shaking my head, as I lift my hand to return the gesture. Pulling forward, she parks next to Kolton's truck as she jumps down from her seat.

"Hey, chicky! Don't you look happy this morning," she smarts, taking in my obvious lack of excitement. Walking over to the back, she pulls a long lilac colored gown out of the back hatch, covered in a clear plastic bag. Turning around, she holds it in front of me with a big smile on her face.

"Isn't it beautiful?" she asks, lifting the dress for me to see.

It's breathtaking and, for a second, I find myself feeling self-conscious thinking of wearing anything with such a deep V plunging down the front. I picture the look on Callum's face when he opens the door to see me wearing it and the hesitance I felt is gone.

It's perfect!

I didn't realize I had said the words out loud until I see Kinsley's face light up.

"Callum is going to shit when he sees you in this, you know that right?" she says with a laugh as she picks up another bag from her trunk, slinging it over her shoulder.

The sound of the lawn mower starting interrupts our conversation as we turn our heads to see Kolton with a smile taking over his face. He's really looking to push our buttons today and the way she rolls her eyes, huffing as she turns toward the front steps, shows she's already over it.

Stuffing the mail under my arm, I follow along behind Kinsley as we head into the house.

"Ugh, I swear sometimes he can be such an ass." She sighs, annoyance seeping into her tone.

"Something tells me he would have something similar to say about you." I laugh as I toss the mail on the counter. Kinsley walks in, setting her bag down on the table before hanging the dress from the doorway.

"Do you want something to drink?" I ask, walking over to the fridge.

"No, the only thing I want right now is wine but, apparently, it's frowned upon this early in the day," she grumbles as if considering it for a minute. It's very unlike Kinsley to turn away wine, no matter the time of day.

"What's going on?" I ask, sensing something is on her mind.

Letting out a deep sigh, she starts to unload the contents of the bag, setting two pairs of shoes down on the chair of the dining room table for me to choose from.

"Nothing, just stuff going on with Wes." I can sense there is more to it than what she is leading on.

"Do you want to talk about it?"

Wes and Kinsley have been together for a while. Like any couple, they go through their ups and downs. Something about the way Kinsley said it has me worried there is more going on.

"Yes, just not right now," she says, looking up at me putting on the brave face, trying to reassure me. It's the same look she gave me earlier, but for the first time since I've met Kinsley, I noticed there's a hint of worry buried underneath it.

Respecting her wishes, I nod my head and steer the conversation back to safe territory.

"What'd you bring there?" I ask, picking up the stack of mail from the counter, taking a minute to shuffle through the pile of envelopes and papers. Most of it is junk, credit card offers, flyers trying to convince me to get cable TV. Flipping over an envelope, I stop when I see my name printed on it,

On the front in perfect print is my name, *Ellie Hayes*. A

feeling of panic sets in as my heart starts to pick up its pace.

Hayes.

My heart clenches as I reflect on the name. Ellie Hayes is who I am at the core of my being. The name holds so much meaning, my first name after my Grandma Ellen, and the last name given by my father. She's also the girl I said goodbye to when I left Garwood.

Uneasiness fills my stomach because it's the name no one in Arbor Creek knows me by, except for Hudson and Kinsley. Even then, he didn't know anything beyond my need to keep it private.

This was supposed to be my fresh start.

"Ellie, are you even listening to me?" I hear, breaking through my daze. Raising my head, I see Kinsley looking at me with concern etching her face. "Is everything okay?"

"Yeah," I say, looking back down at the envelope. There is no stamp or return address. I feel the bile rise in my throat. "Just not sure who this is from," I say, turning over the envelope and running my finger under the seal, opening it.

Pulling out the contents, my heart stops when I see an old worn photograph of me from Christmas 2007. I remember the day it was taken. It is one that has been forever ingrained into my memory. It was the last one I spent at home with my mom and Royal before I finally came clean to my Grams.

The way my eyes are sunken in and the forced smile on my face has me aching for the young girl in that picture. This is the Ellie Hayes I remember, the one I've worked so hard to forget.

Turning it over, I recognize the print as being the one on the front of the envelope. The words written once again confirm all my fears.

I can keep running, but not even the edge of this earth could take me far enough away from him.

These bars will only protect you for so long, Ellie.

Seventeen

Ellie

AFTER THE LETTER SHOWED UP IN MY MAILBOX, I knew I needed to find a way to explain it to Callum. I was starting to feel like I was keeping things from him. He still doesn't know the truth about me and why I've kept him at arm's length.

Hearing him talk about the stresses of his job and the impending conversation with his father, I knew I couldn't tell him while he was out of town. He likely would be upset and would jump in his truck, heading back to Arbor Creek. He had too much going on right now, and I didn't want to be one more thing to add to the list. Royal is in jail for another two years, so what's the point when I could wait a little bit longer.

I managed to get a little bit of sleep last night, even with the anxiousness of Callum's return looming. I spent most of this morning and early afternoon out on the front porch reading. The sounds of birds chirping and the soft wind blowing helped relax my racing mind.

Once it was time for me to start getting ready, I drew a warm bath filled with lavender oils. It was so calming, I nearly fell asleep in the tub. I spent extra time lathering my legs and arms up with lotion. Kinsley had insisted I wear my hair down, so I left it curled in soft waves down my back.

Walking into my bedroom, I slide the closet door open and grab my dress, laying it across the bottom of my bed. Unzipping the bodice, I step into it and pull the straps over my shoulders before zipping it up on the side. The top of the dress is fitted, leaving everything from the waist down flowing. The front is detailed with beautiful rosette flowers and plunges deep showing off more cleavage than I normally care to show. I feel confident and beautiful.

Settling on minimal make-up, I opt for the natural look with a hint of lavender eye shadow and a nude lip gloss. Once finished, I take my necklace from the medicine cabinet and arrange the pendant across my chest. Just as I'm spraying a light scent of perfume, I hear a knocking sound rap against the screen door.

Stepping out of the bathroom, I shout a quick "come in" down the hallway before walking into my bedroom to grab the heels I had chosen.

"I'll be right there," I yell again.

Sitting down on the end of the bed, I step one foot into the heel and buckle the strap around my ankle before doing the same to the other foot. Smiling to myself in the mirror, I give myself a once over before picking up my phone from the nightstand. Realizing I don't have anything to store it in, I opt to carry it in my bra. I guess it's a good thing the girls have plenty of room to share, I think, as I laugh to myself.

"I didn't even hear you pulling up," I say, walking down the hall, the sound of my heels clicking against the hard wood of the floor. Walking into the kitchen, I grab the keys as I turn toward the entry way, looking for Callum.

"Callum?" I call, looking down the hallway. For a minute, I consider that maybe he slipped into the bathroom. Noticing the light is off and the door is left cracked open, I turn to my left to see if he is in the living room and come up missing.

"What the hell, Callum! Where'd you go?" I say. A feeling of uneasiness creeps over me, causing me to clutch my keys tighter in my hands. The feeling of metal cutting into my palm draws my attention away from the rapid beating of my heart.

"Seriously! This isn't funny, Callum. Where th-" A strong arm wraps around my midsection, drawing my body in close just before a firm hand clasps around my mouth, effectively stopping any words from coming out. I can feel my eyes bulge in my sudden panic.

The stale smell of cigarette smoke hits me, and I know who it is before even seeing his face. Closing my eyes tightly, I send up a silent prayer for Callum to walk through that door. Tears threaten to escape and the words begging him to save me sound like a chant in my mind. I silently remind myself to breathe, remembering the same mantra that has helped me focus all those times before.

Breathe in. Breathe out.

"My sweet girl," he moans, running his nose along the side of my head, inhaling deeply. "I missed you. I am sorry it took so long for me to find you."

Grunting back at him, I struggle in an attempt to fight him off but the hold he has on me is too strong. His arms are wrapped around mine like a vise, preventing me from moving. His strength is no match for me as I let out of a soft cry of defeat.

"I've been waiting for you," he moans in my ear, and the taste of bile threatens to fill my throat. "I knew I couldn't come back until your little boyfriend was gone. I know I promised you I'd come back for you whenever I got out. I just never expected to find some fucking pussy to be here when I showed up," he spits out harshly.

What does he mean he couldn't come back until he was gone? How does he know who Callum is?

My thoughts race, replaying the last few weeks since Callum started coming around. My heart thumping hard, I'm surprised it hasn't found a way to pound itself out of my chest.

"Now it's time for you to come with me. C'mon," he says, pulling me with him, keeping me trapped against his chest.

Feeling unsteady on my feet, I strain to keep my balance as he drags me with him. I can feel the panic set in. My foot gets caught in the length of my dress, causing my ankle to roll. I wince as the pain shoots up my leg. His grip is tight around my mouth, forcing me to struggle for a breath as my jaw aches.

I haven't forgotten how angry he was after being arrested and subsequently convicted or the promise he made to me that day. I replay the words he had spoken back and the salacious smile that spread across his face.

"Don't worry, sweet girl. I will come back for you and we'll be together. You'll be punished for what you've done. I promise I'll be seeing you very soon."

As soon as we are near the door, it hits me that if he manages to get me out, there's a chance I may never make it back here alive. My body aches, feeling tireless against the strength of his arms. My hand shoots out from where it's trapped against my side, reaching for the wood trim. I struggle against his grip, against his tight hold.

Squeezing my eyes shut, I focus on arranging the key in my hand so that the sharp end points away from me. Jerking my head forward suddenly, I slam it back against his face as I stab the metal key into his thigh.

"You fucking bitch!" he yells in agony, removing the hand from around my waist to cover his bleeding. I faintly recognize the sound of the keys dropping to the floor. Wrapping my arm around my head, I hunch over in pain, trying to regain focus and blink away the spots filtering in and out.

I struggle to take a step away from Royal, the twinge of discomfort in my ankle making it difficult to move. My heart is racing and pain slices through my head as I rub my hand against my forehead.

"You're going to regret that, you little bitch," he spits.

I'm trapped with nowhere to go, a strangled cry breaks free. Wrapping his left hand around my throat, I gasp for a breath as his fingers squeeze, blocking the airway. My eyes bulge, silently begging him to let me go, but I know it's no use.

"Like I said, I promised you I would be back for you and you'd be punished for what you've done. It seems you've forgotten so I'm here to remind you," he says, drawing his right fist.

The next thing I see is his frightening grin, blood streaming out his nose and down his chin, just before his hard fist slams into the side of my face.

Waking up, the first thing I notice is the pounding in my skull, feeling like someone had taken a hammer to my head. With the sound of music blaring around me, I search around me for a clue of where I am. The last thing I remember is the steel-like fist that came directly for my face just before I passed out.

Like a hammer.

My body rolls to the side suddenly as I realize I'm moving. Darkness envelopes me as the smell of gasoline fills the small space. The scent is so potent, I fear that maybe I've been drenched in it.

The volume of the music lowers just as the song changes. I can hear the faint sound of gravel crunching beneath tires. My legs are bound at my ankles with my hands braced together against my chest. Struggling to move, it strikes me that even if I could get loose, I may not be able to make it far.

Closing my eyes again, I picture Callum in his suit as he shows up to pick me up for the wedding. I imagine the way his smirk would take over his face, the look of desire passing over him as he took in the deep V-neck on the front of my dress.

Tears fill my eyes, streaming down my face. My damaged and tattered heart can't bear the thought of never seeing him again. I never got the chance to tell him how I felt about him, what it meant to me to finally open up to someone about my past. I pray that if there is a God, he would find a way to lead Callum to me. He has already saved me once before; I just hope he can find a way to do it again.

The car slows down and makes a turn, causing me to roll from my right side over to my back. My eyes are wide open in high alert, searching for any sounds that would help me clue into where we are. The feeling of vibration against my chest takes me by surprise and my heart jumps to my throat.

My phone.

Keeping my hands clutched together in front of me, I try to turn my hand bringing it closer to my chest. I'm not too far away from where it's stuffed in my bra. I hold my breath as I push my left hand down, bending my right back as I move along my chest feeling the hard case. It's dark but the continued vibration against my chest helps me move my hand along to pull it from the confines of my dress.

As soon as my hand wraps around my phone, I let out a giant sigh of relief. My hands are shaking so hard as I struggle to hold it in my hand and focus on not dropping it. Holding my thumb down on the Home button, my phone unlocks and a pop-up appears before me displaying the missed text messages from Callum.

Callum: Ells?
Callum: Where are you?
Callum: I have tried to call you five times and it keeps going to voice mail. The front door was unlocked, left wide open and I can't find you.
Callum: Text me, please.

Swiping up. I click on the flashlight app and use it to quickly survey my surroundings. There is a blanket beneath me and a bottle of motor oil near my feet. I angle the light down toward my body and see silver duct tape is wrapped around my tightly thighs and ankles, making it difficult to move. The silver shines beneath the light where I see my wrists have been secured together as well.

Clicking the button to turn it off, darkness surrounds me as my eyes readjust. The car comes to an abrupt stop, causing me to roll onto my side. Using my elbow, I brace for the movement trying to avoid rolling forward. The phone slides out of my hand, landing at the other end of the trunk. The light from the screen illuminates the small space.

"No, no, no! Shit!" I whisper to myself with a huff. Moving my legs so they are curled against my chest, I use my elbow to push my body closer toward my phone. The feeling of the rough carpet rubbing against my skin burns. I can see the light dim as the screen locks, making it difficult to see in front of me. Pushing my feet into the side of the wall, I try to shuffle closer as the tears continue to stream down my face as I struggle to not break down completely.

I can't contain the sigh of relief when I feel the hard case against the tip of my fingers. The skin chafes as I use my chin to slide it closer, adjusting it in my grip. Hearing the car door open and slam shut has me frozen in fear, hearing Royal's voice.

"What the hell took you so long? I told you I didn't want to wait all night on your bullshit. Here are the keys," a man says, the sound of his voice muffled, mixed with the jingle of the keys. My mind searches through my memory, hoping to recognize the voice, but come up empty.

"I told you I'd be here as soon as I could. I had shit to do so chill the fuck out," Royal spits in frustration. "Have you heard from her yet?"

My breath comes out heavily as my finger touches the screen. I send off a silent thank you. I can hear keys rustling, drawing my attention away, causing my hands to fumble.

"Focus, Ellie," I whisper to myself. I can feel my body tremble as I pull up the messages and shoot off a quick text to Callum before locking and releasing my phone, just as the key turns and the trunk pops in release.

As soon as the hatch is open, I squeeze my eyes closed tight, fighting off the brightness as I slowly peek my eyes open. The sun has started to set as darkness approaches. Looking behind him, I find we are now alone which makes me wonder if whomever knew I was back here and if I missed an opportunity to get away.

"There she is." He smiles his sinister smile, causing my stomach to roll just seeing him again standing in front of me. "I'm sorry you had to ride back here but you are feistier than you used to be."

I want nothing more than to spit in his smug face.

What he doesn't know or realize is I have more to live for this time around. I'm not going to go down without a fight.

Eighteen

Callum

PULLING MY TRUCK UP ELLIE'S DRIVE, I BRIEFLY CHECK the time on my phone before depositing it back in the center console. Turning the truck off, I leave the keys in the ignition, not wanting to waste another minute. I need Ellie. I need to feel her in my arms, her soft skin beneath my fingertips, and her lips pressed against mine. I physically need her.

Climbing out of the cab of the pick-up, I check my tie as I run my hands across my chest smoothing out my dress shirt. Opting to leave the suit jacket in the backseat, I quickly jog over to the front of Ellie's house, taking the stairs two at a time.

I instantly notice the front door is slightly open, which is unlike Ellie to do.

"Ellie, you ready? Get out here right now and give me those sweet lips," I yell, chuckling as I step into the entry way.

Looking down at the floor, I notice the shoes and rug in a disarray. My brows pull together in confusion.

"Ellie, sweetheart?" I say, leaning down to move the rug back into place. Something sparkling catches my eye. I bend down and use my finger to drag a metal chain toward me.

I know immediately something is wrong when I see the compass pendant dragging along the ceramic tile. If I wasn't looking closely, I would've missed it but there is no mistaking the drops of blood on the floor near the dark colored rug.

Clutching the pendant in my hand, a feeling of unease settles into the pit of my stomach. I quickly run down the hallway toward Ellie's room. Flipping the lights on, I look around for any sign of her but nothing appears out of order.

Running my hand along my pocket, I realize I left my phone in the truck as I race down the hall and out the door. My hands fumble as I pull up Ellie's number and click the call button. The phone rings and rings, going to her voice mail every time.

My fear sets in as my anxiety escalates, realizing something is very wrong. Ellie and I have been texting throughout the day, sharing her excitement over the wedding, and my anxiousness to get back to her. Sweat drips down my brow as I pull up my messages app and shoot off several texts to her.

I stare at my screen, praying I see the confirmation she has read the message and the bubble appearing to show she is responding back, but come up empty after what feels like an hour. I quickly shoot off a text to Kinsley, in hopes that she has seen or talked to Ellie recently.

Not waiting for her reply, I call the only other person I can think of. When the line connects, the gruff voice that comes through fills me with relief before the reality of the situation hits me again.

"Reid, son! Everything okay?" Hudson grunts, concern evident in his tone. Growing up, Hudson was always looking out for me. Ever since I was young and my dad left, I remember him challenging me to be a better man than the example I had set in front of me. If he only knew how he has impacted me.

"I'm not sure. Have you talked to Ellie recently? Do you happen to know where she is?" I rattle out, holding my breath in hopes he knows and that she is okay.

"No, I haven't talked to her since she was at the store yesterday. What's wrong?" Hudson is the type of man that doesn't show fear, but I know he has caught on to Ellie and glimpses of her past she works to keep hidden.

Without hesitating, I replay everything to him since showing up at Ellie's house. The pendant is still clasped tightly in my hand, feeling like a solid weight to match the one sitting in the pit of my stomach.

"Is it possible it's him?" he asks, drawing my attention. As if reading the expression on my face through the phone, he clarifies his question. "I know you know what I'm talking about, son. Is it possible he was released and she's somehow in danger?"

Not wasting time wondering if she told him or how he found out, I focus on his question before responding.

"She told me he was in prison, but I don't know. FUCK! Hudson, what if he was? God damn it!" I yell, squeezing my phone in my fist, worrying I will crush it. My mind races through every detail Ellie has told me about Royal.

"I'll be right there, son. Call the police!" he shouts, a rustling sound comes through the line followed by the sound of his truck starting. When the call ends, a ding comes through notifying me of a text message.

As if on cue, I look at the text message from Ellie and it's as if everything around me comes crashing down.

Ellie: 911

By the time I disconnect from the emergency operator, Hudson is pulling into the driveway behind my pick-up truck. Emotions that I've fought off well up in me. Seeing Hudson standing in front of me, clasping my shoulder in his strong hand, is nearly my undoing.

The realization of everything creeps in as I replay over and over what I saw. Ellie's text message reaching out for help fills me with dread, fearing what she could be going through right now.

I pray the blood that marred the floor is not from her. I silently beg that she fought him off, that she fought to come back to me. I swear to God if he lays a hand on her or harmed her in any way, I will fucking kill him. I will kill him and not care or feel bad about it for even a second.

Hudson doesn't say anything but he doesn't need to. A few minutes later, a patrol car pulls into the driveway. Bending down, I rest my hands on top of my knees as I force a deep breath into my lungs. Tears fill my eyes and flow down my face. Using my thumb and index finger, I rub my eyes and use the back of my hand to dry the tears.

"You're Callum, right?" a strong voice asks, commanding my attention. Standing up to full height, I reach my hand out in front of me to shake his.

"Yes, sir," I say, concern and anger lacing my words. Living in a small town, I recognize the man standing in front of me. I've seen him around Wes's shop before but I haven't talked to him or know his name.

"My name's Detective Keller. Dispatch relayed the details of your call. I understand your girlfriend is missing and you have reason to believe she was abducted. Can you tell me her name and what you know?" he asks.

"Her name is Ellie Ryan. I was coming in from out of town and I was here to pick her up for a wedding we were attending together tonight. When I got here, the front door was left open and the rug and shoes in the foyer were strewn all over. If you know Ellie, it's unlike her to leave the house open like that, especially if she was not home."

"I'm sorry," Hudson interrupts. "Her last name is Hayes," he says, not making eye contact with me. I can feel the confusion lining my brow, mirroring the same look as the detective.

"I'm sorry, Mr. Hudson. How do you know this woman?" he asks, narrowing his eyes looking between the two of us.

"Ellie works at Hudson's and is renting out this property from me," he shares, pointing toward the house. "She goes by the last name of Ryan, but her last name is legally Hayes. This information was disclosed to me when she began working for me at the same time she became my tenant."

Hudson looks back at me with sympathy in his eyes. "I'm sorry, son, but it wasn't my information to share with you."

Nodding my head, I acknowledge what he says. I still can't help the questions that are swirling around in my head. I know after talking to Ellie there was a lot she did to hide her past out of fear it would chase her down.

"Can you tell me why you believe she may have been abducted, sir?" Detective Keller asks.

"Ellie texted me '911' just before I called to report her missing. I also found her necklace broken on the floor with blood spots on the tile in her entryway," I say, sharing with him the pieces of the puzzle that has my heart heavy with concern. "I believe someone from her past may have found her. I can't be sure though." I sigh in frustration, nothing is adding up. "I don't know what is going on but I believe someone took her and that she could be in some real danger."

I give him a brief rundown of the history Ellie shared with me not long ago. I am not surprised when the information I share doesn't seem to strike Hudson as news. The way he rattled off his name confirmed he has already done his homework. I don't believe for a second Ellie shared it with him, but knowing her he knew there was more to it.

"And we're sure that this Royal Carter is in prison, correct?" Detective Keller asks Hudson. His concern matches mine. The uncertainty behind this confirms everything that I'm feeling.

"Yes, sir," Hudson says. I know we both agree, if someone set out to hurt Ellie deliberately, the only person it would be is *him*.

"I'm going to put in a call to check into Royal Carter and see what information I can find on him. While I'm doing that, you said she sent you a text from her phone. It's a long shot but I'm going to see if it's on and if I can put in a request to track her location."

The words hit me like a smack in the face.

When Ellie came with me to buy a phone, I insisted she register it in case she ever lost it. She thought it was bullshit, but I told her she wasn't used to carrying it and that I wouldn't be surprised if she ended up leaving it somewhere.

Truth be told, I wanted to protect her in every way possible.

Pulling up the Location Services, I glance up at him and say, "I can do you one better. I have access to her iCloud account. I should be able to track her phone from here."

I just hope when we find her it isn't too late.

Ellie

"Wake the fuck up, bitch!" The harsh words come out as a muffle just before the loud smack strikes the side of my face. The pain ricochets through my skull. A strong hand wraps around my jaw, forcing my head back as I struggle to breathe through my nostrils.

"There she is," he says as I peek my eyes open. The damp, musty smell is so pungent it causes my stomach to roll. A small light hangs from the ceiling, doing little to brighten up the room but it doesn't matter.

I could spot the useless piece of garbage standing in front of me from a mile away.

The sinister smile is back, leaving me with the urge to wipe it right off his sick fucking face.

"I'm sorry, what'd you say? I can't hear you." He laughs, enjoying my agony. "Listen, we're going to make this quick. I have someone showing up here soon. It's a bit of a surprise for you. I have a feeling you're really going to like it."

The way he says surprise tells me it's the kind I will want nothing to do with.

Shuffling to move, my wrists strain against the duct tape holding them together. The resistance cutting deep, reducing the circulation to my fingers. Attempting to turn my wrist, I try to loosen the duct tape and ease my hand out. It's no use though, the duct tape is wrapped so tight, I'm not able to move my hands even an inch.

"I've waited a long time for this, Ellie. I'm going to remove the duct tape now because seeing you tied up like this doesn't do it for me. I much prefer you compliant," he chuckles. "I promised you would pay for putting me behind bars. So, it's time you come to terms with your punishment. I'd wait until later, but well… I can't leave you hanging. After all, you are all dressed up for this special reunion," he moans, bending closer.

His breath comes out in heavy pants against the side of my face.

"If I remove this, you better not try anything. I'll have no fucking problem slitting your throat, so don't even tempt me."

My eyes connect with the sharp object in his hand, causing my heart to pound. He runs the blade over the chiffon of the dress, down to the exposed skin on my chest.

Nodding my head, I lower my eyes as I hold my wrists out in front of him. If he's going to remove the tape, he needs to think I'm the same broken down girl he left behind. Sliding the knife between my wrists, he uses the sharp edge to cut away the tape. I don't move right away, knowing he'll expect it if I do. Instead, I bide my time and wait as he pulls the tape away, loosening the confines.

"While I was locked away I thought a lot about what you would look like all grown up. Your long blond hair and creamy pale skin," he groans, lowering his hand to adjust himself. "So beautiful."

My stomach rolls with dread. I'm not the same girl I once was, and I won't make this easy for him. I know if I'm going to get out of this basement, it's going to be because I put up a fight. I'm done letting him control my life. I refuse to let him put his hands on me again.

I swallow nervously as I attempt to calm my racing heart, thinking through my next move. I know I can't overtake him with his strength, he proved it earlier. I just know if I can find a way to get out of this room, surely, I can get to my phone and call for help.

"Alright, now that I've done you this favor, I have something for you," he says, taking a step back as his hands return to the button on his pants.

I can't even hold back the tears streaming down my face knowing what's coming next.

"Open up your pretty little mouth for me. I'm only going to warn you once, if you try to fucking bite me, I'm going to knock your teeth down your throat. You hear me?" he barks.

Wrapping his hand around my jaw again, he wrenches my head back as he forces his fingers into my mouth, prying it open. The movement causes me to gag against the intrusion.

Bending my legs beneath the chair, I get into position as I wait for the opportunity. As soon as he moves the knife away to lower his pants, I make the move I've been counting on.

Shooting my arm out, I slam my forearm against his wrist, knocking the knife out of his hand, taking him off guard. Royal snaps his attention up to me. Using every ounce of strength in my body, I use my fist to connect with his groin. His hands move to protect himself causing the knife to slide across the floor in the process.

"You little bitch," Royal grunts, dropping his knees to the floor.

Not missing the opening, I dive toward the knife. I don't make it very far with the tape wrapped around my ankles but I don't let that deter me. As soon as my hand is wrapped around the handle, I clutch it in my fist to avoid losing my grip, rolling over to face Royal.

He's hunched over as he howls in agony. With all the force left in my body, I push on. The sharp edge of the blade hits him in the side of his stomach, as a look of shock takes over his face.

Pulling the knife out, I don't let myself think about the blood covering my hands. Sliding back, I put some distance between us. My hands shake as I try to quickly cut away the tape wrapped around my ankles and thighs. Pulling the tape away, I hurry to stand. My legs feel unsteady beneath me, but the adrenaline coursing through my body spurs me on.

Looking over at Royal, blood continues to pour out of the wound, turning the light gray shirt a dark burgundy. His eyes are barely open. They lack focus as he stares up at the ceiling.

I know counting him out would be my biggest mistake. Shuffling along the side of the basement, I press my back against the cinder block wall. As soon as I've inched past him, I break for the stairs running up them. Checking the door, I'm surprised when I see it unlocked.

With nothing but the knife in my hand, I hold it out in front of me as I take a step out of the dingy basement and into a short hallway. With a quick look to the left and right, I'm startled when I see the rest of the house is empty. Whomever he was talking to earlier must have left. Spotting the front door, I make a quick run for it. As soon as it opens and the cool breeze hits my face, I take a deep breath.

Against my better judgment, I take one last glance behind me. I don't see her standing in front of me, at least not until my bare foot hits the front porch step. It takes a second before my mind registers the green eyes shining back at me, matching my own, just before everything goes black.

All this time I've spent running, hoping someone would come along and save me. For the first time in my life, I realized the only hope I had was to save myself.

Nineteen

Ellie

THE SOFT HUM OF THE LIGHTS ABOVE FILTER IN through my mind, waking me from unconsciousness. They shine bright above me, almost like they burn through my eyelids as I fight off the urge to squeeze them tight.

My limbs feel heavy. Even if I wanted to lift them or try to move, it would be no use. The pain I feel throughout my body is more of a dull ache, barely through the surface as I try to register where I am. My thoughts come back to me in pieces, but focusing on one thing.

Royal. He is here.

My head starts to pound as I replay the events I can remember. Royal showing up at my house, ending up in the trunk of a car, finding myself tied up in a disgusting basement.

Fear and panic creeps. Maybe Callum couldn't find me

213

like I hoped.

A beeping sound next to me flits through my mind as I start to register where I am.

The creak from a door opening followed by a soft click jolts me from my thoughts. Footsteps approach me as someone slides something across the floor. The sound as it creaks is followed by a soft click. The footsteps approach me as someone moves something. I try with everything in me to turn my head and open my eyes. Fear creeps inside me, settling in the panic. I want to know who is here.

Until I hear my name and relief envelops me, melting everything away.

"Ellie." The soft words come out with an ache, and I feel my eyes well up.

Callum.

I feel his hands wrap around mine as he peppers a soft kiss on the back. I would know the feel of his calloused hands around mine anywhere.

"If you can hear me baby, I want you to know I'm here. I'm not going anywhere." The sadness laced with worry has me fighting once again to do anything to let him know I'm here. It's useless, like every part of my body is weighted down. I want to shout from the top of my lungs, tell him I'm okay, but I can't.

Callum lets out a deep sigh and I know it's because he was hoping for some sort of response from me, too.

"It's okay, baby, it's going to be okay. I know you need your rest. You fought hard, so fucking hard. I will stay right here by your side, I'm not ever leaving. Not now… not ever."

I can hear the soft hiccup accompanied by a sob unleashed from his throat as his lips find the back of my hand once again. My heart breaks just thinking about how broken up he sounds. I ache to find a way to let him know I'm here, but my body is growing more tired by the second.

The last words I hear as my subconscious pulls me back under are the three words I thought I'd never hear, but have longed to tell Callum.

"I love you, Ellie."

Callum

I feel like my heart has been ripped out of my chest since I first saw her. Cuts and bruises covering her face, arms, and I'm sure other places I can't see. Seeing someone as sweet and kind as Ellie hurting like this has rage coursing through me unlike anything I've ever felt before.

As soon as he got the confirmation Royal had been released, I had been coming out of my skin at the thought of where she could be and what could've happened to her. Once they picked up a signal on her cell phone, they were quick to move in. I was about to insist I come with him, wanting to get my hands on this motherfucker when Detective Keller told me I needed to stay where I was. If Ellie were to separate from her phone, the first place she would likely go is home.

Where she knew she would be able to find me.

Kinsley joined us, along with another patrol officer in case Ellie were to show up. Kinsley couldn't control herself or the emotion racking through her body. Standing in the driveway, I wrapped my arms around her as sobs shook her small body, the worry and fear overwhelming us both.

I felt like I had shaved a fucking year off my life waiting for the phone call that they found her. Hearing Keller's gruff voice on the other end of the line, instructing me to meet him at the hospital where he would fill me in on the details.

I just needed to know three fucking things, now. That my girl was safe, she would be okay, and that they caught him. I knew by the tone of his voice I wasn't going to like what I heard next.

Keller wouldn't tell me what he saw when he found her, which looking back on I'm grateful for. I don't think I would be able to keep it together hearing what kind of hell she had lived through. The only information I got from him was she was going to be okay and he would find him.

The only thing stopping me from running out of this hospital and finding him is knowing she's the one who needs me right now. I promised her I would be here, that I wouldn't leave her side. When she opens those beautiful green eyes, I want to be the first person she sees.

Staring down at her, I lift my right hand and run my thumb along the soft skin of her cheek. Tears fill my eyes and I don't even try to hold them back, letting them flow down my face. Leaning over the side of the bed, I clutch her small delicate hand in mine.

Running my fingers along her marred skin, I study her hand. Several of her nails are broken, as if they were ripped from her fingers. I know she put up a fight, hell, she broke the wrist of her other hand trying to escape. A small, yet sad sense of pride fills me just knowing my girl fought.

She fought to come back to me.

Raising her hand to my mouth, I press a soft kiss against

the back and hold it there for a moment, just appreciating she's alive and will be okay. I send up a silent prayer of thanks to God for bringing her back to me.

I never got the chance to tell her how I felt about her before I left town. Waking up with Ellie wrapped in my arms that morning, I knew what I was feeling. I loved Ellie and I wanted to tell her but the time never felt right and then before I knew it I was out of town. At the time, I wanted to be able to tell her in person. I told myself that when I got back, when I had her in my arms, I would tell her everything.

I wanted her to know how brave she is and how much I admire her courage to start over. I want to tell her thank you for bumping into me at the bus station and how today I still remember how beautiful she was that day. I never saw her coming. I need her to know how much I love her and how, unlike everyone she has loved in her life, I am going to make a promise never to leave her.

I wish she would wake up so I could tell her, so she could see all the people around her who care about her, who haven't left her side.

Kinsley, Hudson, and Halle have been up here just as much as I have been. The first two days, Kinsley and Halle closed the salon, rescheduling their appointments to be here by her side. My mom and Randy have been up a couple of times to be here for me. My mom insisted she wanted to be here for Ellie, but decided to stay out in the hallway. She didn't want their meeting to happen while Ellie lay in a hospital bed, unconscious.

The doctor has continued to be reassuring, reminding us that her body went through a great deal of trauma. That word hit me hard, even though I know he only meant to explain she has been through a lot and her body needs time to rest.

Kinsley and Wes show up a little while later. Feeling someone shaking my shoulder, urging me awake, has me sitting up right. My eyes are wide and wild with panic as I look at Ellie in hopes she's awake.

Looking up, I see Wes and his ugly mug grinning at me, shaking his head.

"Dude, have you showered since you've been here?" he asks, laughing. "You're not going to wake your sleeping beauty when you smell bad enough to make her pass out."

If anyone else said something like that to me, they would be laid out.

Grumbling low, I throw a "fuck you" back, glaring at him, earning me a small chuckle.

"You might want to stop while you're ahead, unless you want to end up sleeping on the couch today." Kinsley chastises him, which has me throwing out a laugh of my own.

"I figured you would want a change of clothes so we stopped by your place," Kinsley says, holding a bag out to me with a sad smile on her face. "How's our girl doing?"

"No change," I mutter solemnly, rubbing my hand over my face.

I know this has been incredibly hard on Kinsley, the look on her face says she is probably getting about as much sleep as I am in this uncomfortable fucking chair. She's continued to push me to go home, get some rest, and shower. After an hour of trying, she must've caught on that it was no use, which is why she showed up here with a bag of my things. I guess she figured if she brought my shit up here, it would help me change my mind about that part of it.

"She's going to be okay, Callum. Ellie is a fighter, and

she hasn't given up yet. Give her time and she'll be back here with us." Bending down, she wraps her arms around my neck. Leaning into her embrace, I let myself accept the warmth of her hug.

"Thanks, Kins, for bringing this up here for me," I grumble. I meant for it to come out a little softer but I just can't find it in me.

"You're welcome. Now seriously, why don't you do you and everyone else in this room a favor and take a quick shower and head down to the cafeteria to get yourself something to eat? You're not helping her get better any quicker if you're not taking care of yourself." She reprimands. I want to put up a fight and I plan to when I look up at Kinsley from my seat and see her standing there with her arms crossed. The indignation on her face tells me this isn't up for discussion. If I want to avoid her laying into me, I need to get up and do as she says.

Standing, I grab the bag from the chair. Seeing me follow through has a smile shining brightly on her face. Wes, however, is back at thinking he is the funniest shit on earth as I flip him off.

As soon as my eyes meet Kinsley's, she softens as if reading my mind.

"I promise, I won't leave her side, neither of us will. If she wakes up, the first thing I'll do is call you," she promises as she moves to take my place next to Ellie.

Leaning down, I run my nose along the side of Ellie's face toward her ear. I have a niggling feeling inside me, taking in the scent of Ellie. It's still there, she's still her. But it's not the same.

The smell of this clean, sterile room seeps in taking away everything that makes her my Ellie.

After I've showered and gotten dressed, I head down to the cafeteria in search of something to eat. I've ate here and there, mostly food people have brought by. The nurse even brought me a bowl of soup last night. She didn't say anything but it was clear she was just as worried about me as Kinsley is. At this point, I'm just grabbing a bite to get everyone off my back. I know if I go back without eating something, Kinsley is likely going to end up pulling my ass down to the cafeteria herself and sit me down with a plate of food in front of me.

I don't know how Wes puts up with all her sass.

After I settle on a bowl of chili with crackers, I turn to take a seat at one of the tables in the corner of the room. Turning on my heel, I'm hit with a wall of emotions when I see who is standing in front of me. I haven't talked to him since the night of the bonfire, but in this moment, all the bullshit falls away.

Setting the tray down on the closest table to me, I take two steps and wrap my arms around my brother's shoulders. The emotions surge through me, losing the battle to contain the sobs that lets loose. Wrapping both arms around me, I'm grateful for his support as I can feel I'm slowly starting to fall apart.

"It's good to see you," I say, breaking the silence, meaning it. "I wasn't expecting you." I grunt as the emotions rise in me again.

With a clap on the back, I take a step back running my thumb and forefinger over my eyes. The stress of the last three days weighing down on me, feels like a ten-ton boulder pressing down on me.

"Yeah, well as soon as Mom told me what had happened, I knew you could use some support. I know we never talked about her nor have I had the chance to meet her, but I know she's important to you," he says, taking a step back.

For the first time, I notice Brea standing behind him with her eyes focused on the floor, looking uncomfortable and giving us our space to have our moment in the middle of the cafeteria.

"Hey, Brea. Thanks to both of you for coming. It's, uh.. It's really good to see both of you," I finish, letting the emotion come through in those words, trying to shake it off.

"Of course, man," he reassures, clapping me on the shoulder again. Lifting his arm to Brea, he ushers her closer to the table where I left my tray sitting.

"How's she doing?" he asks, a look of concern lining his brow.

Moving to take a seat, I fold my hands together in a fist.

"She's okay. She hasn't woken up yet so there are still a lot of unknowns, but the doctor is optimistic," I say, letting out a deep breath. "All the tests they've ran show signs she is responding. Right now, it's just a waiting game, just waiting for her to wake up."

Hearing the words come out of my mouth, they carry so much weight. More weight than I realized I was carrying. It's as if hearing them out loud brings the reality of the situation back to the forefront of my mind. I keep telling myself it could've been worse; the whole situation could've been a lot worse.

"That's good to hear, man," he says, clasping his hand over the top of mine.

Growing up, I did so much to take care of him, to seclude him from the shit going on between our parents. He was so young, he didn't deserve to have to deal with their bullshit. I think in my mind it was my way of protecting him.

Having him here, showing me support through something that is quite possibly one of the hardest things I'll ever have to face means a lot to me. We have a long way to go to mend the shit between the two of us. We are all given second chances, but I'm starting to learn you may never know when.

"How long are you in town for?" I ask, taking a bite of my chili while taking a minute to let my eyes roam over to Brea. Since we hadn't talked, I wasn't sure what was going on with them. The way her hands are tied in knots in her lap and the sidelong glances he is shooting her way, it's clear something is going on with them.

"Through the weekend. She was originally planning to head home to visit her family but I convinced her to come along for a road trip. We'll probably head back to Chicago on Sunday morning," he says, looking over at Brea, flashing her a small smile like there's some kind of inside joke I'm missing.

For the first time in as long as I can remember, he looks happy.

We chat for a little bit as I eat my chili. While I'm glad to see them both, my mind keeps thinking back to Ellie and getting back up to see her. The topics are safe, never mentioning the situation between him and our father which I'm grateful for. Today, I just need for everything to be okay.

Until Ellie opens those beautiful green eyes, I just need for everything else to be okay.

Twenty

Ellie

IF I DIDN'T KNOW BETTER, I WOULD'VE THOUGHT I WAS waking up in heaven. The deep husky sound of Hudson's laugh filtering through as I can vaguely make out Kinsley's voice.

"It's not my fault. I didn't realize you were so sensitive. It was a frickin' bet. Your Cubbies won the World Series, what more did you want," Kinsley retorts, earning a laugh from Callum.

The sound reverberates through me, deep into my heart and soul healing me in the process.

My eyes flutter and I catch a peek of the bright fluorescent lights shining overhead. God, these things really do make my eyes burn. It's like looking directly into sunlight as I squeeze my eyes shut, flinching in the process.

"Oh my god, did you see that?" I can hear Kinsley gasp as

she whisper-shouts, trying not to be too loud but the relief is evident in her voice.

"I swear I just saw Ellie move."

Two hands wrap around mine. I can smell Callum's scent as he leans in, whispering against the shell of my ear. His breath against my skin causes goose bumps to spread across my arms.

"Baby, can you hear me? Wake up for me please, I want to see those beautiful green eyes," he whispers, the words filled with so much hope.

"Bright," I mumble, coming out hoarser than I expected. My mouth is dry, as I move to run my tongue along my lower lip, wetting it, while hoping Callum will understand my plea to turn down the lights.

I hear Kinsley mutter "I got it" as her feet shuffle across the floor just as the light clicks off.

My body feels so worn down, making even the slightest of movements hard as I struggle to pry open my eyes. I notice the look of relief that passes over Callum's when my eyes connect with his. Dark circles are visible beneath his eyes.

"Hi," I mutter. His bright smile nearly takes my breath away. Running his palm along my cheek, I relish the feel of his warm skin against mine.

"How are you doing? Does anything hurt?" he stresses. Looking around the room, my eyes land on Hudson and Kinsley who are both standing at the foot of the bed. Kinsley has her arm wrapped around her grandfather's as she leans into him, wearing the same look of worry on their faces as I see on Callum's.

"I'm okay," I say, hoping to put them all at ease. "Tired."

"I'll let Dr. Kline know you are awake," Kinsley says,

moving quickly and disappearing out the door.

I want so badly to say more but I feel like my mouth is the Sahara Desert. Running my tongue along my lips again, I can feel the prickly skin beneath it. The sting mixed with a hint of blood as my tongue slides across the cut, splitting my bottom lip.

"Let me get you something to drink," Callum says, setting my hand down on the bed and moving to stand. Hudson waves him off, telling him to have a seat.

"We missed you, Ells." He smiles, patting his hand over my feet at the bottom of the bed. I can see the emotion in his eyes as he blinks through it, then turning toward the sink to grab the water pitcher.

A second later he's back, handing Callum a small Styrofoam cup with a straw. Holding it to my face, Callum bends the straw so it's in front of my mouth as I lean my head forward to take a drink. My head feels heavy, like a ton of bricks on my shoulders. I can't help but groan as the liquid slides down my throat.

Two knocks sound at the door as Kinsley enters followed by an older man. By the way he is dressed, I'm going to guess he's Dr. Kline.

Immediately, Kinsley is at my bedside sliding in close to give me a small hug.

"I love you, Ells," she whispers as she steps back mumbling an apology.

"Hello there. It's good to have you awake and back here with us. My name is Dr. Kline," he says, tipping his head toward me with a warm smile on his face.

"Can you tell me your name and how old you are?"

He's an older man, dressed in khakis and a button up

shirt. The hospital badge hanging from the pocket of his shirt shows his name, Dr. Andrew Kline.

Andrew. Just like my father.

Looking back up at him, I can't help but think of what my father would look like if he were still alive.

"My name is Ellie," I say, my voice still sounding hoarse. "I'm twenty-two."

With a smile and a nod of his head, he leans down using a small flashlight to check my eyes.

"You were found unconscious after taking quite a hit to your head. It left a pretty big bump and some swelling, which has gone down significantly since you arrived a few days ago. Your wrist was fractured. You'll have to wear a cast for a little while until that heals. You'll have that on for about four to six weeks."

At the mention of that, my mind flashes back to being in that basement and fighting hard to escape. While the dress I had been wearing is now gone, I can still smell the musty scent from the basement.

"We were concerned about the lasting effects of your injury and have been running some tests. Now that you are awake, I would like to get you up for a head CT and run some other tests." I see Callum pacing next to me with his arms crossed, a lot like he had the day in the emergency room. Holding my hand up to him, he looks down at me before pulling up the chair next to my bedside.

"I'm going to have the nurse come in to take you up for the tests and then we'll get you settled back here for some rest. How is your pain?" he asks as he leans over, checking the IV fluids on the side of the bed.

"I'm really sore and my head feels like it's going to

explode," I groan. Even talking leaves me feeling worn down and physically drained.

"I'm going to have Ms. Glenda come in and get you up for testing. The detective has been by hoping to speak with you, however I will advise him to come by later. Once you get back in the room, we'll give you some pain medicine to help you get some rest." With a nod of my head, I mutter a thank you as Dr. Kline leaves the room.

Leaning back, I turn my head toward where Callum is sitting.

"I'm sorry," I mumble, remembering his friend's wedding.

"What for, baby?" Callum asks, confusion etches his face, waiting for me to respond.

"I thought it was you," I say, thinking back to when I thought Callum had shown up to my house to pick me up. "I wanted to see you in a suit." I smile, missing how handsome I am sure he would look.

"Don't you worry about it. I promise I'll make it up to you." I can hear his smile through his voice, although the sadness is still there.

"I have plenty of other dresses you can wear, Ellie. Once we bust you out of here, they're yours to choose from." Kinsley smiles softly.

"Knock, knock!" As I turn my head, I see an older woman enter the room. "My name is Ms. Glenda, I'm your nurse. How you doin', honey?" she asks, her voice just as warm and welcoming as her smile. Telling by her accent, she isn't around here.

"I'm alright," I mumble, trying to return her smile.

"I'm going to get you upstairs to get checked out. Don't you worry, you don't have to move a muscle," she says. Bending down to unlock the wheels on the bed, she begins moving over the monitors so they are hooked up to the side of the bed.

"I am going to take your girl with me for a little bit, but I promise she'll be in good hands." She smiles reassuringly at Callum as he stands up, leaning over the bed, and running his nose in my hair before pressing a soft kiss to my forehead.

Turning my head, I see both Hudson and Kinsley approaching. Hudson doesn't say much, always wearing a strong exterior but I can see the worry on his face he is working to disguise.

"I'm going to be okay, guys," I say, smiling. Tears fill Kinsley's eyes, as she hurries to wipe them away before they fall. As they both approach the bed, Kinsley leans over to give me a hug. I lift my hand to try and return the embrace, fighting to hide my discomfort.

"I'm so glad you're okay," she whispers. "Don't ever scare me like that again." I can't help but laugh at Kinsley's way of trying to put on a tough front.

As soon as she leans back, she gives me a small wave and promises she will be back to see me later. As Hudson approaches, I know I am going to have to work harder to keep my emotions in check.

"You had me worried. This old heart can't take that kind of stress," he says, wrapping his hand around mine as his laughter filters through the air. "I didn't get a chance to tell you this before but I want you to know how much everyone here loves you. You have a family here," he chokes, the words coming out more broken up than he expected. Clearing his throat, he continues, "June and I will be by to see you tomorrow. Get some rest."

With a squeeze of my hand, he takes a step back as Glenda

promises to have me back with them soon.

Callum

It took a couple of days before Ellie was released. The doctors were concerned about the swelling and the possibility of a brain bleed, which resulted in several more tests. As much as I hated she was there laid up in a hospital bed, I was relieved she was resting safely in a place where they could give her something to help with the pain.

The day after Ellie woke up, Detective Keller stopped by the hospital to talk to her and to take her statement.

I wasn't prepared for the details that would come with it. Hearing Ellie replay the assault to how she ended up in the trunk of Royal's car and brought to an old house, was hard. We ended up learning the house she was at belonged to a family member of an inmate Royal had met when he was locked up. It was sitting empty, which made it a perfect hideout.

Keller shared with us that Royal had been released from prison nearly six weeks ago. Since Ellie was the victim in the case putting him behind bars for molestation, the Department of Corrections attempted to reach her but when she left town, she never gave a way to track her down.

Royal hadn't shown up for his meeting with his parole officer, which ended with a warrant being issued for his arrest. The feeling of unease sits in the pit of my stomach, churning now just picturing of how bad it could've been.

I couldn't help feeling grateful that I was able to convince

Ellie to get a cell phone. The one thing she worked hard to avoid having ended up leading us to her and ultimately saved her life.

I didn't miss how her hand squeezed mine when she shared other details, like how she found a pile of cigarettes behind her house and the picture she got in the mail of her as a kid. It pissed me off and hurt to hear her rationalize it. I think in her mind Royal was still in prison so she didn't believe he could hurt her. I was just upset to hear how much she had hidden from me.

The way she turned her head, licking along her healing lip and met my eyes, I could see the apologies written there.

"Have you tried to track down my mother, too?" Ellie murmurs.

"Do you think she would have some information related to the investigation?" Keller asks, his voice coming out soft but with an edge of firmness there.

Nodding her head, I could sense her hesitance for what she was to say next, but hearing the words come out of her mouth only broke my heart further.

"She'll have information for you. I saw her just before I was hit from behind."

A mother is supposed to be someone who loves their children, takes care of them. For Ellie, the woman who gave birth to her is the same one who was now helping this fucking monster. To think, he was right under our noses for the last two months and I had no idea, had my blood simmering. I could hardly contain the rage coursing through me hearing that.

It wasn't hard to convince Ellie to stay with me, at least until they both had been found. Kinsley and Hudson had stopped by her place. Hudson wanted to change the locks on the place after everything. Kinsley ended up packing up for Ellie. Ellie was more worried about getting her wallet, wanting to have the photo she kept tucked away of her father with her.

Pulling in the long drive of my property, I squeeze the top of the steering wheel hearing the gravel crunching as we ease our way toward the back of the land. I'm grateful the house sits back about a mile off the road, far enough away from anyone passing by to see. There is only one road in and out, giving us the privacy and security we both need right now.

"How you doing, baby?" I ask, looking over at Ellie as I put the truck in park and turn off the ignition.

"I'm okay," she sighs, turning her head to look out the windshield, lost in thought. She hasn't said it, but knowing they are still out there has her nervous and on edge.

"Talk to me," I beg, wrapping my hand around hers, bringing it to my mouth kissing along her fingers.

"I'm sorry," she whispers, tears forming as she runs her other hand along her cheek. Not wasting a second, I lean over and pull her closer. She comes easily as she slides into my lap.

"Need to feel you sweetheart," I mumble, running my nose along the side of her face, pressing a small kiss against her temple. "You have nothing to be sorry for. Tell me what's wrong,"

"Have you ever thought about what would make someone turn their back on their child? Why our parents left us like this? How could my mom let him do this to me again?"

Hearing her search for the same answers I spent years wanting is like a knife to my heart. The jagged edges piercing something so deep in me. Pressing my hand against the side of her face, I turn her head until her eyes meet mine.

"I don't have those answers. I don't think we will ever have those answers, baby. I hope you know that none of this is your fault."

Her mother blamed her for what happened to her dad. Ellie wears the guilt of her father's death because of it.

"I have accepted what happened to me growing up. The role Royal had in my life. He will pay for what he's done when he rots in hell." The anger in her tone a stark change against the soft words spoken just a moment ago. "It was easier when I believed she just thought I was lying. She's really gone now. The mother she was when I was young is gone."

"I think family comes in different shapes and sizes. The people we should be able to trust are not always the ones we can. The family you have are the ones who love you through the good and the bad, unconditionally. You have that here now."

I can feel her tremble beneath the palm of my hand as the tears continue to stream down her face.

She moves her head to my shoulder, pressing her forehead against my neck as her emotions take over. Her heart is breaking in front of me, and all I can do is wrap my arms around her, hoping to keep all the pieces in place.

I don't know how long we sit here wrapped together. I know how fragile she feels, both physically and mentally, right now. I'm not going to move until she's ready. This is something she needs to help heal the invisible scars of her past.

A few minutes later, she mumbles she's ready to go inside and I help her out of the truck, leading her inside the house. It's crazy to think this is the first time she will be coming to my house. Although I wish it were under different circumstances, I can't help but feel like she's coming home.

She doesn't know this yet, but I don't plan on letting her move back to Hudson's. I want her here with me always.

As soon as everything is in the house and unloaded, I walk down the hallway and back into the living room, searching around for Ellie but coming up empty. When I walk into the kitchen, I find her sitting at the high-top bar with a glass of water. She's staring out the window, once again looking lost in thought.

"Would you like me to draw you a bath?" I ask, sweeping her hair out of the way off the nape of her neck. Peppering two small kisses along her shoulder, I let myself enjoy the feel of her soft skin beneath my lips as she sighs in content.

"A bath sounds wonderful," she says, leaning back, pressing her head against my shoulder.

Pressing one last kiss against her shoulder, I turn the chair to help her down. With her hand in mine, I lead her down the long hallway and into the master suite.

The bathroom is one of my favorite rooms in this house. Bending down, I turn on the water testing the temperature, letting it warm up. What I find behind me when I turn back around nearly knocks the wind out of me.

Ellie's face holds a sadness, it hasn't left since our moment in the truck, but the look in her eyes says so much. The pull, this connection between us, is undeniable.

"Thank you for letting me stay with you. I'm not used to being cared for like this, at least not like you do anyway." The missing smile from her face is back but not nearly as bright.

"I want you here with me, right by my side," I say, closing the distance between us. "I'm not going anywhere, baby."

With my face pressed against her neck, I lean back and whisper, "Let me help you get undressed."

Nodding her head, she turns and faces the mirror. I can see Ellie looking up, taking in her own reflection. Grabbing the hem of her t-shirt, I ease it up and over her head as her hair falls against her back.

Seeing the bruises and cuts marring her beautiful skin has the anger I was feeling earlier roiling until I look up and meet her eyes. Wrapping her arms around her waist, she tries to cover herself.

Running my lips along her shoulder and down her back, I kneel behind her as I slide her pants and underwear down her legs. I press my mouth against the marks on her legs and lower back, not leaving one untouched before I move to stand behind her.

Stepping around her clothes, Ellie turns to face me as I continue to run my lips along the bruised skin on her cheek. I can feel her body tremble beneath my touch as goose bumps appear.

"You're absolutely beautiful," I say, wrapping her arms around my neck, pulling her naked body against mine. "I've already told you this, but there isn't a single inch of you that I want you to keep covered. Every scar, every bruise. Remember?"

Running her fingers along the hairs of my neck, I lean back until I am once again looking her straight in the eye. I didn't expect to find the look of desire shining back at me.

Leaning forward, she presses her soft mouth against mine. I want to pull back, change the direction this is going, but when she parts her lips and whispers she needs me, I break. Just hearing those words, the desperation in her voice, I know I can't tell her no. I want to be certain but I know I won't deny her this.

"Are you sure?" I ask, my breath coming out haggardly against her mouth. With a nod of her head, I close the distance once more as my tongue eagerly seeks hers.

"I want you to replace every bad touch with memories of yours. I want your hands everywhere so the only thing I remember is the way my body tingles as I come apart beneath you."

With her body pressed against mine, I lift her legs off the floor and wrap them around my waist. Just the feel of her heat pressed against me has me feeling unsteady on my feet as I move to set her on the edge of the counter. My body reacts as she rocks against me, causing me to force down a groan.

Moving my hand down between us, I run my finger along her wet folds, inserting one finger into her. I can feel her body come alive beneath my touch as her breasts are pressed against my chest. Pulling back out, I insert a second finger curving it until I feel her tighten around me, then I pull out completely.

Taking a step back, I unbuckle my belt and ease my pants down over my hips.

"Callum," Ellie mutters, feeling the loss of our connection.

"I know, baby," I groan, feeling my hands shake. Stepping back in front of her, I run the head of my cock against her entrance as I wrap my arms around her. Pulling her closer to me, I press on until I'm fully seated in her tight pussy.

"Ellie," I moan just as she lets out a soft whimper. A surge of emotions pass over me, remembering just a few days ago, I was worried if I would ever see her beautiful green eyes again.

Moving my hand back between us, I let my finger skate across her tight bud. The movement causes Ellie to gasp as she grinds against me. Her fingers dig into my shoulder as she grapples to hold on. I can feel her pussy clench around me as

I grit my teeth, thrusting deeper.

"I will give anything to keep you safe and in my arms," I say, moving my hand back to her hip, "just like this." Each word punctuated as I lean forward, bringing her mouth to mine in a punishing kiss.

"Yes, Callum!"

I can feel her release coming and with one last thrust, we are both falling as our orgasms take hold as I wrap my arms around Ellie, trying to stay upright. I run my hands over Ellie, loving the way she melts for me. With my head pressed against her neck, I force air into my lungs as the aftershocks race through my body.

"It's a good thing the bathtub isn't filling up, sweetheart, or we'd have a swimming pool on our hands." I laugh, pressing one last kiss on her shoulder as I pull out.

I can feel her eyes rake over me as I walk back over to the tub putting the stopper in, letting it fill. Looking at her over my shoulder, I catch her staring at my backside. Realizing she's been caught, her cheeks brighten with embarrassment as I give her a playful wink.

"C'mon, baby, let's get you in the water before it gets cold." I chuckle.

Twenty-One

Ellie

I'VE HAD A HARD TIME SLEEPING AT NIGHT SINCE BEING released from the hospital. Sometimes, I wake up in a panic thinking I am back in the trunk or in the basement of the old house. Feeling the weight of Callum's arm draped over my waist and his breath against my shoulder had me sliding closer to him.

I've been a ball of nerves at the thought of Royal being out there. I feel like at any moment I'm going to break into a million pieces, unable to hold myself together.

Callum has been out of his mind with worry, hardly letting me out of his sight. He has been spending most of his time at home with me, even working from home. I hate to tell him this but I'm thankful for the times when he is working. When he's not hovering, I feel like I get a break from my thoughts.

Kinsley has been stopping by regularly to see me, bringing me magazines and checking out books I put on hold from the library. Hudson and June stopped by last night to see us, bringing a homemade enchilada casserole she prepared and some pumpkin bars she had been testing out.

I can't help but feel like I've flipped everyone's world upside down. Callum hasn't been into work since before he was out of town, Hudson has been left in a tight place without a lot of employees since Kinsley had recently went to working at the salon full time. She's been helping him out lately, which I appreciate, but I know it puts a lot on her between two jobs.

I told myself if Royal was ever released or found me, I wouldn't stay in Arbor Creek. I couldn't bring these people down with me, which is what I feel like I'm doing now. I didn't expect for the people I've met here to have had such an impact on who I am. They really have become my family.

The sound of the doorbell ringing followed by three loud knocks breaks me from my thoughts as I absentmindedly flip through a magazine. Tossing it on the coffee table, I head over to the front door, checking through the peephole, seeing who it is.

Looking down the hallway, I can see Callum standing in the doorway of his office dressed in nothing but a pair of jeans. His hair is disheveled in a fresh-out-of-the-shower sort of way. With his phone pressed to his ear, he covers the speaker as he mouths "it's his mom." With a small grin, he turns and strides back into his office.

His mother? His mother is here and he's just going to leave me alone to answer it?

Looking down, I take in my appearance and quickly check the mirror. My hair is looking wild and unruly, having just woken up a little bit ago. The black shirt I'm wearing is one of Callum's old high school football jerseys. It's worn and smells like him.

It's safe to say I'm not in any state to be meeting my boyfriend's mother.

The sound of knocking returns, forcing my feet to move.

Fuck, I'm all worried about what the hell I'm wearing, and I'm doing a shit job of welcoming his mother, instead leaving her standing out on the front stoop.

With a quick peek through the peephole, I unlock the door and swing it open to find a warm smile shining back at me. Seeing the woman in front of me, I know without even meeting Callum's father who he inherited his natural charisma from. This woman radiates joy and happiness.

"Good morning, Mrs. Whitt. C'mon in." The smile on my face matching her own.

"Ellie, sweetheart, please call me Connie or Momma if you prefer. How are you feeling?" she asks, running her hand down my arm until it finds my hand.

Wrapping her warm hand around mine, she squeezes it, giving me a reassuring smile. The concern on her face as she looks me over looks a lot like the one June gave me when she and Hudson stopped by. Taking a step back, I make room for her to enter as she bends down picking up the bags she brought with her.

"I'm okay, starting to feel a little more like myself, but still sore," I mutter, following along behind her.

"Can I help you carry something?" I ask, feeling like my manners have left me as she walks into the kitchen with two large brown paper bags nearly busting apart at the seams.

"Nonsense, honey. Please have a seat. You should be

taking it easy. I'll be in and out of your hair in no time at all."

Taking a seat at the breakfast bar, I watch as she deposits the bags and gets to work fluttering around the room. The way she moves through the kitchen, unloading items, preheating the oven, it's clear she has done this a time or two.

While Callum is a grown man, more than capable of taking care of himself, there's something about the way she looks after him. You can tell by the genuine smile she enjoys taking care of her family.

"Can I get you something to drink?" she asks as soon as everything is unloaded and put away. Pushing up her sleeves, she turns on the sink and starts filling it up adding dish soap.

"I'm okay, thank you though," I say, watching as she sets out to clean the dishes we had left in the sink from the night before. I immediately feel terrible, thinking she probably feels I'm going to make a horrible wife or mother.

"There is just something about washing dishes," she says, looking at me with a smile. "So many of the simple and mundane things have been replaced with modern technology. There are just some things that don't beat how they used to be."

The look of happiness sets in, the warm smile she had when she first arrived stretched bright across her face. Her long dark hair, curled in waves, clipped back in a barrette.

"I'm not much for technology myself. Until I met Callum, I had never even owned a cell phone. Even today, I still have a hard time keeping track of the darn thing." I laugh, folding my arms on the countertop.

After I woke up in the hospital and Detective Keller stopped by, he returned my cell phone. I didn't know until I got home but Callum told me they were able to use it to track me down. I guess there's one thing about technology I can be thankful for.

"I didn't want one, never had a reason to have one, until I met him. I guess now, looking back on it, I'm glad I listened."

"Don't let him hear you say that. He has a thing about always wanting to be right," she jokes with a knowing smirk on her face.

"Yeah, and he doesn't like to take no for an answer either," I say, recalling our conversation in my kitchen the day I fell. The way he pushed me to go to the hospital to get my head checked out and then followed it up by telling me we were going to make a trip to the cell phone store the next day.

"He always has been that way, you know. I know he told you about him and his father," she says, stopping to clear her throat. The sudden change of direction in the conversation brings me back to the here and now as I nod my head.

"He has always been a go-getter. It's one of the things about him I've always been the proudest of. He doesn't sit by and let life pass him by. When he sees something he wants, he isn't afraid to go after it."

My heart softens just hearing the pride in her words, just hearing them and knowing them to be true. Since I met Callum, he has always shown me, if I let him in, how fiercely he would love me. Even from the first day at the bus station.

"I know you have a lot to fear outside that door," she says, dipping her hand beneath the water to wash the suds away, picking up another plate. Running the scrub pad along it, she cleans it off before running it under the water faucet.

"I won't bring it up or ask you to relive the horror of what you've been through, but I just hope you know you don't have to spend your life running anymore, sweetheart. My boy, even though he probably hasn't told you yet, he cares about you.

Those three words, if I had to guess are scary to hear on your end, but are even scarier for him to voice. So, if he hasn't told you yet, just promise me you'll be patient. Only a special woman would be so lucky to be on the receiving end of that type of love. You deserve it, too, you both do."

I know how close Callum and his mother are, so I shouldn't be surprised to hear he has told her about our relationship and shared a hint of my past.

The sound of a throat clearing behind us draws us out from the seriousness of the conversation. Hearing Callum's mom tell me she knows how he feels about me, only to have him walk into the room, has me wondering just how much of the conversation he had heard.

"Morning, Ma. You know you don't have to clean up after me," he says, coming up behind me, running his hand along my shoulder. His fingers massaging into my skin, helping ease the tension of the conversation from me. Running his nose along my head, he mumbles a small "hi" in my ear before pressing a small kiss there. Walking around the counter, he greets his mother with a hug as she takes a step back from the sink drying off her hands.

"I'll do whatever I want to do," she says, looking at me with a wink, turning to give her son a hug.

She runs through all the stuff she brought over, smiling when she shares she made his favorite lasagna for us. She also picked up a prescription for me at the drugstore called in by the doctor to help with my pain and anxiety.

Callum looks over at me before bringing his attention back to his mother. "I just got off the phone with Mason a few minutes ago," he says. I know this has been a long time coming between Callum and his brother. He told me about the argument that had them on the outs while he was visiting Chicago. What he didn't explain to me was why he had let so much time pass before he had reconciled with his brother.

"With everything going on, I forgot Steven was coming into town this weekend. He's wondering if we would be up for dinner tomorrow since Mason will be in town." Callum's eyes meet mine, and I see the storm of emotions swirling beneath the blue irises. I know how he feels about talking to his father. It's been a long time since he's had a conversation with him, a rational one at least.

"I think it would be good for you," Connie says encouragingly. "It's time for you to talk to both of them, put this all behind you. I don't like seeing my boys fight, not talking. It's gone on for long enough." I know Callum is secretly searching for the approval he needs, knowing a lot of his anger is for the way his father treated his mother growing up.

"Your father's not a bad man, Callum. He has his faults and he didn't always treat me right. He could be a stubborn bull, but I think that's something you get from him, too," she says with a laugh. "I've made peace with the past. I think for the sake of taking care of you, it's time that you made peace with it, too."

Callum nods his head as he turns to look at me. I know he wants to at least see what his father has to say.

"Yeah, I never have been one to take no for an answer," he says, catching me off guard before he flashes me a wink.

With his comment, my heart starts to beat out of my chest, wondering just how much of our conversation he heard before he walked in.

Callum

I certainly didn't need something else to fucking stress over. Spending a few days inside the house had Ellie and me nearly clawing to get out. So when she said she was going to spend the afternoon out on the dock, I knew there was nothing I could do to stop her.

When we made plans for dinner with Mason, Brea, and my father, I made a condition it would happen if we could host it at my house. Knowing the police hadn't made any arrests, I wasn't willing to take any risks when it came to Ellie's safety. It's obvious they both have a few screws loose and I'm fearful that, at this point, Royal will think there isn't much left to live for. Until the police have them, I was prepared to take every step necessary to keep Ellie safe.

Opening the sliding glass door, I step out onto the back patio of the house facing the pond. It's early September and while it's a little cool, it's the perfect weather to grill out and enjoy dinner outside. Moving to the steps, I stand here and watch Ellie from where she sits with her feet hanging just above the water.

As if she can somehow sense I'm watching her, she turns her head as she closes her book in her lap. Moving to stand, she makes her way up the hill toward the patio with a smile on her face. She looks beautiful with her long golden blond hair blowing in the wind.

"How are you doing with everything?" she asks, climbing up the stairs, making her way over to me. Once she reaches me, she wraps her arms around my waist, resting her cheek against my chest.

"If I'm being honest, I'm ready to just get it over with."

"Don't you think maybe it's worth giving him a chance and hear what he has to say? You never know, it could be worth listening to," she assures, leaning back to look up at me. "I'll be here every step of the way. You're always the first to remind me that you're here by my side, but I hope you know that I want to be there for you, too."

"I can get through anything if I have you by my side, sweetheart." I smile, leaning forward, pressing a soft kiss to Ellie's lips, running my hands along her back.

I can hear the doorbell ring from inside the house as I press one last kiss to Ellie's lips.

"C'mon, baby, let's get this over with," I mutter, wrapping my hand in hers.

Heading inside through the sliding glass, I leave it open for Ellie to follow as I pad my feet along the floor toward the front of the house. Just as I move to unlock the door, I can feel Ellie approach as her hand runs along my back, silently offering me her support.

"Hello, son," my father says. As always, my father is dressed in a suit and tie. Steven Reid is always a businessman, even if it's a family dinner on a Saturday afternoon. I wouldn't expect anything different today.

"Hello, father, Mason," I say sternly. "Brea, it's good to see you again." The soft smile on her face looks uneasy, meaning I'm sure my brother has told her about the tension running through us.

Remembering my manners, I run my hand along Ellie's spine introducing her to everyone. Although Mason and Brea had been to the hospital, she hadn't been awake for me to introduce her. Taking a step back, I smile as I wave them in. I hope the smile on my face is as welcoming as I intend for it to be, although I can't help but feel like it's forced.

"This is a nice place you have, man. I haven't seen it since I was home for Christmas but a lot has changed," Mason says, looking around. Brea and Ellie are both talking and smiling with each other. As Ellie shows her around, they make their way into the kitchen.

"I agree, this is a really nice place you have, Callum. Thanks for having us," my father says, moving his hand out in front of me to shake my hand. Returning the gesture, I feel his hand envelop around mine as he wraps his arm around my shoulder. "I hope you know how proud of you I am, son."

I can't help but feel taken by surprise by his compliment. Leaning back, I make it a point to look him directly in the eyes, and that's when I notice something different about him. The bloodshot glossy look in his eyes I'm used to seeing for so many years is gone.

Nodding my head, I return his smile. "Thank you."

After taking some time to show them around the main floor, we make ourselves comfortable on the back patio. Firing up the grill, we make small talk about Mason's school, how things are going at Whitt's, and how Florida is treating my father. Although the conversation continues to flow, I can't help but think some of the topics are awkward. We are skating around everything, but not acknowledging the way we left things in Chicago.

Ellie and Brea are seated at the patio table as I overhear Ellie tell her about how we met outside the bus station. I can't help but smile when I look over at her. She moves to take a drink and my eyes find hers over the top of her glass. When she sets the glass down on the table, she flashes me a smile, tipping her head toward where my father and Mason are talking about school. I know it's her way of encouraging me to break the tension hovering in the air around us all.

Turning back to them, I listen intently as Mason talks about the Criminal Law classes he is taking next fall as my father nods his head listening. Looking down at the glass in his hand, I watch as he takes a drink of his ice water holding the glass in front of him. The usual habits he always had when he had been drinking are gone; the way he would insist on a whiskey and coke at dinner, the way his words would slur, or he would barely listen to your conversation.

It's clear my father hasn't been drinking. If I had to guess by looking at him, I'd say it's been awhile since he's picked up a drink.

"What brings you back to town? Mason mentioned yesterday that you were staying in Des Moines," I ask, curiosity getting the best of me.

"The same thing that brought me to town when you were visiting Chicago and the same reason why I've been trying to get in touch with you now." The mention of Chicago causes my shoulder to tense, preparing for this to turn into an argument. I can see Ellie out of the corner of my eye turning her head toward me, making sure I'm okay.

"Son, I know I wasn't a good father to you growing up. Hell, I was an even shittier husband to your mother. I was lucky to have had her, and I was a bastard who didn't value her like I should've. I had my own problems, and I'm sorry you had to witness them and the burden was put on you. I understand why you feel the way you do about me and why you were upset with me back in Chicago."

Looking at my father and hearing the words, I see

something I haven't seen since I was young.

My Dad.

"What's changed? I don't get it," I say. There is a hint of a bite in my tone I didn't mean to come out. I know Ellie can sense where this conversation is going as she pushes her chair back from the table.

Walking around the edge, she mumbles they're going to get the sides prepared. She looks at me, making sure I'm okay before she does as Brea follows along behind her into the house.

"A lot has, Callum. Six months ago, I almost lost my license as an attorney and damn near put myself in the hospital. The only option I had was to put myself through rehab." He sighs, rubbing his fingers along his forehead as he takes another drink of water. Mason has his back turned to us as he takes over flipping the burgers on the grill.

"I know how bad it sounds. I lost my family and moved to Florida but it took almost losing my job before I turned it around. It's fucked up and I know that, but I'm glad I finally did it. It's the first time in a long time I've had a clear head."

Taking a drink of my own, I let the weight of his words sink in. Am I mad that almost losing his job was the final straw?

The answer is no. I'm just glad he is getting help and taking care of himself.

"You look good, healthy. I'm happy for you. Regardless of how we left things when you were in Chicago and everything that's happened between us, I'm glad you sought out help."

"Thanks, your approval means a lot. I got a job in Des Moines, I'll be moving up here in a couple weeks. I'm up here wrapping up the closing on the house I just bought. I thought it would be good for me to come back home and be closer to family."

I can hear it in his tone, the hope. Like my mom said, it's time for us to make peace with the past. I don't want it to hold me back anymore.

"I'd like that," I say, clapping him on the shoulder. The sliding glass door opens as Ellie and Brea walk out with glass dishes in their hands as Mason heads over with the platter of cooked burgers. We all move to take a seat around the patio table. I can see the worry on Ellie's face as her hand finds mine under the table, her eyes taking in my face trying to read me. Squeezing her hand in mine, I flash her a reassuring smile.

The conversation flows through dinner, keeping the topics light. I can feel Ellie relax as she notices the earlier tension in the air is now gone.

My father asks Ellie how we had met, and I can't help but smile as Ellie recounts for the second time tonight how we ran into each other at the bus station leaving Chicago. When it's Brea's turn to answer the same question, I can sense the unease as she struggles to explain her relationship with Mason, settling on them being friends. The look of frustration that passes over Mason's face and the glimmer of sadness in Brea's eyes at the admission says there is more going on between them that isn't being said.

The sound of the doorbell ringing inside has me excusing myself from the table. With the way the night has went, I could use a minute to step away and take a breath. It isn't until I'm wandering back through the house that I wonder who could be here.

Peeking through the peephole, the tension sets in again when I see who it is.

Twenty-Two

Callum

"**D**ETECTIVE," I SAY AS I OPEN THE DOOR. MY EYES immediately float to the man standing behind Keller, recognizing him as the detective as his partner. He had been at the hospital after Ellie had been found and brought in. Holding his hand out to me, I return mine, shaking it.

"Detective Duluth," he says with a nod.

Taking a step back, I let them in. "We're sorry to bother you. I hope this is a good time. Is Ellie here?" Keller asks, looking around the living room.

As if Ellie can sense we are talking about her, I turn to hear her enter from the patio as she calls for me.

"Ellie, can you come in here?" I know they're here to talk to her but I'm not about to let her go through any of this shit without me next to her every step of the way.

"Good afternoon, Ms. Hayes. We wanted to stop by and give you an update on your case." Ellie took some time to explain to me after she moved why she kept her name private. As much as it hurt to hear, I knew she wanted to start over in a new town, and her identity was something she felt she needed to keep quiet to remain under the radar.

I understood why. That doesn't mean I liked it, but I understood.

"Thank you for stopping by," Ellie says, lacing her fingers in mine. On the outside, she may look broken down at the hands of Royal, but she has proven just how strong she truly is. Squeezing her fingers, I silently offer her support and remind her I'm here with her.

"What can we do for you?" I ask, encouraging this conversation along. I'd be lying if I didn't say I'm ready to get this over with.

"I wanted to tell you in person we were able to locate both Royal Carter and Lynne Hayes. They are both in custody. Royal is currently being treated at the local hospital while under the custody of the Everton Police Department. He was suffering from an infection from an untreated stab wound to the abdomen. Once he is released, which should be soon, he will be detained and booked in Pearl County."

I can't help but smile at the pride rushing through me just knowing how he received that stab wound.

My girl, the fighter.

"Have you been able to get information from her? Do you know why she was there?"

"While Royal was in prison, we know that they still maintained their relationship. She would regularly come to visit him. In her statements, your mother has said that after he was released he turned up missing which we know now is when he came to Arbor Creek. We believe she was coming to see him and wasn't aware that you were here."

"Please," Ellie says, holding up her hand, stopping him from talking. "Please don't refer to her as my 'mother' anymore. Her name is Lynne. She's been anything but a mother to me."

I can see the remorse written all over his face as he nods his head, acknowledging his mistake.

"He is being held on kidnapping and assault with intent to commit sexual abuse. Royal will be lucky if he ever walks free again." I can hear the audible sigh of relief come from Ellie as I let go of her hand, moving to wrap my arms around her.

"I should let you know he is arguing this wasn't an abduction case and no abuse has taken place. He is saying you knew he was coming for you, the abuse was at the hands of Mr. Reid, and he was there to get you out of that situation."

"Are you fucking shitting me? The piece of shit said I did this to her?" I can feel the rage coil in me, boiling just under the surface. The pent-up emotions I've kept in check over the past week searching for a way out.

"That's correct, sir. However, we have evidence proving otherwise. We can first start off with the fact you were out of town. We also found personal artifacts and photographs in the vehicle left on the property, the one he used to transport Ms. Hayes, proving he had been stalking her for quite some time. Photographs that have clearly been taken without her knowledge and, if I had to guess, without her consent."

The audible intake of breath and the sob that follows nearly breaks my heart. This man, this piece of shit, continues to do everything he can to break her.

Wrapping my arms around Ellie, I can feel her shake as her body is pressed against me. Leaning my head in close to hers, I whisper, "it's over."

"I want those photos burned. I want them to appear as though they never existed, do you hear me?" I spit. I know I'm running the risk of getting myself in deep shit talking to the detectives this way but I will not have these pictures of Ellie anywhere for anyone to see them.

"I understand, sir. At this point, they are being used only as evidence in the case to put him behind bars. I know it won't be easy for you to have to face this man," he says, turning his attention to Ellie, "but the best chance we have of putting him away for life is if you testify. Do you think you could do that?"

My chest hurts just thinking about all she has endured at the hands of this cocksucker. With my arms still wrapped around her, Ellie turns her head so it's resting against my chest.

"It's going to be okay. I'm going to be there with you every step of the way," I whisper. "I'm never going to leave your side."

Taking a deep lungful of breath, she leans back and looks me in the eye. "I know that now," she says. I can see the love in her eyes. "I'll do it," she says with so much conviction as she turns to look at Keller.

"He has put me through hell for most of my life. I'm ready to send him there to rot."

Pushing her hair away from her face, I press my lips against her temple. Keeping my arm wrapped around her, I move to stand at her side as we face the detectives together.

They fill us in on what to expect on his upcoming arraignment, reassuring Ellie he will remain behind bars until the trial begins. With the promise to keep in touch, we see the detectives out and plan for Ellie to stand before the judge on Monday.

As soon as the door closes, I hear Ellie's sigh of relief as I wrap her back in my arms.

"How are you doin', baby?" I ask I know this is a lot for her to take in.

"I'm okay," she says, wrapping her arms around my waist as she rests her head against my chest. "The pain doesn't hurt any less knowing she still thinks I lied about the past. What kind of mother would still be in a relationship with someone who abuses their child?" she mumbles, burying her face into my neck. I can feel her body tremble through the emotions.

"I don't know, baby," I mutter, hearing my voice crack as I press a kiss against her temple.

"I hope now she sees the pain he put me through. She'll have to live with it because I won't ever forgive her for this. In a way, I almost feel relieved. Before I knew Royal had been released, I felt like the date was looming out of fear of what was to come when he did. I just want to get the trial over with so I can finally feel like I can move on. I'm ready to focus on my future," she says, leaning back letting her eyes find mine.

"I'm looking forward to what the future has in store for us, sweetheart."

Sliding her hands up my chest, she wraps her good hand around my neck as I lean forward, pressing my lips against hers. Running my tongue along her lower lip, she opens her mouth for me.

The sound of someone clearing their throat behind us breaks us from our moment. Looking up, I can see my father, Mason, and Brea standing off to the side in the dining room across the room from us. Both Brea and my father look uncomfortable for breaking up our intimate moment but Mason can't help but enjoy the awkwardness with a shit eating grin on his face.

"Sorry about that, the detectives stopped by to give us an update on the case," I say, using the opportunity to change the subject.

"Everything okay?" my father asks, hearing the concern in his tone.

"He was found and locked away, which is all we can ask for right now." I reassure him, keeping my arm wrapped around Ellie's waist and pressing her against my side.

"That's good to hear. I'm sure you're ready to put this behind you."

Feeling Ellie nod her head against my chest, she replies, "More than you could ever know."

"Well, I really should get going. I have an appointment tomorrow morning to wrap things up at the bank. Thank you for having us, Callum. It was nice to meet you, Ms. Ellie."

As we say our goodbyes, I wrap my brother in a hug. Neither of us apologizes for the shit over the past few months. Looking back on it now, I know it was his way of trying to bring us together.

"Thanks, man, for coming to town. For being here for me with everything at the hospital. For today," I say, slapping him on the back.

"Of course, bro. You better start answering your phone now or I'll be back sooner than you expect," he jokes. Ellie laughs, promising she'll make sure to keep me in line.

I don't know what the future looks like with my father or if I can trust his rehab has done enough to help him change. I guess I'll leave the ball in his court and see where it goes.

Ellie

One thing I absolutely love about Callum's house is the bath tub. The thing is big enough to swim laps in.

Okay, maybe not quite, but it's huge.

After all the events of today, from Callum's brother and father coming over to the detectives stopping by, I needed some time to myself doing nothing but soaking in the tub.

I could tell Callum was worried about me. He's concerned how I'm taking the news about Lynne and how I'll handle testifying. I was being honest when I told him I was ready to move forward. As many questions as I had for my mother, I know Callum is right. I may never get the answers I'm searching for. I've thought a lot about that since the conversation we had the day we came home from the hospital. Like Callum, I think it's time I make peace with my past.

If I've learned anything, it's that I'm stronger than I give myself credit for. With everything that's happened, I only feel more grateful to have Callum by my side. I don't think I could get through this without him. He gives me the strength I didn't know I had.

Lying back, I use the loofah to rub the body wash over my body. I'm careful to keep my cast out of the water, which isn't easy to do, but I manage. Thinking back to the time in the hospital and the conversation I had with Callum's mother, I can't help but think about my feelings for Callum and the words I heard him whisper.

"I love you, Ellie."

I haven't told Callum I heard him that day. I know how I feel about him but a part of me still worries that maybe he said those words given everything going on. He was worried about me, and I was in the hospital. You say things when your emotions are running high.

That's what he meant, right? He just wanted me to know he loved me out of fear of thinking it could be the last time he would ever have the chance to say it. Emotions were high.

Hearing a knock on the door, I turn my head as Callum peeks in.

"You coming to bed soon or are you planning on sleeping in the tub tonight?" he asks, a small smile taking over his face. He can't see me over the high walls of the tub, but it doesn't stop him from letting his eyes wander as I look over the side.

"I'm getting out in just a minute; the water is starting to get a little cold," I say, lifting my hands above me to wrap my hair in a top knot.

"If you're not out in five minutes, I'm coming in for you." He winks. Knowing how much time I've been spending in this tub lately, he obviously thinks he'll have to haul me out.

With a nod, Callum turns to leave, pulling the door closed behind him.

Stepping out of the tub, I quickly dry off. Lathering my legs and arms with lotion, I slip on my tank top and shorts. Hanging my damp towel on the rack, I step out of the bathroom and find Callum lying in bed. His shirt is off, leaving his broad chest on display, and I smile at how relaxed he looks.

Walking around to the other side of the bed I've taken over as my own, I pull back the comforter before I bend down to plug in my cell phone. It takes a second before it hits me just what I'm seeing, causing my hand to fly to my chest.

"Callum," I say. It comes out as more of a question than I originally intended. "Where did you find this?" Leaning over, I pick up my necklace from Grams draped over the side of my picture frame. The picture of my father and I that Callum insisted I put next to the bed, instead of tucking it in my wallet.

Tears fill my eyes as relief fills me after thinking I would never find it again.

"When I showed up at your house to pick you up for the wedding, I found it on the floor in the entry way. It had broken, so while you were in the hospital I had Kinsley take it to the jewelry store to have it fixed."

Needing to feel closer to Callum, I turn and walk back around to the other side of the bed. I can feel his eyes track my movement as he makes room for me. Not wasting another second, I move in close to him, pressing my lips against his. Leaning back, I leave just a breath between us as I whisper a "thank you."

"You don't have to thank me, baby. I know how much this necklace means to you," he says, running his hand along the side of my face.

Leaning into his palm, I take a minute to appreciate the feel of his hands on me. "My Grandma Ellen gave me this necklace right before she passed away," I say, looking down at the compass engraved in the pendant. "She had always wanted me to get out of Garwood, to finally have the strength to put the past behind me. I'm ready to finally do that."

Callum runs his hand down the side of my face, over my shoulder, and down my arm until he wraps his hand in mine.

"I'm so glad you did, Ellie." The words wrap around me, giving me the courage to say what I've wanted to say for so long.

Nodding my head, I continue on, "I believe I was meant to run into you that day at the bus station and again that night at the bar. In my heart, I know I was supposed to come here to Arbor Creek. I believe my Grams was hoping this is where I'd end up. This is my home now and it's where I found you."

The words are barely out of my mouth before Callum's lips are on mine. They are soft, yet urgent, and they feel like home. Callum wraps his hand around the necklace, setting it on the nightstand next to the bed as I slide my hand around his neck.

Running my tongue along his lips, he opens for me and as soon as my tongue meets his, I can hear the groan unleashed, vibrating beneath his chest. Leaning back against the headboard, he wraps his arms around my waist, mumbling about needing to feel me. With both of my legs positioned on either side of him, he wraps both his hands around my face as he runs his thumbs along my cheeks. It's the words he says next nearly stop my heart from beating in my chest.

"I love you, Ellie. I believe I was meant to love you. I made a promise to you that I would never leave your side. For as long as you'll have me and as long as I live, I'll spend every day right here loving you."

Before I can even stop it, tears roll down my face. Running his thumb underneath my eyes, he whispers for me not to cry.

"I love you, too, Callum."

With my hand pressed against his heart, I can feel his steady heartbeat against my palm. I know he feels this, too. With my body pressed against his, I don't leave any space between us as I press my lips back against his.

This time it feels different. For the first time, I feel hopeful when I look at my future. I know through the trial and family problems, we will always be by each other's side.

I can't help but look forward to getting through it all together.

Epilogue

Callum

Three Months Later

A LOT CAN CHANGE IN THREE MONTHS AND A LOT HAS changed. Ellie never did go back to staying at the house she rented from Hudson. Things weren't easy through the trial.

Preparing her testimony resurfaced a lot of her old memories and the nightmares that plagued her often kept her up at night, but we got through it. She's started seeing a counselor because as much as she tried, there are still days she struggles to cope with the losses in her life. Including her mother.

Ellie never again acted like her time in Arbor Creek was temporary. If anything, her relationships only continued to grow after the wall she had built started coming down. Her friendship with Kinsley and Halle only got closer. It made me happy to see her continue to get closer to our friends, planting her roots here in Arbor Creek.

The same could be said about the relationship and bond she had developed with Hudson. In a lot of ways, I think she looks up to Hudson in a grandfather role and we often attended their family lunch once a month. She is still working down at the grocery store for Hudson during the week, something she enjoys doing.

Rolling over, I move my arm out in search of Ellie but only find the cold sheets beneath my palm. Glancing up at the alarm clock on the nightstand, I see it's a little after eight and based on the sounds coming from the kitchen and the soft music playing, I'm guessing Ellie is in there trying to cook us breakfast. She can be incredibly messy when she cooks, but I don't complain.

Mostly because I love it and I never want it to stop.

Wearing nothing but my lounge pants, I pad down the hallway toward the kitchen. Lifting my hand, I run my fingers along the muscles of my arm, stretching as I work to wake up. Leaning against the doorway, I can't help but smile as I watch Ellie standing in front of the stove with a spatula in her hand. Music is playing through the Bluetooth speaker as she sways her hips along to the beat as Marvin Gaye sings, giving me all kinds of ideas about where this morning could go.

I can't move, my body rooted in place as I watch her move to the music. It isn't until she turns around to put the eggs and butter in the fridge when she spots me, causing her to drop the butter on the floor as she covers her heart in surprise.

"Baby, it's good you didn't drop those eggs. I wouldn't want you to go all footloose on me again," I say, laughing, as I walk over and pick up the butter from the floor.

"How long have you been standing there?" she asks as I

stand and take the eggs from her hand, turning to put them in the refrigerator for her. Turning back around, I smile when I see her cheeks are red with embarrassment.

"Long enough." I smile, moving toward her and grabbing her hand, pulling her closer to me. "I love watching you dance like that. I want to wake up to you like this every day," I whisper, wrapping my hands around her waist, pressing my lips to her forehead.

Wrapping her arms around my neck, she is careful of the spatula still in her hand as she looks up at me. "I do, too," she says, smiling as she presses her lips against mine. Her lips are soft as she opens her mouth for me, her tongue seeking out mine.

Leaning back, I smile down at her as I continue.

"The little swivel you do with your hips, too. You can do a little dance like that for me whenever you want," I say, raising my eyebrows suggestively.

"You keep making fun of me and I won't be doing any little dances for you for a while," she says playfully, smacking me on the chest as she turns back around to tend to the food.

Reaching my hand into my pants, I grab the ring I snuck from my dresser drawer and bend down on one knee. She doesn't even sense my movement as she starts talking about her plans to meet up with Kinsley later today to get a haircut. Grabbing her hand, I pull her away from the stove, turning her in the process.

With the spatula still in her hand, I'm not surprised when it flies to the floor when she sees me on my knee before her.

"Callum," she whispers, moving her hand back to her chest once again, as if trying to steady her heartbeat, but this time she doesn't stop until it's clutched around her necklace.

"Ellie, baby, I love you. I want to wake up next to you every morning and go to bed next to you every night. I want you to be the one I dance with at Brodie's and the one who's ridin' shotgun in my truck. I want you by my side for the rest of my life. Marry me."

It isn't a question because there is never a question who Ellie is to me.

She is my everything and soon, she'll be my wife.

Coming Soon!

Heart's Compass Series
(Each book can be read as a standalone)

Lost Before You (#2)
Mason & Brea ~ Coming Late 2017

Until I Find You (#3)
Halle & Graham ~ Coming 2018

Wherever You Go (#4)
Kinsley & Wes ~ Coming 2018

Playlist

Think A Little Less – Chris Lane
Mind Reader – Dustin Lynch
Smoke – Florida Georgia Line
Drunk On Your Love – Brett Eldredge
Make Me Miss You – Sam Hunt
Take Your Time – Sam Hunt
Yeah – Joe Nichols
Hard to Love – Lee Brice
From The Ground Up – Dan + Shay
Love You Like That – Canaan Smith
Footloose – Kenny Loggins
Hurt So Good – John Mellencamp
Lets Get It On – Marvin Gaye

Listen to the Playlist on Spotify

Author's Note

Dear Reader,

Thank you so much for reading *Where I Found You*. There is a little bit of Callum and Ellie in who I am so it was a big step for me to write their story and click publish. I'm so grateful that you took a chance on their story.

If you enjoyed this book, please consider taking the time to leave a review or recommend it to a friend. Reviews are incredibly important to authors, especially new authors like myself. Reviews not only help other readers decide whether to buy my book, but they also inspire me to continue following my dream.

Thank you again for your support!
xo, Brooke

Acknowledgements

First and foremost, thank you to the readers and bloggers who have taken a chance on me and read my book. To the amazing bloggers in this community, I love the hell out of all of you! You put so much time into reading, reviewing, sharing, and spreading the word about books. I hope you know how important you are to this community. Without you, I never would have fallen in love with all the books I've read or found myself on this path in life. THANK YOU!

Derek – Thank you for being my rock and partner in life. And to my boys, everything I do in life is for you. I love you three more than I could ever put into words.

Mom, Asha and Gram – Your endless support and encouragement throughout this journey means a lot to me. Thank you for always pushing me to go after my dreams.

Kate and Kelsey – Point blank, I don't know if this book would have been finished without the two of you. Thank you for always being my shoulder to lean on when I needed it the most, encouraging me and inspiring me to write even hotter scenes. We are, after all, the Dirty Trio! ;) I can't until the day I get to meet you in person. I promise, vodkas on me!

My AMAZING Beta's, Barb, Dawn, Giovanna and Julia – Thank you so much for reading Callum and Ellie's story when it was a little rough and for your help throughout this entire process. Your feedback has been invaluable to me. The amount of support and encouragement you have shown me means EVERYTHING to me. I'm so grateful for your friendship!

The Real MVP's – Thanks for being there for me. For encouraging me, listening to me vent, and cheering me on every step of the way. A special thanks to Nicole for loving Callum as much as I do and for inspiring me to write Halle's character. LOL!

A special thanks to:

My editor, Roxane LeBlanc. You have taught me so much. I appreciate you being patient with me. Thank you for your keen eye and honest feedback. I can't thank you enough!

Lindee Robinson, for the beautiful cover photo, and Najla Qamber, for designing the perfect cover to fit Callum & Ellie's story. I look forward to working with you both on my future books.

Natalie and Stacey with Books & Boys Book Blog, for your support, helping me promote my cover reveal and release, and for answering my numerous questions.

My formatter, Stacey Blake, and my proofreader, Julie Deaton. Thank you for helping put the finishing touches on my book. I appreciate you both!

All the amazing authors that I've met in this community for reading my book, liking, and sharing my posts. Thank you, Abigail Davies, Danielle Dickson, Aurora Hale, Nicole Richard, Kim Reese, Katie Fox, Brooke May, AW Clarke, Eleanor Lloyd-Jones, and Liv Moore. I am so grateful for the friendships I've made. I look forward to watching all of us continue to grow in our careers.

About the Author

Brooke lives in the Midwest with her high school sweetheart and their three children (both human and furry). Growing up Brooke always had a love of writing; she started out writing poetry when she was young and began journaling her thoughts as she grew older. Diving head first into a good book has always been therapeutic for her. Now her two passions have collided.

Brooke believes that any bad day can be cured with chocolate and a good book. She enjoys spending time with her family, collecting paperbacks, going to the movies, and watching basketball and football.

Connect With Brooke

www.authorbrookeobrien.com
www.facebook.com/authorbrookeo
www.instagram.com/authorbrookeobrien
www.twitter.com/authorbrookeo
bit.ly/NewsletterBrookeO

Follow Brooke on Amazon and Goodreads to stay updated
on upcoming releases.
www.amazon.com/author/authorbrookeo
www.goodreads.com/authorbrookeobrien

Join Brooke's Book Babes for sneak peeks, giveaways, and
more: www.facebook.com/groups/brookesbookbabes

63526856R00156

Made in the USA
Lexington, KY
10 May 2017